AREA 51: EARTH ABIDES

By

BOB MAYER

www.bobmayer.com

This is a work of fiction. Names, characters, places, and incidents either are the product of the author's imagination or are used fictitiously, and any resemblance to actual persons living or dead, business establishments, events, or locales is entirely coincidental.

Area 51: Earth Abides by Bob Mayer
COPYRIGHT © 2020 by Bob Mayer

ISBN: 9781621253464

AREA 51: EARTH ABIDES

By

BOB MAYER

THE SERIES STORY
(AS FAR AS WE KNOW, SO FAR)

Feel free to skip if you've read the previous books and remember the story, or if you don't want spoiler alerts for previous books. To skip, jump to the opening of this book, with the chapter **LAST STAND OF IMPERIUM, PART I,** or scroll through a few pages and you'll be there.

Aliens, called Airlia, came to our solar system over 10,000 years ago on a mothership. They established their headquarters on an island in the middle of the Atlantic Ocean they named Atlantis. This was an outpost in their ongoing war against a species known as the Ancient Enemy, or more concisely, the Swarm.

The Airlia leader at Atlantis was Aspasia. After time passed, he felt secure from the interstellar war and stopped reporting to the Airlia Empire. A police force was sent, led by Artad on a second mothership, to determine what had happened. In the meantime, two humans, Donnchadh (who would become known as Duncan) and Gwalcmai from another Airlia colony where the people had instigated a successful revolt against their Airlia overlords, arrived on board a small spacecraft, the *Fynbar*, after being dropped outside the Solar System by a mothership commandeered by the rebel humans. They had left behind their own world which had been damaged beyond repair during the revolt. On earth, Donnchadh and Gwalcmai began to sow the seeds which eventually initiated a Civil War between Artad and Aspasia.

Atlantis was destroyed and Aspasia and his followers were banished by Artad to a base at Cydonia on Mars. Artad established his base underground at Qian-Ling in China where he ruled as the first Emperor. Others of his followers established the First Dynasty in Egypt, where Airlia ruled over men before our human recorded history. During that reign, half-breeds, the spawn of Airlia and human consorts, were born. These became known in human legend as the Undead, or more colloquially, vampires.

A covert civil war was fought through the ages by various agents of both Airlia sides, including humans, clones, the mentally controlled (Guides) and hybrids, until it exploded into World War III when an attempt was made by Guides to fly Artad's mothership, hidden at Area 51. The details of all of this are in prior books, with Book 1 in the series, **Area 51**, covering the attempt to fly that mothership and why it had to be stopped at all cost: because engaging an FTLT drive would draw the attention of the Swarm and a Reaping. That would be bad, as we learned in **Area 51: Invasion**.

Humans succeeded in defeating both Artad, Aspasia and their corrupt followers, but that didn't end World War III. Rather than coming together as one species, various nations and factions fought each other. The leaders of the revolt against the aliens, and the protagonist of this series, a Special Forces soldier,

Mike Turcotte, and Lisa Duncan (as Donnchadh was now known) were forced to destroy the last attempt by surviving Airlia on Mars to finish a Faster Than Light (FTL) transmitter to contact the Airlia Empire and summon help. In doing so, Duncan sacrificed herself by crashing Artad's mothership into the array on Mars.

(A lot of other stuff happened over the course of nine books, such as King Arthur, the Great Wall of China, Jack the Ripper, Excalibur, the Great Pyramid, the Sphinx, the Grail, an attempt at spreading a second Black Death, etc. etc. but you get the drift).

Back when Atlantis fell, Duncan and her mate had founded a small group of humans called Watchers. Their mission was to keep tabs on the Airlia and their minions throughout the ages. To watch and wait until humanity grew powerful enough to rebel. A splinter segment of Watchers (the *Myrddin*) broke off, led by the man known in legend as Merlin. This group was determined to do more than watch. They believed their mission was to insure the survival of mankind. In ***Area 51 Redemption***, Turcotte and his team tried to determine what the *Myrddin* were up to.

The leader of the *Myrddin*, Mrs. Parrish, had established the Facility, a self-sustaining, underground eco-system in west Texas, where they kept the Chosen: 5,000 children who were destined to be the future of mankind. Even before World War III and the overthrow of the Airlia, the *Myrddin* had determined that Earth was doomed. Pick your poison: by climate change, disease, nuclear war, the Airlia, the possible arrival of the Swarm—in sum, the odds were against sustainability of the human race on the planet. The plan was to seize Aspasia's damaged mothership in orbit, repair it, load the Chosen, and then wipe out Earth-bound mankind with a combination of three lethal viruses combined in one airborne superbug: the *Danse Macabre* which had a life span of six days; long enough to spread around the world. Then land and repopulate with the Chosen.

The plan was well underway when one of those 'end of human life' factors arrived at the edge of the Solar System: a massive Swarm Battle Core came out of FTLT.

As the Core traversed the Solar System toward Earth, a desperate race emerged for the future of mankind. Turcotte and his team managed to get some people on board the mothership although the Chosen had been loaded. A woman claiming to be Nikola Tesla's granddaughter, Professor Leahy, joined with them and helped move a group of apparent cast-offs from the Chosen—the Metabols—into the Facility, once the Chosen were on board the mothership.

Nosferatu, one of the Undead, and his partner Nekhbet, joined forces with Turcotte and came upon the means by which the *Myrddin* planned to disperse the *Danse Macabre* around the world.

As the Swarm Battle Core arrived in orbit, that one mothership, holding allies of Turcotte and Tesla's 'granddaughter' and the Chosen, escaped via FTLT to an unknown destination, leaving Turcotte in the *Fynbar* covering for them. This leads to **Area 51: Invasion**.

The Swarm began its Reaping process, systematically destroying the militaries of the world from orbit. Unknown to the Swarm, and everyone except Nosferatu and Nekhbet who allowed the *Myrddin* plan to proceed, the *Danse Macabre* was spread world-wide during this attack.

From orbit, the Core launched warships carrying the results of the Metamorphosis. These were genetically engineered creatures designed to 'reap' humans by capturing them with a parasitic organism and returning them to the Core for amalgamation. These creatures carrying the parasite were the monsters of our legends: dragons, kraken, Naga, Cthulhu and more.

Over seven billion humans were enthralled by Swarm parasites, marched onto the warships, flown up to the Battle Core, and absorbed into the primal ooze that is the 'blood' of the Core and the source from which the monsters are made and the Core regenerates its hull. Unfortunately for the Swarm, almost all of these humans were infected with the *Danse* and thus the Core was fatally infected. The Swarm flew the Core into the sun as a purge, leaving behind some warships and scout ships and clusters of monsters and Swarm on Earth that hadn't made it up to Core in time. There are also human survivors including Turcotte in the *Fynbar*, and the Metabols hiding in the Facility.

Area 51: Interstellar picks up on another world, Earth15, that is still under the control of the Airlia. There is a revolt brewing among the humans and they manage to overthrow the Airlia. As they celebrate their hard-earned victory, a mothership arrives overhead: the one that escaped Earth. As a curious side-note, at the end of Interstellar some humans who had been captured by the Swarm from other planets, had not been amalgamated into the organic base of the Core, but rather transferred to another type of Swarm Core, a Life Core, the interior of which was adapted to their survival and resembled their home world. What is the Swarm planning for them and the other Scale life forms inside?

Got it? A lot of other stuff happens in the books, but this is the main storyline.

This book takes us back to Earth at the end of *Area 51: Invasion* and Turcotte, the Metabols, Fades, Nosferatu and Nekhbet, Swarm monsters and the other survivors. All are left on an utterly ravaged planet.

But, Earth Abides, does she not?

And before we go forward with our story, we need to go to the distant past, close to a beginning that was also an end. To an empire of humans who ruled countless worlds from our planet and Solar System.

TALIANT FLEET BASE.

MILLIONS OF YEARS AGO

"It's a trap." Fleet Admiral was adamant, as he pointed at the message displayed on the screen in the front of the Star Chamber.

"Flexibility of thought has never been Fleet's forte," Librarian commented from her front row seat. "Or else we would still have a Fleet docked here. A single Armada at least. But I understand all we have remaining is one squadron?" She was a short, diminutive woman with a loud, deep voice. She was white-haired, with surprisingly bushy eyebrows that were her trademark. She dressed in the drab, unadorned grey pants and smock of those who attended the Compendium. The only adornment of rank was the pin of a scroll on her left collar.

The leaders, the remaining leaders, of Imperium were in the Star Chamber in Prime Ring on the equator of Taliant on the exterior of the station's outer hull. Besides Fleet Admiral in his medal bedecked black uniform, and Librarian, there was VicDep, who was nominally the leader of Imperium and other functionaries. Fleet Admiral wore the bright red of his position and five small black star bursts on his collar. Aides stood along the wall behind them. There were others with some power, but those were the three that mattered.

As Prime Ring rotated, they had an excellent view of Jupiter beneath their feet where the hull was clear. Earth, their home planet, was currently on the other side of the Solar System which seemed apropos for the grim tone of the meeting. While Earth still existed, Imperium City had been destroyed five years ago, which explained why VicDep and not the deceased PrimeMin, now ruled.

Taliant is in orbit between Mars and Jupiter. It is a sphere with the shell hull 1,200 miles in diameter. At full capacity, the interior could hold three Armadas, meaning its docking capabilities was three times that of the next largest fleet base in the far-flung Imperium. It is also the primary ship-building facility. Now it held the remnants of one battered squadron. These were the ships that had limped home after the last disastrous battle with Unity. There were also older ships of the line that had been decommissioned and awaited rendering, but were now being retrofitted and brought back to operational status. Despite the string of defeats, there were more shiny medals on Fleet Admiral's uniform than there had been before hostilities with Unity had begun.

Besides Fleet headquarters, Taliant is home to the three Academies: the Political, Military, and Science, each with their own storied histories and legacy of distinguished graduates. It had not been the seat of the Imperium's government; that had always remained on the home planet, Earth.

Had.

Imperium City, the center of the Imperium, had been built on an artificial island in the midst of a wide ocean. Five years ago, though, after the beginning of the Unity Rebellion, a sleeper cell of Unity activists had detonated a chain reaction of fusion bombs, utterly destroying the city.

The surprise attack had stunned the Imperium just months after rejection of the report from Unity of the Awakening. The outer colonists claimed that a unit from Fleet had caused the event by violating the law with an experimental weapons test. Fleet's version of events was that one of its recon squadrons had been ambushed by Unity Militia and wiped out.

Oddly, at least for those remaining leaders at Taliant, rather than turning most of the outer colonies against Unity, the destruction of the capital had rallied many subordinate star systems to the rebel side, including most of Fleet Militia.

Unity, of course, denied responsibility for the attack on the squadron, claiming the squadron had been conducting illegal weapons testing and had, and here's where the story got strange, been destroyed by that very planet, Light-Union-Twelve, the weapon had been deployed against. According to Unity, the planet had become sentient: aka the Awakening. Unity also claimed one of their ships had been destroyed during the Awakening and that it had initiated a quarantine of the L-U-Twelve system, and, furthermore, from here on out, all of Unity space was off limits to Imperium Fleet. Which Fleet, of course, immediately violated and thus all-out war between Imperium and Unity had begun.

Five years of brutal interstellar war had left those initiating events and claims murky, as many wars do, and it no longer seemed relevant to most on either side as billions were dead. The rapid escalation was the result of millennia of simmering resentment among the colonies who'd been loosely organized under the Unity banner. They'd always felt they weren't on equal footing with the home world and its earlier, inhabited planets that made up the center of Imperium.

"This is not the time for squabbling," Admiral said. He was a tall, distinguished looking man, which raised the question of how much of his rank was due to ability and how much to appearances. It had been a long time since Fleet had engaged an alien species. There had only been sporadic battling with other humans in troublesome colonies or quadrants and, the ever-present pirates in the outlying quadrants. There were many who whispered Imperial Fleet had grown soft with peace and failed to anticipate the rebellion.

Unity had been a political force among the colonies for thousands of years, spreading outward along the ever-shifting Boundary, representing those far from the center of Imperium. There had been occasional flare-ups by planets, but Unity had never turned on Imperium. The various fleets of Unity's assorted militias had always answered Fleet's call when needed to battle an alien encounter. Again, though, that had not occurred in hundreds of years and the ties between Fleet and Unity Militia had grown cold and distant.

"I'm not squabbling," Librarian said. "I'm pointing out the obvious. If only we had seen the obvious five years ago, acknowledged and dealt with the Awakening, perhaps we'd be in a different situation?"

Fleet Admiral stuck to the party line. "We've seen no proof of the Awakening. It's preposterous. A planet cannot be sentient. Unity ambushed our ships then sealed their space against us, which is illegal under Magnus Charter."

"You've never quite been able to explain the why of that encounter," Librarian pointed out.

"Why doesn't matter," Admiral snapped.

"Why not?" Librarian asked, in her own peculiar way of non-linear logic.

Admiral was confused. "Why not what?"

"Why can't a planet be sentient?"

Admiral waved a hand, dismissing the concept. "Unity are traitors."

"Unity has seen enough of something to rebel against us and seal their space," Librarian argued. "It began out there—" she gestured at the transparent hull beneath their feet. Visitors to Taliant were often disoriented by the arrangement where 'up' was inward, not outward on the station. "They said they have proof but we didn't want to see it."

"The 'proof' was the destruction of a squadron," Fleet Admiral said, "on a peaceful resource reconnaissance mission in that quadrant. There was an ambush by Unity. They have not changed their traitorous colors. They have always desired to be free of Imperium. Of course, we didn't hear that during the Sloth Wars."

"That was quite a while ago," Librarian said. "Unity has a different story about current events. They say your resource reconnaissance mission was a test of a dangerous new weapons technology along the Boundary and it triggered the Awakening."

"You've been making that baseless accusation since this began," Fleet Admiral said. He glared. "Some might say your words are treason, Librarian."

"Are *you* saying that?" Librarian challenged.

Taliant had some natural gravity because of its mass, but not anywhere near enough, so the Rings on the interior of the outer hull rotated at a speed sufficient to maintain approximately 1G. Ships of the Line and transports docked in huge interior bays where there was no atmosphere. They reached it through portals spaced around the hull. Along the inside of the outer hull in the various Rings, were the Academies, factories and other infrastructure that made Taliant self-sufficient. Except, of course, for the raw materials every civilization consumes. The planets of the Sol System had long been stripped of that and it required an unending stream of space-freighters from other systems to keep the Solar System, and Taliant, functioning. Most of those came from worlds under the Unity umbrella. While some black marketeers now braved Unity blockade, Imperium relied heavily on those worlds closer and still loyal. It wasn't enough for long term sustainability.

Here on the equator, in Prime Ring, which was the only one that rotated on the outside of the shell hull, were made the decisions that decided the fate of Imperium. Prime Ring was slightly over 1,200 miles in diameter, to fit outside Taliant Hull, and two miles wide. Above their heads, the hull was stationery as the Ring circled around it. All the other rings were inside, varying in widths in order to avoid the others, and with different orientations and velocity to maintain 1G. If one stood at the very center, which one could not do because of the fusion reactors there, and looked outward, it would be a dizzying array of massive turning rings inside a hull, except, of course, for Prime Ring.

It wasn't exactly certain who was in charge in practical terms. Fleet had taken command after the destruction of Imperium

City. After all, that was an act of war, the soldier's province. The ranking political officer still alive, VicDep, was a weak man. Although by the terms of Magnus Charter he was in control, he preferred to delegate authority regarding the war, and thus responsibility, to Fleet Admiral.

This had caused Librarian, the head of the Compendium, to become more and more vocal over time. Especially as Fleet suffered defeat after defeat and Unity grew to be the predominant power. From the beginning Librarian had urged a truce with Unity. She'd been adamant that the Awakening needed to be investigated. But almost everyone in Fleet, and on Taliant, indeed in Imperium, had lost loved ones in the war and the point of no return had been passed a long time ago.

Today, though, there was a most unusual development and the reason for this meeting: an unexpected request from Unity for a truce.

"I am speculating about treason," Admiral said, "based on your words."

VicDep finally stirred. "The first issue is whether we should reply to Unity."

Librarian was dumfounded. "Why wouldn't we? What do we have to lose beyond what we've already lost? Is there some secret plan to win this war we are currently losing?"

Fleet Admiral had been waiting for that opening. "We're not losing. We have interior lines, always a strategic advantage. We control most of our space."

Librarian raised a bushy, grey eyebrow. "For how long without resources from Unity space? And interior lines might be an optimistic way of saying we're surrounded."

Fleet Admiral gestured at his assistant and a holograph control pad appeared in front of him. He waved his hands through a couple of hexagons. A three-dimensional star map flickered into existence. It was one they were all familiar with: Imperium and the surrounding space. Bright orange indicated the region Imperium still controlled. It was slightly more than half what it had been at the start of the war which allowed Admiral his 'most'. Almost completely surrounding it was the fluorescent green of Unity, the colonies that had rebelled. Outside of that was the shimmering red line that marked the Boundary: the edge of known space. It probably wasn't up to date since Unity wasn't checking in with the latest their surveillance and exploration ships had discovered.

"This request for a truce does not come in a vacuum," Admiral said. "Here." There was a yellow spark. "Here. Here. Here." Three more sparks. "Our stealth probes report Unity Militia is withdrawing. Numerous FTLT drives engaged. That's four systems their warships are pulling back from."

"How do you know they're not advancing?" VicDep asked. "Or maneuvering for another offensive?"

"Because a stealth probe picked up all four squadrons assembling here." A yellow glow lit and remained, deep inside

Unity space; near the Boundary. The system containing Light-Union-Twelve.

Librarian immediately saw the significance. "That's where they claim the Awakening began. You've had a stealth probe there ever since your so-called recon squadron was wiped out, haven't you?"

"That's not important at the moment," Admiral said. "What's important is they are pulling back. Very quickly. In a manner our simulators say is not planned but reactionary."

"Why are they pulling back?" VicDep asked.

"We don't know," Admiral said.

"Why do you assume it's a good thing?" Librarian asked.

"It gives us time," Admiral said. "We will have a second squadron ready soon."

"We've lost Armadas," Librarian pointed out. "What difference will another squadron make?" An edge in her voice indicated she already knew, and feared, the answer.

"We are arming our refitted ships with a newly developed weapons system," Admiral said. "One that is capable of obliterating entire worlds." He waved his hands and a small flame lit up. "While Unity is distracted, we will take out Foolshome. The very heart of their resistance. Kill Speaker and the other leaders of Unity."

"You fool!" Librarian was on her feet. "Doing that will only harden their resolve, much as losing Imperium City hardened ours. Increase the brutality. We must make peace. This is a negative sum procedure."

Admiral ignored her and turned to VicDep. "I assume I have approval from Political to proceed with planning."

It was not a question., but VicDep nodded.

*****

"Are you afraid?" Librarian asked as she walked quickly along the corridor toward her executive office, not far from the Star Chamber.

Captain Tai was senior to Librarian, whose real name he didn't know. It was such an important position in Imperium that his supervisor was always called by her title. Tai had stood along the back wall during the meeting, with the other assistants.

He was dressed in Fleet Black with the red dagger pins indicating Marine on the high leather collar, one on either side, over the jugular. He was a solidly built man, well-muscled with that peculiar gait that indicated he came from a grav-heavy world. There was the slightest hitch to it because his right leg was artificial from just above the knee and despite being the best technology, the weight wasn't quite the same. His head was shaved as if he were on deployment, and tattooed hashmarks starting on the crown and extending back over his skull toward his spine indicated combat patrol deployments to the Boundary and against pirates and rebellious planets. His chest boasted no medals like Fleet Admiral. Marines didn't do medals.

"No, Librarian," Tai answered.

Compendium was the library for all three Academies, holding the accumulation of knowledge of Imperium. Tai's assignment was unusual for someone from Fleet, particularly a Marine. Normally a graduate of the Science Academy who had served Compendium for decades held the position.

"I knew that a Marine would say that, especially one as experienced as you, but you should be concerned at the very least, Captain," she snapped as they entered her office. The door slid shut behind them and she went behind her desk, sitting in the elevated chair that put her on eye level with visitors. "Fleet Admiral just admitted, without directly doing so, that they did try to test a weapon out there five years ago. And whatever they did brought about the Awakening. They didn't just invent a planet killer in the past week. They've had it all along. Have they not?"

Tai straightened. "I have heard nothing of such a weapon. Not then. Not now. However, it is certainly possible for Fleet to keep such a thing secret at one of their dark sites. The Code is very strict about security lapses."

"I was not accusing you, Captain," Librarian said. "I was asking if you agreed it's likely they've had it all along."

Tai nodded. "Yes. It is. But—" he hesitated.

"Continue," she snapped.

"How can a planet be alive, Librarian?"

"I don't know." She drummed short fingers on her desktop, frowning. "Not good. Not good at all."

"A planet being sentient?"

"No." She grunted. "Well, I suppose that might not be good either."

"The new squadron with the weapon, Librarian?" Tai asked. "It doesn't sound as if it's ready for deployment."

"No," Librarian snapped. "The new squadron is an old squadron that's been sitting in Taliant for five years. They've had the same technology ever since they sent the supposed recon squadron to the L-U-Twelve system to test it. They haven't used it again, which means?" She waited for Tai to fill in the answer.

"They're afraid of it," Tai said. "They also suspect it might have had the effect Unity claims."

Librarian nodded. "Very good. It scares Fleet. Admiral might be a fool, but he's not stupid. There is a difference. That he wants to use it now shows desperation. He's seizing what he views is an opportunity. That scares me."

"It *is* a desperate situation, Librarian," Tai pointed out. "Fleet is trying to minimize it, but the losses have been high. The honored rolls are getting longer every day." His eyes grew slightly unfocused. "It is hard to remember friends lost just five years ago with all that has happened since."

"It is worse than Admiral realizes," Librarian said. "Unity pulling back to L-U-Twelve. Asking for a truce. Something is happening out there and he's not concerned about that, only seeing the immediate tactical gain and not the strategic picture. They *do* still teach strategy at the Military Academy, do they not?"

Tai was used to Librarian's digs. "They do, Librarian. All five years. Required for all cadets."

She sighed. "This squadron with supposedly new weapons isn't good either. There is a simple question Admiral has apparently never considered: if L-U-Twelve became sentient and wiped out his squadron and the Unity ship, what does it mean in the greater scheme of things? Can any planet come alive? Earth? We still have many planets loyal to Imperium. Think of the carnage if this spreads? It will be a war unlike anything Imperium has ever experienced. How can we live without worlds?"

"What can we do?" Tai asked.

Librarian laughed, transforming her face for a moment into the benevolent grandmother that she also was. "That is what I like about you, Captain Tai. Your drive." She tapped a finger on her desk, then made a decision. "Our ancestors, long ago, when humanity was confined only to Earth, were, of course, primitive. There was much they didn't, couldn't, comprehend."

Librarian saw the confused look on his face. "Bear with me, Captain Tai. Because we think we know more than we know and that is the path of folly. The path Admiral is running down full tilt. Because one thing we don't know, and it's fundamental, is where did this all come from?"

"All what?" Tai asked.

"The universe."

THE PRESENT: AFTERMATH OF WORLD WAR III AND REAPING

THE EARTH

The wound wasn't deep on a planetary scale, barely three miles into the lithosphere. But it had occurred at a junction of plates, a subduction known as the Cascadia Zone off the northwest coast of the North American continent. The zone is roughly six hundred miles long and seventy to one hundred miles wide, in the ocean stretching from Northern California to British Columbia.

The detonation, over 100 megatons, had been the largest man-made explosion ever. A pittance compared to what the planet was capable of. For example, the Mount Toba super-volcanic eruption 70,000 years ago, was 100 times greater than the largest volcanic eruption in recorded history at Mount Tambora. Toba threw so much ash into the air that it brought a year-round winter to the world for over a decade and almost wiped out the human race as temperatures dropped and sunlight was blocked; rather similar to what was occurring now as a result of the nuclear weapons that had been utilized.

Mount Toba produced a genetic 'bottleneck' where the entire human race was reduced to less than ten thousand people. Everyone who came afterward was descended from this fragment. Sadly, there were less than that many humans left alive now. Between World War III and the Swarm Reaping, there were now less than a few thousand humans alive.

But Mount Toba happened *by* the earth, not *to* the earth and went upward, not inward. Toba had been a necessary release of power from the inside of the planet. Part of a natural evolution that has occurred as long as the planet has been in existence. Change is the one constant.

This man-made explosion had occurred underwater where the planet's crust is thinnest. It penetrated the outer surface of the planet into the mantle, just a scratch in the geologic scale, a half mile into a band over eighteen hundred miles thick, making up eighty percent of the Earth's volume and consisting of magma and rock. The deepest mine ever dug by humans had never come close to breaking through the mantle, halting at two and a half miles into the crust. The underground nuclear tests conducted by various countries in the previous century had been subsurface events, none deeper than a half mile. Never before had humans penetrated into the mantle.

The explosion was the result of another human sacrifice against the invading Swarm. The aliens, while mostly focused on Reaping the human population and bringing it on board the Battle Core to be amalgamated, had also sent a single warship deep into the Cascadia subduction zone with a cargo of hadesarchaea. These are genetically designed thermopile microorganisms that can exist in places where other life would perish from the heat. Their mission had been to invade that fault line, multiply, and spread along the fault lines around the planet to degrade them and make the crust unstable, putting the finishing touch on wiping out all life on the planet.

The Swarm made sure that no remnant of Scale life was left after it Reaped a planet and this was the final touch. In essence the hadesarchaea was to be a planetary virus infecting Earth. By consuming the mantle as it spread, it would destabilize the fault lines between all the continental plates. This would cause dozens of Mount Toba's, filling the sky with so much ash, a deep ice age would result. The planet would eventually resettle and reboot, but only after millions of years.

More importantly, it would not be a natural event.

A Russian submarine, the *Sarov*, carrying a 'doomsday' weapon, the 100-megaton torpedo Poseidon, had obliterated that Swarm warship and the hadesarchaea when the courageous captain detonated it while diving his command deep into the subduction zone.

It might be considered a severe cauterization of a potentially fatal wound for life on the planet. However, the warhead had also been seeded with Cobalt-60 because it had been designed to be a doomsday weapon against fellow humans. While this killed the hadesarchaea, it left that point in the Earth's mantle contaminated with radiation. Was the cure worse than the virus?

Both events had been noticed. And felt but not yet understood.

Forces long dormant were awakening.

THE SOLAR SYSTEM

After the self-destruction of their massive Battle Core, the remaining Swarm warships and scout ships were vectoring toward interstellar space in a random pattern, each on its own. They faced an interminable journey at STL speed in interstellar space since none were capable of FTLT: Faster Than Light Transit. The Swarm, however, was never in a hurry. The individual Swarm inside the small scout ships were capable of going into dormancy that lasted centuries if needed. Those in the larger warships could do the same, and many did, with a handful maintained as duty crew, that would live and die and regenerate anew as time passed.

Scale (intelligent) life had never sacrificed itself so completely in order to battle the Swarm as had just happened. Over seven billion reaped humans, infected with a trio of deadly human invented viruses, the *Danse Macabre*, had been absorbed by the Core, with the Swarm realizing its mistake only after it was also infected. To prevent spreading the contagion, the Supreme Swarm had flown the Battle Core, a spaceship 6,000 miles in diameter by 4,000 miles polar, into the system's star, a brutal, but effective containment.

No Swarm Battle Core had ever been destroyed in battle and technically, one might consider this self-immolation a draw since almost all humans had been reaped and humanity's own wars brought on nuclear winter on their planet. Still, it was an unprecedented event.

The surviving Swarm on the smaller ships all shared one thing. A message about this solar system to relay to any Swarm Battle Core they came across. The message was simple. It consisted of a warning:

Beware this place. Here there be humans.

However, one warship, with its attendant scout ships hangered on board, remained behind, lurking in the Asteroid Belt. Its mission was to observe and record what would happen next.

DAVIS MOUNTAINS, TEXAS

"Here there be monsters," Sofia whispered as she surveyed the valley. One could not help but notice the large, two-legged Swarm-generated beast slowly making its way below them. "Curious."

Sofia was pre-teen, with gangly limbs she'd grow into. She had dark, Latino skin and long, thick black hair. She wore a light gray jumpsuit, like all of the Metabols. There were one thousand, five hundred and twenty-four Metabols in the Facility. Two dozen had accompanied Sofia and her mentor, Asha, outside of their underground Facility to see the Fades disappear into the ashfall and find a dog, as they had been instructed by a dying wish.

"We should get back to the Facility," Asha said, not quite an order from the adult because Sofia, and the other youngsters were Metabols, adjusted to be 'different'. The problem was that Asha, and the other scientists who'd overseen the project, weren't quite sure what the differences were. There was one thing that was certain: Sofia, and her pre-teen comrades, displayed an intelligence and composure far beyond their years. Thus, the trepidation in Asha's voice about telling them what to do.

Asha was lying next to Sofia, peering over the top of a ridgeline near the entrance to the Facility in the Davis Mountains of west Texas. The other Metabols were gathered behind them, all within a few years of Sofia's age. Seated among them was a dog, Rex, a German Shepherd/Chow/ mutt, once owned by the very first Metabol, Darlene, who had allowed herself to be reaped aboard the mothership to relay important information about the nature of the Swarm. On the dog's collar was a USB key which Darlene had let Sofia know was important. How she had been able to impart this information telepathically across the distance between the Battle Core in space and the Metabols hidden in the Facility was another aspect that Asha didn't understand.

"We should see what's on Darlene's USB," Asha urged in a low voice, hoping some of the answers were on it. She wore a biological hazard suit, in fear of the *Danse Macabre* viruses, but the hood was pulled down since Sofia and the Metabols had eschewed safety and confirmed that the viruses had burned out after six days as they'd been designed. Asha was a tall woman with ebony skin. Her skull was shaved and scrolled with faint tattoos.

They were covered by ash drifting down from the sky, the results of an all-out nuclear exchange on the other side of the world between India and Pakistan that left all their major cities burning proving the theory of mutually assured destruction. Asha's handheld detector indicated the radiation level was acceptable for a short period of time. She knew it was not the radiation that would doom all on the surface, but the pervading cloud of ash that would usher in a long winter. Their only hope for long term survival was the self-contained ecosystem of the Facility.

"We shouldn't stay out here too long," Asha said.

"It is odd that the beast is still functioning with the Core destroyed," Sofia noted, ignoring Asha's discomfort and exhibiting no fear, just curiosity. "Darlene said there was a single, master brain of the Swarm on the Core. A Supreme Swarm. That is gone now."

"Who or what's controlling it then?" Asha asked.

Sofia shrugged. "Instinct." She frowned. "There are Swarm left behind, though. Those that didn't make it onto the Core before it left. Not many, but they are out there. I can sense them." Sofia glanced at Asha. "The beast is Cthulhu. It is odd that H.P. Lovecraft knew of this specific type of creature and even drew a rather decent approximation of it. One wonders which came first: was it part of a deep genetic memory he drew upon or did the Swarm create these monsters drawing on our own fears?"

The creature she was referring to was thirty-five feet tall and an anthropoid in that it walked upright on two legs and had two arms, but little else resembled human form. The legs were bent backward at the knee and the feet ended in splayed claws that dug into the sand as it stalked along the valley. The arms ended in similar claws and were webbed to the body from shoulder to elbow. The skin was rubbery, scaly, mottled dark green and black. The head was the stuff of nightmares: a lump of writhing tentacles around a large, gaping maw. Two of the tentacles were so long they reached the ground. Two red, beady eyes were just above the mouth and the entire head slanted back to a large bulb with a drooping sack that extended down the back to the waist.

The Cthulhu paused, shifting back and forth on its legs, several tentacles wavering in the air, then it set out with a purpose toward the far side of the valley.

Sofia pointed out its destination. "A Fade."

A boy, the same age as Sofia, and dressed in the same type of jumpsuit, was two hundred yards from the Cthulhu. There had been forty-two Fades in comas in the Facility, apparently failed Metabols. But Sofia and other Metabols had placed their hands on the unconscious children and brought them back to some form of awareness. The Fades had exited the Facility without a word, going off into separate directions. Despite all her schooling and work in the Facility with the Chosen and Metabols, Asha was accepting she was out of her depth scientifically with whatever had happened to these children, both Metabols and Fades.

The Fade made no move to run as the beast approached. In fact, he showed no fear, no emotion, in the presence of the Swarm monster. The Cthulhu reached him. Two tentacles grabbed the boy, lifted him high, then stuffed him into the maw.

All without a sound or movement of resistance or protest.

"My God," Asha whispered as the boy's form appeared inside the sack on the back of the Cthulhu's head. He was not struggling. Indeed, the boy was outlined against the rubbery skin, arms and legs spread wide, as if embracing his horrid captivity. As they watched, the human form slowly dissipated.

"He is part of," Sofia said, turning away from the reaping and sliding down a few feet before standing.

Asha joined her. "Part of what? The Swarm?"

Sofia shook her head, her ponytail swaying. "No. The Core is gone. There are their beasts, like the Cthulhu and others, along with some individual Swarm on the planet, several not far from here, but without the Core, they have lost direction. Before she became part of, Darlene let us know that the Swarm had a single, controlling brain, somewhere deep inside the Core. That's gone now. The Fade is part of the Cthulhu, which is an extension of the Swarm, but the Cthulhu is now part of the Fade."

"He's dead," Asha said.

"He is part of," Sofia repeated. "He still lives. Just in a different way."

She was looking past Sofia and the cluster of Metabols and stiffened at what just appeared overhead. "We have to run for the doors!"

Sofia looked over her shoulder. A dragon, another of the Swarm's engineered monsters, had just flown over the mountain that was on top of the Facility. With a wingspan of eighty feet, it was a black figure outlined in the grey downfall of ash. It banked and went into a dive, directly toward Asha and the Metabols.

Asha knew they would never make it to the doors in time, nor should they attempt to, because that would reveal the hidden entrance to the Facility. She subconsciously hunched over, waiting for the dragon to breath snake-like parasites rather than fire. Parasites which would overwhelm and slither inside her body, take over her nervous system, and put her in the thrall of the Swarm.

"Be calm, Asha." Sofia reached out and grabbed Asha's hand in hers, as the other two dozen Metabols also joined together.

A blast of air as the dragon's wing beat hard, slowing its descent as it came within fifty feet. Its mouth opened to spew forth the parasites. At that moment, something large leapt over Asha and the Metabols heads.

Cthulhu landed with a heavy thud on the slope between them and the dragon, reversed knees bending far to absorb the shock, then straightening. The dragon's wings beat harder, trying to halt its attack, but it was moving too quickly. The dragon, much lighter in weight, slammed into an immovable object. With one clawed hand, Cthulhu grabbed the dragon by the throat and held it, red eyes staring into red eyes.

While Cthulhu's hand squeezed the throat, forcing the dragon to open its mouth, a tentacle reached into its own maw and withdrew a mass of squirming snake-like parasites. It stuffed them into the dragon's mouth, the tentacle sliding deep down the throat, then coming back out, empty.

The beating of the dragon's wings began to slow, its efforts to escape lessening.

Then it became still. Cthulhu let go of its neck. The dragon folded its wings in and stared at them with dark red eyes. As did Cthulhu.

"What are they doing?" Asha whispered to Sofia.

"They are part of," Sofia said.

"Why aren't they attacking?" Asha asked. "Did the Fade take it over?"

"They are merged," Sofia said. "They are one."

"What are they going to do?" Asha asked.

Sofia shook her head. "I don't know. But they won't harm us." Sofia let go of her hand and reached down, running her fingers through Rex's fur. She looked up at the dark, foreboding sky. "You are correct. We must go back inside the Facility."

AIRSPACE, NORTH AMERICA

Mike Turcotte, ex-Special Forces, and the leader of the battle against the Airlia, the alien race that had secretly controlled humanity since the time of Atlantis, had now helped guide a victory over a second, and even more deadly alien race, the Swarm.

The victory, however, had been the ultimate in Pyrrhic. Most of the world's population had been reaped and incinerated aboard the Battle Core as it self-destructed into the sun. Almost all of those not reaped were dead from the *Danse Macabre*.

He flew the *Fynbar* into the atmosphere, having witnessed the end of the Core. Mission accomplished, but again, at what cost? The lone bright spot was that just before the Swarm assault, the Mothership, containing the Chosen, specially selected human children originally from the Facility, had punched into Faster Than Light Transit with the spaceship controlled by his Russian friend Yakov and Professor Leahy, along with the Airlia, Nyx.

Destination unknown.

The *Fynbar* was human designed and built, and brought to Earth by two humans who'd been part of a successful planet-wide revolt against the Airlia from a different colony. The male, Gwalcmai, had died at the Battle of Camlann during a battle between Airlia proxies posing as Arthur and Mordred. The female, Lisa Duncan, had perished recently, crashing the second mothership into the Airlia communication array on Mars, preventing an emergency signal for help from being sent out.

Saucer shaped, the *Fynbar* had a bulge in the forward center and two large pods in the rear, which housed the STL engines. It was dull gray and designed with two seats inside, actually depressions, for pilot and co-pilot in the forward center facing the displays and controls. There had been two deep sleep/regeneration tubes in the rear of the cabin, but one had been given to Mrs. Parrish in order to get Yakov, Leahy and others on board the mothership. There was one tube remaining and a man's body was in it, a blank slate for whatever consciousness was uploaded into it.

Turcotte was descending over Seattle, where he'd left Nosferatu and Nekhbet. His muddled plan was to collect the two Undead and then head to the Facility in Texas and link up with the Metabols. Beyond that, the future was dark. Turcotte was tired to the bone from the nonstop action since he'd been assigned to Area 51; which seemed like forever ago. It seemed he'd been fighting all his life.

While returning to Earth, he'd seen that the dark smear of ash originating from the Indian subcontinent was now covering most of the planet. His mind churned questions that he had no answers to. How would that affect the weather? Of course, humans had been doing a number on the climate for a long time anyway. Would the lack of industry and cars and planes and all the rest offset the ash cover? Would nuclear winter offset global warming in some ironic way?

How many were left alive on Earth? Asha and the Metabols. Who else? Perhaps some submarine crews. Some survivalists in the middle of nowhere? Turcotte had no idea how thorough the Reaping had been. Pile on top of that the *Danse* and the odds were downright lousy.

Turcotte keyed the radio. "Nosferatu?"

Nothing but static. Had the two Undead lived up their moniker or had they perished? He could see devastation along the shoreline of Puget Sound when it came into view at five thousand feet and he had visibility through the ash. The tsunami from Poseidon's detonation had obliterated the shoreline. Turcotte briefly wondered about radiation levels, not just from Poseidon, but the various nuclear exchanges during World War III.

Turcotte gasped as the implant in his brain pulsed with power, sending a spike through the center, between the two hemispheres. It was so severe that for several moments it blinded him. When he could see again, as the pulse receded, he was less than five hundred feet above ground level. Vampyr's island, where he'd left the two Undead, was too far away given his altitude and the uncertainty of when he would lose consciousness. He was above another island to the north of it, Whidbey, and he chose the ferry parking lot on the south end as his destination.

The *Fynbar* slammed into the pavement hard as another bolt of pain cleaved through Turcotte's brain. He let go of the controls and the spaceship powered down, leaving him in complete darkness. As the pain lessened, he leaned forward, resting head in hands. He had no idea what the implant was or how it had been emplaced. In fact, given recent discoveries, he was uncertain *he* was who he'd thought he was. His entire past might well be a lie.

Who was he? What was the implant? Why was it coming alive? Duncan has said it was possible she'd put it in but had no memory of doing so or what it was. Given the fact she'd denied her own past to herself, Turcotte saw no reason to believe, or not believe, her speculation.

Who had done this to him? Why?

A third spike of pain, greater than any before caused him to scream and then he passed out, head in hands as he slumped to the side of the pilot's depression.

Blood dribbled, drop by drop, from his nose.

PAINE FIELD, WASHINGTON STATE

"If I can't feed," Nekhbet complained, indicating the two Russians, "what is your plan for them? More importantly, what is your plan for us in this forsaken place?"

Nosferatu indicated one of the many airliners parked on the tarmac of the Boeing Factory. "We have transportation. There will be survivors. More than just these two." He put an arm around Nekhbet's thin shoulders. "We will make do. Don't you trust me, my love?"

"You use that line too often," Nekhbet said. She was as tall as Nosferatu, a tad over six feet, and they both had pale, white skin. Their eyes set them apart from humans, with red pupils. Given the dimness of the ash laden sky, they had dispensed with their usual wraparound sunglasses.

The two humans Nekhbet wanted to dine on were the only survivors from the Russian submarine, *Sarov*; allowed to leave by the captain before he took his command on its fatal dive. Tasha and her boyfriend were young, terrified, and utterly lost as to what was going on.

They were standing outside the largest building in the world, the Boeing Everett Factory, which sprawled over the land for one hundred acres. It was from here that the planes carrying the *Danse Macabre* had taken off to deliver their deadly loads. Flown by *Myrddin* pilots who had not been aware their planes were rigged to blow up as they attempted to land at major airports around the world.

Numerous airliners were parked all about along with a helicopter. The ground was covered with a thickening layer of ash. The trees surrounding the assembly building and runway were also coated with them. While the Puget Sound area was known for being overcast, this was darker, grimmer.

Nosferatu cocked his head. "Do you hear that?"

"You've always had better hearing," Nekhbet said. "I, on the other hand, was granted the talent of—"

"Hush," Nosferatu snapped.

Nekhbet pouted while Nosferatu scanned the sky. "There!" He indicated the *Fynbar* dropping toward Whidbey Island, just a few miles across Puget Sound. "Turcotte."

"Isn't that a bit fast?" Nekhbet wondered as it disappeared from sight behind the trees lining the Boeing runway.

"Something is wrong," Nosferatu said, which caused Nekhbet to burst into laughter and the two Russians to huddle closer together.

"Really? You are the master of understatement, my dear. Which something?" She spread her hands, taking in the ash drifting down from the dark sky. "At least we don't have to worry about the sun anymore."

"We must get to Turcotte," Nosferatu said. He gestured to the two Russians. "What are your names?"

The girl answered, looking far too young in her sailor's uniform. "I am Tasha. This is Peter. We are from the *Sarov.*"

"Let me have Tasha," Nekhbet said, not bothering to lower her voice. "You can have Peter. He looks like a healthy young lad."

"What are you?" Peter demanded, stepping in front of Tasha and raising his fists. "What do you want of us?"

"*I*," Nekhbet said, "am the daughter of Osiris and this is the son of Horus. We are of the First Age of Egypt, when the gods ruled and humans obeyed." She sighed. "Things have gone downhill from there, obviously. Personally, I would like to drink your blood."

"Quiet," Nosferatu said. "Be nice."

"I've never been nice," Nekhbet said, "but I am always hungry. Really, you should accept me for who I am."

"We will not drink your blood," Nosferatu assured the two Russians. He turned to Nekhbet. "You are making—" he paused as she leapt past him.

Nosferatu wheeled about as Nekhbet blocked Peter's knife thrust toward his back. She had the arm holding the knife in her grip and snapped the forearm, the knife falling to the ground.

Nosferatu forced himself to hold back as Nekhbet spun the Russian man about and opened her mouth wide, teeth clamping down as his neck.

"Peter!" Tasha cried out, taking a step toward the couple in their bloody embrace.

"Stay," Nosferatu ordered, getting between her and their respective partners. Tasha dropped to her knees; hands held up in supplication. "Please save him."

Nosferatu shook his head. "It's too late."

"He was only defending me," Tasha pleaded.

"As was Nekhbet for me," Nosferatu replied. He knelt and lifted her chin with his hand. "Do you want to live?"

Tasha nodded.

"Good," Nosferatu said. "We need people who want to live." He stood and waited until Nekhbet was done.

His partner dropped the Russian's lifeless body, her face flush. "You're not going to take her?"

"No," Nosferatu said. "And she's mine. Under my protection."

Nekhbet shrugged, sated for the moment. "The time may come when she will be needed." Nekhbet smiled, revealing blood stained teeth.

Nosferatu pointed at the helicopter he'd flown over from Vampyr's Island. "We must go to Turcotte."

"And then?" Nekhbet demanded.

"One crisis at a time," Nosferatu said.

GEOLOGIC RESEARCH STATION, CALIFORNIA

When Gina Tarranti was eight years old, her father had forced her to camp alone in a pup tent in the alley between their apartment building and the next one in Brooklyn. She'd been embarrassed and scared to be alone in the wilds of New York City. She hadn't known, until years later, that he'd spent the night on the fire escape two stories up, keeping watch over her.

She'd spent the night wide awake until exhaustion overtook her around three in the morning.

When the sun rose the next day and she crawled out from under the canvas tarp, she'd been relieved. And also, a tiny bit more confident about her place in the world. As the years went by until she went off to college, he'd layered more and more tasks on her. Once he'd rented a car and they'd driven 'upstate', which for a New York Native meant north of Westchester County. He'd left her in a cave in the Adirondacks for an entire week armed with just a knife, a canteen and a poncho and the survival skills he'd taught her. She'd practiced those skills with an urgency she'd not experienced before, but also explored the cave, going far into the darkness until she came up a narrow crack in the rock. Cool air blew up out of the crack, indicating it went somewhere and came back out on the surface. She reached in with her arm, feeling as far she could. She'd finished the week ten pounds lighter, but confident in her abilities. And with a deep fascination in what lay deep beneath that crack.

She'd never thought any of his various tasks were unusual until she arrived at college and was telling her room-mate about them. The look of astonishment had taught her to keep that part of her childhood close to herself.

It had been a fluke of scheduling that she'd been on duty two hundred feet below ground in the San Andreas Fault Geologic Research Station when the Swarm attacked. She wasn't supposed to be here, but a fellow PhD candidate had decided to elope and Gina was covering for her.

She was that type of person.

And now she was alive. She had to keep reminding herself of that fact despite the stale, hot air and darkness. The fact that she had no idea what was currently going on above her and was alone were problematic, but underneath it all, she had a feeling she was fortunate to be here.

She'd followed the approach of the Swarm Battle Core on her computer via the fiber optic cable to the University. Not long after the Core went into orbit, that feed went dead. She'd made the decision after the link was cut to remain until someone came to her, because the size of the Battle Core had more than enough to convince her that things were not going to turn out well.

Better safe, two hundred feet down, than sorry. She could take care of herself for a while.

Her instruments were designed to pick up the slightest of tremors in the Fault and the planet. She'd noted the string of explosions and although she'd never seen the like before, knew from past records that they were nuclear explosions on the planet. Most on the other side of the world. Not long after, she'd felt the rock around her shudder from some powerful event on this side of the world. Unbeknownst to her, it was the detonation of Poseidon, the Russian nuclear weapon, far to the north, off the coast of the Pacific Northwest.

That had strengthened her resolve to stay deep. She was safe here. There was a steel hatch in the floor of small building on the surface that covered the entrance to the shaft. The lab was a chamber ten feet long by eight wide. Half of that space was filled with monitoring gear, including the emitter which fired powerful electromagnetic pulses into the planet for research and monitoring. The bounce back was recorded not only here, but with sister-stations all around the world. Depending on the strength and wavelength of what was received, they could extrapolate the composition of what it passed through.

Gina had her sleeping pad and day pack. There were also several gallon jugs of water she'd hurriedly filled before securing the hatch. She had her small camping stove with a couple of bottles of gas and freeze-dried meals, so in essence, other than aliens invading overhead, this wasn't much different than any other camping trip.

Despite the loss of the main line providing internet and electricity, the chamber had power provided by an array of solar panels on the surface. Gina allocated based on priority: keeping the monitoring instruments running and recording data. She also kept to the research schedule, sending out pulses into the planet as required.

The data wasn't making sense.

There was a lot of surface activity. Explosions at varying distances, all over the world. But there was also unusual subsurface activity. Earthquakes, tremors and other readings she'd never seen before. It would take months back at the University to make sense of it all.

Four days ago, there'd been banging on the hatch and she'd climbed the ladder. When she got to the top and reached to unlatch it, blood-curdling screams had given her pause. They'd lasted for several moments, then there'd been silence. She'd hung there, one arm looped through the top rung of the ladder, the other hand on the latch.

The screams nor the banging reoccurred. She'd just made the decision to open it and see what had happened when another sound caused her to pause. A slithering noise on top of the hatch caused her to pull her hand back. That had lasted a few minutes and then there was silence.

For the first time she was scared.

Gina had climbed back down and inventoried her supplies, focusing on the water as that was the most critical. She'd been rationing and now tightened that restriction. With her new plan she estimated she could last another eight days before she would need more.

The power from the solars was steadily diminishing, forcing her to reduce the amount of time she ran the instruments, something she regretted because it was all so unique.

Sitting cross-legged in the dark, she had a moment of inspiration. If the other geologic stations were still on line, they would be picking up her pulses. Her father had made her learn Morse code, among many other seemingly arcane skills. Dots and dashes could certainly be manifested via pulse. She powered up the emitter, the glow from the screen the only illumination in the lab. She began tapping an SOS, something she figured even someone not trained in Morse might understand. If she got an answer, she could open a dialogue and learn more. But for now, it would suffice to know she wasn't alone.

She tapped for two minutes, sending powerful pulses into the earth. Then the screen flickered and died, having drained the backup batteries. She'd have to wait for the feeble draw from the solars to recharge them.

She lay on her sleeping mat, staring up at absolute darkness.

Ten minutes later, a distant noise, more a vibration in the rock itself, roused her from a half-slumber. She turned on the small light. Cocked her head. Put a hand to the rock floor. A definite vibration, but not anything she'd ever experienced before. She leaned over and placed her ear to the rock. A distant, rolling, rumbling noise from—Gina frowned—below. Far below. She didn't know how she knew that, and it wasn't particularly scientific, but it was deep.

Was the fault active? Gina glanced up at the ladder. The vertical tunnel was lined with corrugated steel but if the quake was strong enough, that would crumble like paper and she'd be trapped. She'd been in here for a half-dozen minor quakes, but this was different. Deeper. There was something about it that was disturbing in a way she sensed but couldn't quite figure out.

Gina stood. She slung her daypack over her shoulder, turned on her halogen flashlight, using some of the precious battery.

She reached for the ladder as the entire chamber began to vibrate. Not intermittently, but steadily. The rumble escalated to a keening noise, as if the Earth itself were screaming. As Gina pulled herself up the first rungs, the stone floor of the lab ripped asunder just beneath her feet.

Clinging to the ladder she looked down. The chasm was a foot wide but strangely ran perpendicular to the fault, east-west.

Gina climbed as fast as she could amidst ear shattering noise as the rock split below and to the side, adjacent to the shaft. She desperately gripped a shivering rung with both hands, dropping the flashlight. One of her feet slipped off and she scrambled to regain her footing.

That was when she realized that even without the flashlight that she could see. A faint red glow. From below. She didn't want to, half-knowing, half-fearing what she would see, but she looked down. The widening crack, unlike her first cave, was bright red deep inside. As she watched, she realized the red was approaching. Fast.

Gina scrambled up the shaking ladder. Now she could feel the heat. Her up hand slipped, missing the next rung. She pushed up with her feet to compensate, grabbed the one above, continued, halfway to the hatch. She could barely think amidst the crescendo of noise surrounding her, but all her focus was on making it to the top.

Hotter.

Three quarters of the way. There was no point looking down. She had to get out.

She reached the hatch, sweat pouring off her body. The heat blistering. Grabbed the hatch and began turning it.

Sizzling, boiling. The magma lapped over her feet.

Gina screamed. Luckily the magma was surging upward so swiftly, it enveloped her in less than a second, terminating her agony. It blew off the hatch and sent a spout of red-hot molten rock thirty feet into the air and dumping her cindered corpse to the side.

The magma stopped and then retreated down the shaft.

The earth was still.

For the moment.

MONS OLYMPUS, MARS

An Airlia mothership is shaped like a black cigar, a mile in length and a quarter mile in diameter. The impact of such a craft on the surface of a planet at high speed is a significant event. However, when it crashes into the largest mountain in the Solar System, the scale of the result is diminished somewhat. Mons Olympus is over fifteen miles high. The base of the extinct volcano is three hundred and fifty miles in width. It, along with the other mountains in its range, make up the Tarsis Bulge, a terrain feature so massive it affects the rotation of Mars.

Lisa Duncan, formerly Donnchadh, had crashed the mothership into the FTL communications array the surviving Airlia from the Cydonia outpost had been building to send a message to their fleet for assistance. The resulting crater was a half-mile deep. There were pieces of the ship, none very large despite the fact the craft had been capable of withstanding the interstellar stresses of Faster Than Light Transit. There was, however, one battered, but intact portion. The bridge of the mothership was specifically designed to maintain integrity under the worst possible scenarios, even such a crash. Though the cockpit had maintained integrity, the g-forces of the crash reduced Duncan and Artad to splattered goo.

Lisa Duncan had been at the helm of the mothership when it impacted Mars. Artad, the leader of the Airlia police, the Kortad, who'd come to Earth to learn why Aspasia had taken the outpost off-line, had just entered the cockpit of the mothership seconds before the crash, the hatch automatically shutting behind him.

The assumption by Turcotte and the others on the Mars mission had been that Duncan was killed in a crash nothing could survive, even having partaken of the Grail. They were correct. Even the Airlia virus couldn't pull together a body that had disintegrated.

But Duncan had had more than just the virus in her. She'd also had an implant in the base of her brain like Turcotte's, something she'd been unaware of.

The implant, a dark sphere just a quarter inch in diameter, lay in the lowest spot in the compartment, where it had rolled to after her skull atomized in the impact. Incredibly thin tendrils of metal extended from it into the closest molecules of organic and inorganic material. It drew what it needed. Like a metal weed, additional tendrils spread out, sliding along the floor and walls, now searching for the remains of Lisa Duncan. They also found the remains of Artad, the Airlia who'd been in here when she crashed the ship. It ignored that.

The largest piece of her was barely visible, but each was carried along the line to the sphere where it was pulled together.

Cell by cell, the implant was rebuilding what had been Lisa Duncan.

THE PAST

PRIOR TO THE CRASH OF THE MOTHERSHIP INTO MARS

WEEKS EARLIER, GULF OF MEXICO

The Swarm controlled human interrogator worked quickly, ignoring the blood that was splattering everywhere. He'd removed a three-inch diameter section of Lisa Duncan's skull, exposing the interior. He'd then made a slit through the three protective membranes surrounding the brain. He didn't blink as he sliced through the pia mater, the innermost layer and a spurt of cerebrospinal fluid hit him in the face.

He continued into the cerebrum so he could get to the artery that was continually rupturing due to extreme conditioning. It was short-circuiting his attempts to discover the location of the planet Duncan had come from. He couldn't stop the conditioning impressed into the very cells there, so he did the next best thing. He put a shunt into the artery and bypassed that section.

As he did this, new flesh was already regenerating, beginning to reseal the protective membrane, a result of Duncan's partaking of the Grail. He got the shunt in place and exited the hole. He watched as the damage was repaired internally and bone began to grow around the opening in the skull. When the wound was closed, he picked up the drill and turned her head so he had access to the rear. He drilled, repeating the process of entering her brain. He found a metal sphere, a quarter inch in diameter. Using surgical magnification, he could see that several small filaments ran from the sphere into Duncan's brain.

This was unexpected.

He grabbed a set of long narrow pincers and slid the thin tongs into the hole, seizing the sphere. He yanked it out, the thin wires ripping free. Then the *Fynbar* lifted, to make the long journey to Mars and the FTL array being assembled by the surviving Airlia.

SPACE, CLOSING ON MARS; STILL PRIOR TO CRASH

"What kind of weapons does this ship have?"

Duncan stared at Garlin, the human who'd been torturing her and was in the thrall of the Swarm tentacle inside of him. "None."

"You lie."

"Why do you need weapons?" Duncan asked.

"What kind of weapons does this ship have and how are they activated?"

Duncan shook her head, trying to clear the pain of the most recent probe. "This ship has no weapons."

The drip of blood from Garlin's left ear was a steady trickle. His skin was paler than it had been. The side of his face was constantly jumping from a nervous tic as the tentacle exerted its control.

"Nothing? Particle beam? Plasma? Arrayed pulse?"

Duncan laughed bitterly. "Those were all beyond our capabilities."

"Then how did you overthrow the Airlia on your planet?"

"Blood. Lots of it. And we helped them defeat themselves."

Garlin remained still as the tentacle inside him absorbed this information. Her answers were not acceptable. The Swarm controlling him and flying the *Fynbar* had detected a Mothership closing, with an intercept coming shortly. A scan of the oncoming craft revealed its weapons systems were off-line, which reduced the threat considerably. The Swarm was evaluating options.

"Defensive capabilities?" Garlin asked.

"Is someone chasing us?"

"If this ship is destroyed," Garlin said, "you will be adrift in space. You will die, come back to life and die again. For eternity."

"Who is after us? The Airlia?" Duncan's eyes widened. "Turcotte. He's coming."

"It would do you well to tell me about the ship's capabilities."

Duncan laughed. "I will never help you."

"Then you will suffer until you tell us." Garlin picked up the saw he had used on her head. He slashed down with it across Duncan's right arm, cutting through the forearm.

Duncan screamed and thrashed against the straps holding her down.

Just as Garlin finished cutting through her arm, there was an explosion and the ship canted hard left. He fell forward, the saw cutting into his own chest, splattering his blood on top of Duncan's. Garlin staggered back from the gurney, looked at the hole in his chest, and died.

Duncan felt the throb of pain from her right arm. Then the ship rocked once more. There was smoke billowing from several panels. She looked down at the straps holding her to the gurney. Her right arm was severed halfway down the forearm. The spurt of blood ceased as she watched, but the jagged edge of the two bones poked out unevenly due to Garlin's aborted cut. She jerked back on the arm, slipping the shortened length under the restraints. She twisted her body and jabbed the end of the bone into the restraint on her other arm. The sharp end punctured the nylon. She began sawing, using her own bone to cut, ignoring the throb of pain.

She heard a cracking noise and turned her head to the left as she continued sawing. Garlin's mouth was wide open and the tip of the Swarm tentacle appeared, forcing its way out of the dying host.

Duncan sawed faster. She cut through the restraint across her chest as the tentacle cleared Garlin's body. She sat up and used her good hand to unbuckle the other straps. The tentacle slithered to the floor and crept toward the Swarm orb which was at the controls of the *Fynbar*.

Free of the gurney, Duncan looked about. She could see the display screen in front of the orb. A Mothership filled the view. There was an open hatch near the front of the large ship and several figures dressed in TASC-suits waited at the edge. There was another open hatch to the right of it and some sort of machine in the bay. A machine that suddenly began sparking.

Duncan realized it was a weapon, getting ready to fire. She looked about wildly and made her decision. She crawled toward the empty regeneration tube, next to the one that held the blank body that vainly had awaited the memories and essence of her lover, Gwalcmai, who'd died so many years ago at the Battle of Camlann, his *ka* smashed and denying him another iteration of reincarnation. Unnoticed, one of the tendrils of the implant made a connection with a thin wire extending out of the healing wound on the back of head. The implant snapped forward, hitting her, but the impact was lost in the overwhelming pain from her severed arm as she crawled into the tube.

As the lid shut on her, the implant began to dissolve into nano-sized bits and flow back into her brain.

*****

They had a plan. It wasn't the best, but Turcotte had served in Special Forces and he knew there was no such thing as the best plan. There was taking action.

They were under an hour out from Mars. Everyone else was in the control room of the mothership, watching the array the last of the Airlia were constructing to call out for aid to their Empire. Turcotte went down the main corridor of the large ship until he reached the cross-way leading to the hanger bay in which they had brought the *Fynbar* with Duncan on board. Turcotte went into the bay and up the ramp into the ship.

Duncan was in the tube, eyes closed. A light on the side of the tube was green. Turcotte went over to the other tube. The light on this one was red.

Turcotte swung the lid open and examined the body. The skin was flawless with no scars or other marks. The man appeared to be in his late teens or early twenties, in excellent physical shape at the time of death. He didn't have calluses on the bottom of his feet. It was as if the man had never left the tube.

Which he hadn't, Turcotte knew. He'd seen a tube like this before. Deep under Mount Sinai. The one Aspasia's Shadow had used to regenerate his new body. Apparently, it had two functions, he realized, glancing over at Duncan's tube. It not only could regenerate a new body, it also could put someone in deep sleep—a necessary thing, for long space travel.

Turcotte looked about the interior of the *Fynbar*. The interior was sparse, emphasizing function over comfort, much like a present-day submarine. He walked to the front, where two depressions faced a control console. He sat in the right-hand seat. It felt familiar, which irritated him. What was in his brain?

He scanned the console. If the seat felt familiar, then perhaps other things would strike a chord. A flat screen to the right, set at an angle in the console caught his attention. There were five buttons with markings below it. He reached and tapped one. The screen flickered, and then came alive.

In rapid succession a series of scenes played out on the screen. Turcotte saw Duncan and her companion, Gwalcmai, leaving their son and home world aboard a Mothership. Going into deep sleep. Awakened and departing the Mothership on the *Fynbar* outside the Solar System. Landing on Earth. Burying the ship at what would become Stonehenge. Raising the first stones there.

He then caught quick glimpses of the two of them through Earth history. On a wonderful island with a huge palace in the center that he assumed had to be Atlantis. They were dressed in local garb and ambushing an Airlia in the streets and killing him.

On a ship, pulling away from the island kingdom as it was destroyed by a Mothership.

Returning to the buried spaceship, regenerating new bodies, transferring their essences via the *ka*, and emerging.

In Egypt, sneaking around in the dark, again killing an Airlia in ambush. A confrontation along the Roads of Rostau with what appeared to be Ones Who Wait, human/Airlia half-breeds.

Regenerating.

Greece. In the newly completed Parthenon, listening to orators.

In a field, killing someone—a One Who Waits-- who tried to ambush them.

Regenerating.

In the stands of the Coliseum as gladiators hacked at each other with swords.

The scenes began to flicker by so quickly he could barely comprehend a tenth. Every forty years or so the two would return to Stonehenge and transfer to a new body. The same form of 'immortality' by regeneration that Aspasia's Shadow had had. Duncan had lied to him from the very beginning, which did not surprise Turcotte at this point.

He saw the two of them at Camelot. Duncan in the court, dressed in a white robe. Gwalcmai in armor, next to the king. Aspasia's Shadow as Mordred. Artad's Shadow as Arthur.

Then he saw a brutal battle, the dead and dying littering a field. Swords and spears covered in blood. Duncan's partner taking a sword blow to the chest from Artad's Shadow wielding Excalibur. His *ka* damaged. Duncan dragging him on a travois back to Stonehenge. Unable to pass his essence on to the regenerated body.

Turcotte stopped the screen and turned toward the tube holding Duncan. Quinn was right—she had never been who she said she was. He felt betrayed—as close as the two of them had become, she had still lied. Of course, would he have been willing to accept the truth at any point? Hell, he still didn't know the entire story. Who were the Airlia? More importantly, who were we, humans? Turcotte wondered.

He went over to Duncan's tube. He looked at the buttons and tapped one. There was a puff of air escaping the tube, and the lid lifted. He checked his watch. They were twenty minutes from Mars.

Duncan opened her eyes. She blinked for a few

moments, orienting herself. The severed arm was already half-grown back, the edge a mixture of raw red and pulsing black as the Airlia virus reconstituted the cells.

"Mike—" Duncan sat up, reaching her good hand out.

Turcotte took a step back, shaking his head. "We're past that. You lied and manipulated me."

She sat still for a few moments, before replying. "I had to."

"Why?"

She glanced over at the other tube. "I am sorry. I was alone for so long. And I needed help. After the Mothership was uncovered and Majestic-12 formed, I knew I couldn't keep it under cover any more. And that I couldn't do it by myself"

"'It'?"

"The Airlia. The truth. I knew a battle, this battle that we've fought, was coming."

"And what is the truth?" Turcotte asked.

She shook her head. "I've blocked it from myself."

"What?"

She climbed out of the tube without his aid, using her one hand to support herself. "These tubes—we took them from the Airlia when we defeated them on my planet. They can grow a new body. Transfer memories and personalities—the essence of a person, via the *ka*. They also can be used for deep sleep. But you can program them too.

After he—" she once more looked at the other tube—"his name was Gwalcmai, my husband, I buried him near Stonehenge—that's the body that couldn't be reborn, I knew it was all on my shoulders. I also knew where my home world was. And the Ones That Wait, the Guides, they were after me. Aspasia's Shadow tried to track me down several times. So, I blocked my own memory using the tube. Sealed off parts. My past. My home world. My memories of my son."

Turcotte abruptly realized the pain she'd been in to do such a thing. He understood the need to seal off the information she couldn't give up, but she'd also cut off memories that would cause her emotional pain.

"I want to know—" Turcotte began, but he was interrupted by Yakov appearing the hatchway. "We're less than ten minutes out. You need to suit up." The Russian was staring hard at Duncan.

"What are you going to do?" Duncan asked.

"We need you to help us," Turcotte said.

"Of course."

Turcotte took a step closer to her. "Not 'of course'. This is our plan. To free our planet from the influence of the Airlia once and for all. I killed the Swarm orb and freed you. If we can destroy this array and kill Artad, we've succeeded. Many people have died so far in this war. We need to end it now. I don't know what your hidden agenda has been and I don't care. Will you do what I tell you to?"

Duncan nodded. "My—our goal—was the same."

"All right. Here's the plan."

BACK TO THE MORE RECENT PAST
THE CONTROL ROOM OF THE MOTHERSHIP

Of course, Duncan had hijacked the plan and sacrificed herself by smashing the mothership into the Airlia array. Turcotte's assumption about her 'true death' would have been correct as the remnants of Artad remained splattered organic material. But not Duncan's.

The implant's tendrils had pulled together enough to form a skull and the beginning of a spinal column. It was a base. A starting point. Slowly, very slowly, the implant attracted pieces.

It was an incredibly slow process, but it was a process.

While World War III raged and exploded into nuclear exchanges; while the Swarm Battle Core appeared at the edge of the Solar System and then traversed it to arrive at Earth; during the seven days of the Swarm Reaping; and while the Core suicided into the sun; Duncan's body pulled together.

Finally, after so many days, Duncan's body, curled in a fetal ball, the skin pale and unblemished, was complete.

It was not, however alive. Not in the human sense, because the implant had put her together differently than the way she had been.

LAST STAND OF IMPERIUM

TALIANT FLEET BASE.

MILLIONS OF YEARS AGO

"Chaos," Captain Tai said. "That is what the scientists believe. The Universe came out of chaos."

"Is that what they taught you at the Military Academy?" Librarian asked. She didn't wait for an answer. "Do you agree?"

"It's physics," Tai said. "The universe is expanding right now. Then it will collapse. And expand again. An endless cycle."

"Yes, but where did it all start? What was the start point?" Librarian didn't wait for an answer. "Our distant ancestors believed in an ultimate originator. A being they called God."

"There are still Spiritualists," Tai said. "But it is a philosophy, not a science. There is no scientific basis to their theories."

"Is there a true scientific basis for what came before Chaos?" Librarian asked, but didn't wait for an answer. "For nothingness?

Or for just accepting that the universe always just was? Did you know I studied philosophy at the Academy before I switched to science?" She was referring to the Political Academy, not the Military, which he'd graduated from, second in his class.

"Of course, Librarian. I studied your background before assuming my post."

"As expected," Librarian said. "I wondered about those questions. Did the universe spring from nothingness or was there an overarching intelligence behind it all? And if so, why would it bring forth Chaos? Or was the Chaos a natural result of the collapse of that first intelligence? Or perhaps a failure of the originating intelligence to advance? A flawed God? Or is Chaos a test for intelligences that follow, like us? To see if we can reach the same level?" She laughed bitterly. "We are obviously failing in that regard. I would submit Imperium has been sliding backward for hundreds, if not thousands, of years."

"We've gotten soft," Tai grumbled.

"Perhaps not soft enough," Librarian said. "Intelligent Life, at least what is currently accepted as 'intelligent' life in the Universe by similar 'intelligent' life, doesn't know how they came out of this Chaos. So how smart are we? We've studied the cultures of those alien species we've encountered and they all followed a pattern similar to our own. As their consciousness emerges, each intelligence in its little pocket of a single planet, tries to come up with an explanation for not only their own existence but that of the world around them. They look outside of themselves and invent, and worship, a greater power. Often that power is the planet itself, but eventually they move it to a more abstract power in the 'heavens'. But think. First, they worship the planet. The ground, the air, the water."

"Yes, but the planet doesn't respond to that worship, Librarian," Tai said. "It just is."

"Always my practical Marine," Librarian said. "Doesn't life come out of the planet? Out of its elements? Don't we get sustenance from planets? Food? Water? Isn't that a response?" She didn't wait for answer. "Originally, we wanted to believe that there is an intelligence that created all. Of course, we did so without any proof except of own existence and ego so we made that intelligence in our own image. What was harder to accept, but we mostly did, is the likely reality that we are simply the result of randomness out of Chaos. Intelligent species, including us, don't like the idea it's all chaos and randomness.

"Which could be both correct and wrong. If our existence did come from some intelligence, then the Spiritualists are correct, but if that intelligence is testing us and doesn't really care if we pass or fail, since there is no indication of intervention by that power, then are they wrong? Does it matter? It doesn't respond."

Tai shifted.

"Ah, my Marine wonders why I talk about apparently esoteric things as our very existence is threatened by Unity? Your military training makes you focus on the practical. But consider this. What if Unity's claim about the Awakening is correct? Admiral rejected it without even considering it a possibility. But we, you and I, need to be different.

"The intelligent species who survive and don't destroy themselves or their planets before they are capable of escaping the gravity well of their home world, then slowly progress outward. And we have found several desolate worlds that were home to intelligent species that never made it off planet. They consumed themselves before making that technological leap.

"Even fewer civilizations reach the level where they can master Faster Than Light Transit, even though they truly don't understand that which they've harnessed. They can use FTLT but there's something about it that is beyond their ability to understand. Fleet Admiral uses it, but he doesn't sit around and wonder what exactly he's using. The Science Academy can tell you how to build an FTLT engine or transmitter, but they struggle to explain how it actually works; rather they offer theories because they know it deals with the factor of time itself, which we have not mastered. Not much different than the spiritualists."

"But it does work, Librarian," Tai pointed out.

"Have you considered what FTLT is, in essence?" Librarian said.

Tai frowned. "Travel between points."

"Not exactly," Librarian expanded. "In essence, we are breaking the rule of time. FTLT is time travel. True it's linear, but it is compressed time travel. What if someone has mastered that beyond simply linear?" She waved a hand, dismissing the theory. "Leaving religion behind, or perhaps adjacent, scientists gather data, conduct experiments, and come up with theories about the Universe and its origins. They try to peer into a distant past, so long ago that their theories are little better than guesses, or, perhaps a different form of religion? What I saw at the Academy is that there is a strong tendency to make the data from observations fit the theories rather than the seemingly more logical way of expanding intelligence to try to understand that which one is not yet capable of, which brings into question whether intelligent species are actually intelligent? The meeting we just had only reinforces that.

"Species that survive manage to muddle through this outer view, and not many do, then make themselves the center of all. Until they make contact with another intelligent species. Imperium's first contact was a rather jolting experience. As we have experienced, that never turns out well for one side. At least in our human experience. The winning side, which has always been us, expands. This is what Imperium has managed to accomplish until now. Is there a limit to how far intelligence life can expand before it explodes into chaos on its own? Or ultimately runs into a more powerful life form?"

"There is the legend of the Ancients," Tai said.

Librarian nodded. "There is. What do you think of that?"

Tai shrugged. "I'm sure there were empires before ours."

"And what happened to them?"

"They fell," Tai said. "All empires fall."

"They do."

"Are you saying we're about to plunge into chaos, Librarian?" Tai asked.

"Oh, we're already there, Captain," Librarian said. "Regardless of what happens in the near future, things will never be the same. I know you believe I ramble but change is inevitable. You know that. It's what makes you different from many of your comrades who wear the red dagger." She leaned back in her chair and interlaced her fingers and regarded Tai. "We can speculate on this because we have the gift, or perhaps curse, of consciousness. When and how that gift was bestowed is a matter of speculation as important as the origins of the universe. After all we cannot be conscious of what we aren't conscious of."

Tai frowned as Librarian asked her own rhetorical question based on her own statement: "And what aren't we conscious of?" She popped up out of her chair. "Come, Captain. There is something I need to show you." She paused in the doorway and looked over her shoulder at him. "I trust you, Captain. I shouldn't, but I do. That's a bit of spirituality. A leap of faith. That is what things have come to."

THE PRESENT CONSOLIDATION

THE EARTH

Humans believe they know more about the planet they inhabit than they do. For example, most of the surface of the planet, seventy percent, is composed of water, yet exploration under the surface of that water has covered barely five percent. On land, while the surface has been mapped, what lies just beneath is only known second-hand. There has been no mythical journey to the center of the Earth. More humans have looked to the sky than peered inward at their own planet. This is done primarily through seismic tomography. Unfortunately, the layers of the planet and the varying electro-magnetic fields make such study difficult as Gina Tarrenti could attest to; if she were still alive.

It was only just before World War III that scientists discovered that it appeared the core of the planet, once believed to be a single ball of extremely hot iron, compressed so tightly that despite the heat it was still solid, actually seemed to be two distinct cores with very different properties: an outer-inner core oriented north-south and an inner-inner core oriented latitudinally. Why this was, geologists could only speculate as it didn't make any sense according to what they knew. They needed more data and stations like Gina's had been trying to provide that. Of course, what they knew was overwhelmed by what they didn't.

Unknown to humans, the core of the planet is much more complicated than just highly compressed, extremely hot iron. There are other elements striated throughout, some of which was in liquid form. There are even pockets of gasses flowing. There's a complex, intricate system at the center of the planet including patches of diamond matrixes.

Life on the surface of Earth is carbon based. This is because carbon atoms can form bonds with up to four other atoms simultaneously. This allows it to make long chains of molecules that form life via proteins and DNA. However, to think there is only one type of 'life' is to be narcissistic on a universal scale. Humans have speculated that there might be alien life based on other chemical elements. While we rely on water as the solvent our molecules need, a different type of life might rely on ammonia or methane to support a base material. The most likely candidate for that base would be silicon as it also can bond with up to four other atoms. Silicon is also one of most common elements in the Universe; oddly it is more common in the Earth than carbon which raises the question of why didn't life, as we know it on this planet, evolve with a silicon base?

Perhaps because something else was utilizing the silicon?

There are two spinning cores deep inside the planet, an inner one rotating longitudinally while the core around it goes latitudinally. Slowly, very slowly, the outer was shifting, going from lateral toward vertical.

The deepest that mankind had ever penetrated into the crust of the planet was the Superdeep Borehole on the Kola Peninsula in the far northwest of Russia. Drilling began in 1970 and it took until 1989 to reach the farthest point, 40,230 feet. Even this effort, though, only reached a third of the way through the planet's crust. The hole was nine inches in diameter and commemorated by a special stamp in the USSR. Of course, not long after this, that political entity collapsed and the site was abandoned and a metal plate was welded over the borehole.

While it was open, it attracted scientists from around the world to study the data and material it yielded, particularly in order to develop technologies to face the challenges of future deep, geophysical study. Gina Tarrenti had been just a baby when the borehole was closed. During spring break one year in her graduate studies, she'd traveled to the Kola Peninsula, by way of Murmansk, to visit it. While others might have been disappointed at the rusting metal plate bolted over such a small opening, it fired her imagination.

She'd studied the data, of course. There were quite a few surprising facts. One was that the transition from granite to basalt at seven kilometers that was anticipated due to seismic wave studies didn't exist. The granite continued and the seismic data was, instead, due to a metamorphic transition in the rock itself because of increased and heat and pressure. A fact that seemed obvious in hindsight. Even more surprising was that the rock was saturated with water. Given the heat, it had been thought that any water would have boiled off, but the rock above was impermeable and the water was trapped. Also interesting was that the water came from below, from deep-crust minerals. These basic but unexpected discoveries made clear that much less was known than had been thought.

The core samples pulled up revealed microscopic plankton fossils six kilometers down. Also unexpected was the discovery of large quantities of hydrogen gas. In essence, the deepest hole had yielded a lesson that should have been taken to heart: the interior of the planet was more complex than theories had speculated.

While the Kola Borehole still held the record for deepest, it lost the record for longest in 2008 when economics trumped science. The Al Shaheen oil well in Qatar ended up with a borehole over 40,318 feet long in the thirsty search for black gold. In 2011, the Sakhalin-I oil well, offshore of the Russian island of the same name, broke that record with a 40,502 borehole into the crust. In 2012, Exxon completed the Z-44 Chayvo well with a borehole of 40,604 feet. Despite all that, Kola, still held the record for deepest artificial intrusion into the Earth.

While Gina Tarrenti's ashes still smoldered in California, magma rose in all these boreholes and thousands of lesser ones. Fortunately, or unfortunately considering their fate, the various oil platforms and rigs were deserted, their crews Reaped by the Swarm.

Explosive streams of magma punched out of every borehole, shooting high into the sky. It was the equivalent of arteries spurting blood. It didn't last long, and within minutes, all the holes were sealed by cooling rock.

As those cores aligned, geologic research stations that had responded to Gina Tarrenti's message were similarly obliterated.

METEOR BELT, SOLAR SYSTEM

The Swarm warship was a black sphere two miles in diameter. There were eight, quarter mile long protrusions, evenly spaced around the exterior. These contained weapons, scout ships and sensors.

In the very center of the warship was a Command Swarm. The average Swarm entity is a yellowish orb several feet in diameter with a half-dozen or more eyes evenly spaced around the body, along with a number of semi-autonomous grayish-blue arms also positioned around the orb. The orb contained a minimal set of organs to keep the body functioning and a four-hemisphere brain encased inside a thick bone exoskeleton. The arms varied in length, from inches to several feet. All were tapered to three 'fingers' at the end. Each arm could detach from the orb and invade another species, taking over its nervous system, much as the smaller snake-like parasites did, except the arm stem brain could exert better control over the host. The limb of the average Swarm had intelligence in its stem brain. This stem was subservient to the brain of the Swarm it detached from.

The Command Swarm resides at the center of the warship. It was eighteen feet in diameter. Instead of arms/tentacles, it had thirty-six slender tendrils that extended outward, into the ship, eight reaching to the tips of the ship's pylons and the sensors. All the Swarm on board were connected to the Command Swarm by telepathic proximity.

From individual Swarm to Command Swarm, there was a hierarchy of command, leading to the Supreme Swarm on the Battle Core. The last order from the Supreme Swarm had been transmitted just minutes before it was immolated by the sun, detailing this one warship to remain in the solar system and monitor.

However, the entire Swarm entity, spread across galaxies, had felt the loss of the Battle Core at the same instant. In one case, a Battle Core had stopped in the midst of attacking the Airlia Orion battle fleet and retreated, fooling the Airlia into believing they'd achieved a victory.

On the warship, sensors pointed at the third planet had picked up the large nuclear explosion negating the hadesarchaea that had been seeded to 'reboot' the planet; another defeat. How that had happened wasn't clear. A scout ship was ordered to fly to Earth and investigate.

Nevertheless, because of the devastation and onset of year-round winter, the surface of the planet would become unsuitable to sustain the few surviving humans. The Scale life was also doomed despite its victory. Once humans were extinct, the warship was free to leave this solar system and seek out a Battle Core to be integrated into. It would be able to report: mission accomplished despite the massive loss.

Swarm Battle Cores had the ability to detect when a spaceship transitioned out of Faster Than Light Transit (FTLT), a fact it took Scale species a while to figure out, at the cost of a number of ships and planets.

Why the Swarm Reaped Scale was as much a mystery as where and how the Swarm originated. They didn't occupy worlds. In fact, their form indicated they either naturally developed into creatures that lived in space or were engineered to be such. The latter was under the suspicion that they had been designed long ago by some Scale species to be weapons of ultimate destruction that, once it was released, had turned on its makers. A doomsday weapon. Or perhaps its makers were out there among the stars after having unleashed their creation?

Another big question was what the Swarm did with the Scale it reaped? Rather than simply exterminate, the Swarm collected the Scale and brought it on board the Battle Core. The answer to that was now known by the Metabols on Earth, since one of their own, the very first Metabol, Darlene, had sacrificed herself aboard the Core and let them know that the Reaped were amalgamated into the organic 'stew' that was the raw material of the Core.

Since they had nothing but time on their hands, while most of the Swarm on board the warship went into hibernation, the Command Swarm dispatched several scout ships to explore the Asteroid Belt for replenishment that the organic stew didn't supply, mostly metals, and also to investigate the traces of a previous, ancient civilization that had been uncovered while the Core was inbound.

GLACIER NATIONAL PARK, MONTANA

Thomas Jefferson Waterman, known as T.J. to his business associates (he had no friends), finished his thirtieth lap in the Olympic sized pool. Checked his time on the large digital clock that had stopped when he touched the pad just above the water line in his lane. Eight-tenths of a second faster than yesterday which was satisfying. The pool was in a room lined with marble. Lights that mimicked perfect daylight glowed in the ceiling.

He climbed out, water dripping off his toned, naked body. He was in wonderful shape for a man of forty-eight. The air was kept at a constant sixty-seven degrees in the pool, contrasted with the seventy-nine constant in the pool water. He walked down a corridor and warm air blew out of hundreds of small nozzles had him dry by the time he reached the next room. He paused at a full-length mirror and admired his body, running his fingers over the faint six pack in his stomach. He opened a closet and hit a button. A door slid and a suit appeared on a rack. He put on the suit slowly and deliberately. He stood in front of the mirror and knotted the tie correctly, as his father had taught him with a slap on the back of the head for every miscue.

He checked himself one last time, then proceeded to his office. As he entered the control bunker, on a series of pedestals to his right was a series of displays. A model of a single oil derrick, circa 1890, was first. Great grandfather. That had been the beginning, in Ohio, which few people consider when they think of oil. But Ohio had been the beginning of the oil boom in the United States, until it was surpassed by Texas and Oklahoma. Which led to the second model; smaller scale but many more derricks, each the size of a pencil stub. Over 2,000. Grandfather. Then several models of massive oil tankers. The model of a deep-sea oil platform. The empire expanding. Father. Then a pile of cash encased in crystal: one million dollars.

The fact T.J. Waterman could afford to waste a million like that said what needed to be said. Of course, nobody else was here to see it other than him. He'd never bragged that his ranch in Montana, bordering Glacier National Park, was larger than the state of Delaware. He'd been taught growing up that it was beneath his station in life. But that wasn't why he didn't boast. He was a smart man, always thinking ahead. That's how he taken the eighty-million-dollar business he'd inherited and multiplied it into ninety-three billion dollars.

Thinking ahead meant planning ahead. There were always numerous 'doomsday' scenarios that were certainly within the realm of possibilities. The threat of nuclear war had hung over everyone's head the day the Russians detonated their first bomb. Upon that event, his grandfather had bought the first parcel of land out here and built the first shelter. A crude, pre-fab survival bunker, atomic bomb era.

T.J. would have agreed with Mrs. Parrish's assessment of the future: dismal. He'd hired the best scientists and they had laid out the facts about climate change with more expertise than those academics working for their university or living on grants or for the U.N. He knew the inevitability of climate change and had pushed his subsidiaries to work even harder to extract petroleum from the ocean floor and via fracking everywhere possible. Regulations and laws were for his lobbyists to get overturned or his subordinates to break, under the philosophy it's more profitable to pay fines if caught; and the odds of getting caught were slim given the bribes his companies scattered throughout the various enforcing agencies.

That he was accelerating the very crisis he was also preparing for had never struck him as contradictory in the slightest. It was logical. Most people were doomed but not all. Certainly not him.

While many of his contemporaries bought land in New Zealand and built huge compounds where they planned to ride out whatever disaster might occur, Waterman had thought them quite naïve in believing they could make it to New Zealand. That required a plane and flight crew and while Waterman owned a dozen planes and employed multiple flight crews, implicit in that was trusting that in a disaster those people would respond to his desires and not their own. Central to T.J.'s belief system was that humans were ego driven and, in a crisis, would always protect themselves rather than anyone else.

This facility, built deep inside a mountain overlooking the country on the edges of the Rocky Mountains, had cost three billion dollars to build. The hardest part had not been the money. He'd learned early in life that money was easy; people were always the difficult part of any equation as they rarely reacted logically. All components had been built elsewhere and assembled on site, minimizing the number of workers needed to complete it.

That had been the hard part. The number of workers. Even automating as much as possible, it had still required one-hundred-and-eighty-eight men and women to complete on site. It had taken him three hours and forty-two minutes of valuable thinking time to come up with a solution to the security problem this presented. He took his cue from the ancient Egyptians; or at least what he thought they had done; he hadn't known about the Airlia, the Undead and the rest. Not at first. The story was that Pharaohs hid the location of their tombs and the treasures within by burying the workers who constructed them inside.

Selection of the workers had been the start. Almost all recruited overseas and brought illegally into the country with no paper trail. For those positions for which he couldn't get an illegal, he specifically chose men and women who had no immediate families who would miss them.

Killing them all after the job was done had been relatively easy. He'd had them gather in the main hall of Heorot, which he'd chosen as the name for his survival complex in honor of the Great Hall in the ballad of Beowulf. They thought they were there for a celebration. The tables laden with food and fine wines and champagne, and beer for the coarser of the lot, had certainly reinforced that belief.

Once they were assembled, he'd had them gassed. His security team had then deposed of the bodies in a deep debris shaft those very same workers had dug and used. Then it was sealed with poured concrete forty feet thick. One-hundred-and-eighty-eight murders might seem extreme to others, but he viewed it as a reasonable price for the result. The next problem, of course, had been the security team. Twenty-one mercenaries. They weren't stupid. It was a logical guess for even the slowest of them to suspect T.J. might have the same end in mind for them. He'd promised each of them ten million dollars, cash.

The team leader had made various demands to ensure their safety upon completion of the job. The money had been packed in duffle bags supplied by the team. They'd had him line up all of his planes at his airfield so they could pick which one to fly out on. They'd then chosen the captain to fly the plane, the man they knew was his favorite pilot. They'd inspected the plane for traps. They'd loaded the two-hundred-and-ten-million in cash on the plane and taken off confident that with the money they were safe.

It had never really occurred to them that such a sum was what he considered a trivial amount as compared to his personal security. Also, a mistake which he found rather amazing, was that they didn't realize that the money was lost to him either way. Despite their training, they couldn't have imagined he'd had all his planes rigged to detonate with explosives integrated into the frame of the aircraft when they were built, with a remote that had a biometric control connected directly to only him. It was one of those things a man with foresight did.

T.J. had sat in his control room here in Heorot and tracked the plane as it flew west. He had hit the remote to blow up the plane once it was far over the Pacific Ocean en route to what the team had thought was a safe foreign country.

That had been that. No one alive knew about Heorot except T.J..

Power came from a fusion reactor, the dream of physicists and environmentalists for decades. Before the woman working at MIT could even consider publishing her astounding break through, T.J. had swooped in with millions of dollars, seducing her with whispers of immediate production, ending climate change, stopping world hunger, all those wonderful things that cheap, bountiful power could bring about and foolish idealists dreamed about. He'd provided her with all she needed to produce several working reactors and then she and her family had met a tragic end in a house fire at Christmas along with what appeared to be all her notes and her laptop. An inquiry was easily paid off to ignore the obvious and accept the cover.

He not only felt no guilt about that, but he believed he was the true genius behind the reactor because he'd fed her information he'd uncovered. Because in the course of searching for new technology he'd learned of the existence of Majestic-12 and the fact that alien artifacts had been discovered on Earth. He'd also had an agent infiltrate the Russian Section IV. Information had been extremely difficult and costly to extract. He'd learned much, including data that helped the design of the fusion reactor. Eventually he focused his search on a particular piece of equipment in Egypt that promised what he desired: extending his life.

His agents used a combination of extravagant bribes and force when necessary. They procured an Airlia regeneration tube from the Roads of Rostau underneath the Giza Plateau. The entire operation had cost money and lives but he had plenty of both to spend. His *ka*, loaded with his essence as of his latest update, twenty-three hours ago, rested in the console for the regeneration tube. An implant in T.J.'s chest monitored his health and if his life signs ceased, the *ka* would be inserted and the clone in the tube would boot up and he would be restored.

Minus whatever had transpired between, but what were a few hours?

T.J. sat at his desk. It was semi-circular and the far side was lined with a dozen large monitors. First, he brought up status for all systems and carefully went through a checklist as he did every twenty-four-hour cycle. He found one or two needed some tweaking to operate at optimum and it gave him great satisfaction to make those adjustments. He checked the backups. Then the backups to the backups. He updated his *ka*.

Then he accessed his sensors. High resolution cameras hidden all over his domain showed everything was quiet inside and out. Ash was drifting down over the mountains, staining the snow.

No sign of human life, but animals were stirring, which he viewed as a positive. Before he'd cut his final link to the outside world he'd learned of the various nuclear exchanges. He'd cut back on those links when the first Swarm warships entered the atmosphere. He'd seen one warship Reaping in the distance the previous week. A few dragons had flown by the mountain, but Heorot was buried deep and the main entrance had been completely sealed with an explosion dropping rock over it. It could only be opened from the inside via two other vault doors, and explosives blowing outward.

That wasn't going to happen any time soon. T.J. had supplied Heorot with enough to last him five hundred years. That could be stretched out indefinitely if he chose deep sleep in the tube. Or he could keep regenerating and stay awake, but he imagined this waiting could get quite boring.

He had four seed vaults holding over ten thousand embryos he'd carefully chosen over the years for their genetic potential. He'd chosen the parents carefully, both men and women. Naturally, he had provided a significant amount of seed, staying just below the threshold to allow genetic diversity.

When the time was right . . .

But now he turned to his next task. Taking the data from his various sensors and calculating how long before he could re-emerge into the world and begin rebuilding it in his image with his army of followers?

THE FACILITY, DAVIS MOUNTAINS, TEXAS

When the *Myrrdin*, the branch of Watchers that had waged a mostly covert war against the Airlia while working to ensure mankind's survival, came to the conclusion that regardless of the outcome of any eventual revolt against the Airlia, the planet was already ecologically damaged and most likely doomed, they set about coming up with a solution.

They quickly decided that changing that forecast was beyond their control even though they'd amassed great wealth and power over the many centuries since they split from the original Watchers. Instead, they went in the other direction: write off the planet and figure out how to save a core of people that could sustain the species. Under the leadership of Mr. and Mrs. Parrish, the most recent leaders of the *Myrrdin*, they took that a step further. They prepared a two-pronged plan, prepared to go either way after an initial premise that the key was to have a way to secure the derelict mothership in orbit around the planet and make it habitable. A spaceship program was developed with an elaborate cover story to be able to accomplish that. The second was to develop the capability to have a self-sustaining capability for the minimum number of humans needed to survive and regenerate the human race. The Facility was the result of that.

Located underneath the Davis Mountains in west Texas, not far from the space port, it had taken twelve years to construct. A cavern six miles across and a mile high had been expanded out of a natural cave. Then a contained ecosystem was developed based on prior, much smaller attempts and trial and error.

If the surface world was compressed into this relatively small space with varying environments: a savannah, a rainforest, a fog desert, agricultural lands broken up by copses of trees. In the very center, of course, a town. On one edge of the cavern there was a slice of ocean complete with coral reef and beach. When power had been abundant, small waves had washed up on the beach.

Power was not abundant anymore and the pumps were working at the minimum needed to circulate to keep the underwater life viable. The Facility was designed to be a closed system and had succeeded in that for over two years. Air, water, food, and all the ingredients necessary for life were contained and recycled in here. Could it last indefinitely? Would some small degradation in one area lead to a collapse of the entire system, much like humans had been doing to the planet outside?

Power was provided by wind tunnels cut into the mountain above and solar panels. The latter showed a marked decrease in output. A backup nuclear reactor had been taken off-line prior to the Swarm arriving. The Facility was on the edge of red-lining in terms of the power needed to keep it going.

The town was designed for children, because they were the future. The modified future in terms of the Chosen. Constrained by the capacity of the mothership, the number for the future of mankind had been settled on as 5,000. Not optimum genetically; 10,000 would have been better, but that was where the *Myrddin* program designed to pick the children to be the Chosen came in. They had been selected and brought to the Facility before they were two and had little memory of life outside of it. The ones who succeeded in the program had been evacuated as the Battle Core approached and placed on board the mothership at Area 51. They were now elsewhere, after the mothership went into Faster Than Light Transit and escaped.

The 'failures' were the Metabols and Fades. Those who slipped below the *Myrddin's* threshold criteria for a superior race. Unknown to Mrs. Parrish and the other *Myrddin* though, was that inside of their organization had been a splinter cell, led by her chief scientist Doctor Leahy, working on their own project: the

Metabols. Humans who could meld together in ways our conscious minds had left long in the past. Unfortunately, some of those became Fades, slipping into a coma and then death. Forty-two surviving Fades, though, had become conscious when Sofia and other Metabols lay hands on them. Those Fades were now out on the surface, while the Metabols and the handful of adults taking care of them were in the Facility.

The large LED screens overhead that used to display the sky were dark and lighting was at minimal power. In the town square, an old Native American named Joseph was leading the Metabols in their daily prayer:

"Live your life that the fear of death can never enter your heart."

The children repeated the line, then picked up the rest with him.

" 'Live your life that the fear of death can never enter your heart.
Trouble no one about his religion.
Respect others in their views and demand that they respect yours.
Love your life, perfect your life, beautify all things in your life.
Seek to make your life long and of service to your people.
Prepare a noble death song for the day when you go over the great divide."

When their voices echoed into silence, the group broke up. Most of the children went off to do the chores needed to keep life going in the Facility: planting and gathering crops, tending to maintenance, some attending classes from the handful of remaining adult mentors who'd been in on the Metabol project.

There weren't many, nor were they really needed as the Metabols had gone past the adults in terms of knowledge with their ability to access each other's minds.

In a meeting room in a building on the side of the Square, Joseph and Sofia joined Asha. Rex was lying at her feet, the USB key that had been on his collar in Asha's hand. She had not yet put it into a flexpad, waiting for the others to join her.

"Shall we see what Darlene left us?" she asked the old man and young girl.

Both nodded.

Asha powered up her flexpad. There was no Ethos, the secure internet the *Myrddin* had used, any more. No internet. No contact with the outside world. A blank screen glowed. Asha pushed the USB key in.

The screen flickered and then Darlene's visage appeared. Behind her was blue sky and the Davis Mountains. She was thin and sported poorly cut, short red hair. She wore a t-shirt with the sleeves cut off. A Marine Corps emblem decorated the front of the shirt and tattoos scrolled her narrow, muscled arms. She began to speak:

"If you got this, then you got Rex, and the only way you got Rex is if I'm no longer around. Which is a bummer, I guess. Hopefully however I went, it was worth it. If it wasn't, like I fell in the shower, don't tell Rex." Darlene smiled. "I guess that's kind of the point, ain't it, Asha? What we set out to do with Professor Leahy? Old Mrs. Parrish thought she could just pick the right kids and raise them right, at least her concept of 'right' which ain't right, and make it work, but the data and research weren't exactly rock solid. We knew it would take more than that. The unnatural selection thing for a superior race was tried before in and the results were horrific."

She looked past the camera, gazing out to a horizon only she could see, then focused back and her voice changed, dropping the aw-shucks, hick accent. "Mrs. Parrish used intelligence and physical fitness, along with perfect gene markers, as the criteria for her Chosen. As if that were all that was needed for mankind to evolve. But she was ignoring the most important thing." Darlene smiled wryly. "Maybe 'cause she didn't have an ounce of it herself: empathy. The ability for people to get along." Darlene nodded. "If you're watching this, I'm thinking Sofia is with you. She needs to know the background of why we made the decisions we did. If she isn't with you, please bring her in before proceeding."

Asha glanced at Sofia, but the youngster was focused on the screen.

Darlene explained. "Mankind has been at each other's throats since we could put our hands around them. Once we could pick up a stick or a rock, we had weapons. And we used them. Whether justified or not, we knew this ability, this tendency, held the seeds of our eventual doom. The fact the human race has survived so far is a testament to something else inside of us. And luck. Ever since atomic weapons were introduced, we've balanced on a knife edge; as Oppenheimer quoted upon watching the Trinity test: 'I am become death'. Yet, we've avoided that death. So far."

As Darlene paused to collect her thoughts, Sofia glanced at Asha and Joseph. "Not any longer."

"No," Joseph agreed. "Not any longer. But *we* are here. And we owe a lot of that to Darlene."

The image continued. "Professor Leahy was the leading proponent of trying to institute a fundamental change in the human psyche." Darlene grimaced. "Sorry. That's not quite right. More accurately, to bring out the better angels of our nature among a select group of people. Mrs. Parrish had already selected the people. Despite disagreeing with her methods, we knew that there was a core of exceptional children among the Chosen. What psychologists call the resilient child, but more importantly the empathetic child. Because we also knew, based on the data and what we observed from the start of the Chosen program, was that some of those selected were sociopaths and psychopaths who would sow the seeds of destruction for the rest. They had traits that Mrs. Parrish actually thought were positives because they mirrored her own. A malignant narcissist is always blind to what they are."

The top of Rex's head appeared in the frame at the bottom, nudging Darlene. She scratched his head, then continued. "Most people don't think of it, but given Darwin's theory of evolution, altruism should not exist. Natural selection, if it is exact, would seem to dictate that true altruists should have died out long ago. Think on it: an altruist helps others at their own expense, indeed, in some case, at the cost of their lives. Thus, they are helping ensure the survival of others who are more self-serving. Therefore, the latter should easily dominate and succeed while the former dwindle and die out. Yet they have not." She nodded as if indicating some unknown person out of sight. "There are people who give up a kidney to complete strangers. They want no acknowledgement and think it's perfectly normal. How can people like that still be around?

"Altruism, putting the group before the individual, was the goal of the Metabol program. You and I, Asha, along with Professor Leahy, knew that wasn't going to work with Mrs. Parrish and the *Myrddin* in charge. We couldn't trust them because the *Myrddin* have become more selfish over the centuries. The fact they came up with *Danse Macabre* and intend to unleash it on the world confirmed that. It is the opposite of altruism: to wipe out ninety-nine point nine percent of the population while the Chosen are safely in the Facility or on board the Mothership was evil incarnate."

Lying on the floor of the room, Rex let out a low whine.

Darlene continued. "We know that there are those who can be altruistic to people they are related to. It's called inclusive fitness, which dictates that altruistic behavior can evolve if the person benefiting shares genes with the altruist. While the individual might not survive, their immediate gene pool does.

However, when it involves strangers, this doesn't hold true. One might argue that reciprocal altruism fills the gap. That in helping others, one is helping themselves, especially if there is the expectation of receiving something back. However, that is not altruism. It's a form of delayed gratification. It involves a calculation, not spontaneity. The *Myrddin's* Strategy was the epitome of cold calculation. Both inclusive and reciprocal altruism are necessary for society to function. However, at their core, they are not altruistic, but rather self-oriented.

"What about sacrifice to save strangers? People from whom one excepts nothing in return? This is what we focused on." Darlene leaned slightly closer to the camera. "We quickly learned by surveying the Chosen that altruism and empathy have little to do with intelligence or perfect genes."

Darlene tapped the side of her head. "The brain is the last frontier. It's the seat of our consciousness, yet we don't know how we're conscious. What happened for our species to make that leap? More importantly, for us, is how did we gain the capacity to care about each other? In a significant way, that has little to do with intelligence. There is one species that made a rather startling and amazing genetic change that we barely register but is all around us. If you have Rex with you, you know who I'm talking about. Dogs evolved, branching off from wolves, pack predators, to become a different species whose primary attribute was not only their empathy but their ability to evoke it in humans. We are more shocked by a person being cruel to a dog than another human being."

Darlene paused, as if she knew the listeners were looking at her dog, who lay at their feet, head resting on one paw, dark eyes looking up at the screen of the flexpad as if he understood what his former owner was saying.

"Until recently the study of altruists, and for that matter, psychopaths, was more a guessing game than science. That changed when we could actually look into the brain." Darlene pointed once more at her head. "We learned that the amygdala is where the impulse for empathy resides. We've used social neuroscience and cognitive neurogenetics to determine that by scanning the brains of humans who were capable of selfless acts. We learned that those deficient in empathy, particularly psychopaths, were lacking in that area. We determined that a particular chemical in our brain, oxytocin, helps fuel the desire to be altruistic. While it would be nice to say altruists make the choice to be what they are, the reality is they are wired and juiced to be what they have to be. Perhaps the only decision is to give in to what one is already predisposed toward. Nevertheless, it is a significant decision in the face of the cost in many cases."

Darlene looked off again.

In the pause, Sofia turned to Asha. "Is this what you did to us? Something to our brains? Drugged us?"

Before Asha could reply, Darlene continued. "There was another interesting thing we discovered. Outside of the hardware and software, there can be an external trigger. We found that change among psychopaths could be triggered in response to recognizing another person's fear. The problem is that a psychopath doesn't recognize fear in others. However, when a psychopath is shown an image of his or her *own* fear in a threatening situation, it breaks through the wall of nothingness. While they don't empathize with other people, they do empathize with themselves. In a way, their own narcissism can change them for the better." Darlene gave a sad smile. "If only we could have done that to Mrs. Parrish.

"We also learned that those predisposed to altruism could recognize fear in others much more readily than the average person. There was a startlingly high correlation in the tests on that. We never quite understood what the connection is, but it is there."

Darlene rubbed her forehead, then dropped her hand. She looked up. "The Swarm is coming. I don't know what's going to happen, but there's no doubt Mrs. Parrish will implement the Strategy. The *Danse*. There's no more time. I'm sure Leahy will do her part to help you and the Metabols. You'll have to get the Metabols into the Facility as we discussed once the Chosen are gone to the mothership." She smiled sadly. "They're so smart. Sofia most of all. They can tap into each other in a way even I don't understand and I was the first. But I can sense her and the others. Their power."

Darlene shook her head. "We're missing something, Asha. It's more than just altruism among humans. Dogs do it across species, but on a very basic, emotional level. How do humans reach other intelligent life in a peaceful way? The Airlia? The Swarm? Whoever else is out there among the stars?" She looked up once more. "I can see it coming. The Core. It looks like a star, but its daylight. It's as big as they've warned."

Darlene stared upward for several moments, then back at the camera. "Between us, Asha, I have concerns about Leahy. She says she's Tesla's granddaughter, but there's no evidence to support that. There's no record Tesla ever had a relationship with a woman, never mind marry or have an affair. Some of the things she knows are . . ." Darlene shook her head. "Just be careful around her. I have no doubt she is against the Strategy and for the Metabols. But there's something off about her. I sense something deeper."

Sofia glanced at Asha, then returned her attention to the screen.

Darlene smiled sadly. "I miss you, Asha. I miss the children. I wish I was more like them. More altruistic, but I am afraid. I don't want to die. I talked to Leahy. And we did something. There is a *ka* in her lab in Colorado. We loaded my essence into it. How did she know how to do that? And had the technology? Not that I'm ungrateful, but still." She shook her head. "So perhaps, someday, if I don't survive and you do, and you are able, you might be able to find me. I know there's more to it.

You need a regeneration tube. An empty body. It's a long shot." She looked up, startled. "Something happening. I've got to get back. I love all of you."

The screen went blank.

"She's right," Sofia said.

"About what?" Joseph asked, as a tear slid down Asha's face.

"There has to be something more," Sofia said. "I can feel the other Metabols. Understand them. Empathize. We could feel Darlene across space on board the Core. But I can't feel the emotion of the Swarm. And the Fades. I know where they are, but they are gray figures in a gray world. I don't feel empathy for them or from them."

"But even that is something we cannot do," Joseph noted. "And are they afraid?"

"No, they're not afraid," Sofia said.

"Am I?" Joseph asked with a gentle smile.

"Yes," Sofia said. "Not as much as Asha, but you are afraid. But not for yourself. You're afraid for us, aren't you?"

Joseph nodded.

"A connection, an empathy," Asha said to Sofia, "among your own kind was our goal. We had to start somewhere."

"What did you do to us?" Sofia asked.

She glanced at Joseph, uncertain whether and how to proceed.

"The truth," Joseph said. "She needs to know her truth. I agree with Darlene. They deserve it."

Asha nodded. "It started with assessment and selection for the Chosen. The *Myrddin* scoured the planet for children with above average intelligence."

"What about our parents?" Sofia asked. "I know about my mother, but the others?"

"The *Myrddin* had the entire world to look," Asha said. "The *Myrddin* are, were, in every country. They began with orphanages and—" she paused, then pushed on—"then there were places where children could be purchased for the right price. They also—"

Sofia interrupted. "You keep saying 'they' and 'their' but you were part of it." It was not a question.

"Yes," Asha said. "I was. We surveyed over half a million children."

"And then?" Sofia prompted.

"The base of the Chosen was selected from that," Asha said. "Once brought to the Facility, every Chosen was given an MRI. We noted those with above average amygdala. We also knew oxytocin was key, but keeping you on a steady drip of that wasn't practical. Then Doctor Leahy came to us with—"

Sofia interrupted. "Who exactly *is* this Doctor Leahy? Why did Darlene worry about her?"

"Nikola Tesla's granddaughter," Asha said. "Tesla was—"

"I know who Tesla was," Sofia said. "As Darlene said: there is no record of him having a child, never mind a grandchild."

"Leahy knew more about Tesla than anyone in the world," Asha said. "She rebuilt Tesla's lab and tower at Wardenclyffe," Asha said. "That's what Tesla used to shoot down the Swarm scout over Tunguska in 1908. She started the Chosen program for the *Myrddin* and designed the Facility and then recruited me and your grandmother to secretly build the Metabol program. She opened up Tesla's secret lab in Colorado on the back side of Cheyenne Mountain."

Sofia interrupted with a question. "Did she do the Chosen program *for* the *Myrddin* or did she manipulate the *Myrddin* to do it for her? To ultimately get the Metabol program?"

Asha blinked in surprise.

Joseph nodded. "An excellent question we never thought to ask."

Asha recovered. "Possibly, but it doesn't matter now, does it?"

"Leahy is with my nana," Sofia said. "If she is other than she claimed, that's an issue. It's also an issue if we don't know what her ultimate goal for the Metabols was."

"We can't do anything about where the mothership is," Asha said.

"But we—" Sofia indicated herself and then other Metabols—"are the result. If Leahy had motives we don't know, then the result could be something different than we think." Sofia moved past that. "What did she come to you with about Metabols?"

"A suggestion that Joseph and I thought was crazy," Asha said. "At first." She was reluctant to continue.

"Please, tell me," Sofia said.

"We knew almost nothing about the Swarm," Asha said.

Sofia started. "The Swarm? How do they enter into this?"

"Bear with us," Joseph said. "It surprised us also when Leahy brought it up."

Asha continued. "While *we* knew little about the Swarm, Leahy seemed to know quite a bit. She was aware her grandfather had shot down a Swarm scout ship in 1908. Which raises the question of how did *he* know it was inbound? Know it needed to be targeted? How could he have invented a weapon that could destroy one?"

"He was more than he appeared to be," Sofia said. "As was Leahy. They had a secret."

"Yes," Joseph said. "They did. Unfortunately, we don't know what it was."

Sofia turned to Asha. "What did Leahy know about the Swarm? And what does it have to do with us?"

"She said she gathered data from Russia's Section IV, which had samples of the Swarm from that scout ship. The Germans recovered a Swarm body from the wreckage and then the Russians took that from the Germans archives after the end of World War II." Now that she was started, Asha pushed on without pause. "Leahy thought the Swarm had some very unique capabilities that needed to be examined. The ability for its arms to separate from the host body and infiltrate another creature and take it over was one of them. Their ability to communicate with a hive mentality was another."

Sofia nodded. "Darlene picked that up once she was thralled by a Swarm parasite. She said they were all part of—" the young girl paused, her dark eyes widening slightly. "What did you do?"

"Darlene and Leahy had a sample of a Swarm," Asha said. "They examined the brain stem at the base of the arm. She analyzed the blood. It was, of course, different than human blood. Denser. It contained some material that . . ." Asha trailed off.

Sofia waited.

Asha finally shrugged. "I don't know what the material was. Leahy said it was a mineral compound that was a building block of their cells and also affected the Swarm brain. Not just their blood but something more. It helped their brains communicate."

"You experimented on us," Sofia said.

"No," Asha was quick to say. "Leahy and Darlene worked together. First on monkeys." She glanced at Rex. "Then on dogs."

"Does 'it' have a name?" Sofia asked.

"T-Fourteen," Asha said. "It meant something to Leahy and Darlene."

"And then on humans," Sofia said.

Asha nodded. "It was given in the hopes that it would self-sustain. It has."

"You didn't know what the effect would be, did you?" Sofia said.

"We had an idea."

Sofia sighed and looked out the window at the Facility. "We were experimented on. And the Fades. We were the failures."

"No!" Asha was firm. "You were the successes. The Fades were, well, we thought they were, the failures. Your grandmother and I manipulated the data that went to Mrs. Parrish from the start. The Chosen were smart. No doubt about it. They worked hard. So we passed them off as the successes. The Metabols showed something different. More empathy. A greater ability to work with others."

"Did the Chosen get the T-Fourteen?"

"No."

"The Fades have it, though," Sofia said. She nodded. "That is how the Fade we saw was able to merge with Cthulhu." Sofia turned from the window and looked up at Asha with her dark eyes. "How many Metabols were killed when they became Fades?"

Asha had the numbers imprinted in her memory. "There were eventually two-thousand-and-fifty-seven. Mrs. Parrish insisted those that didn't go into comas or die, be purged. She didn't know about the Metabol program. She just thought they were failures who didn't respond to her various enhancement drugs and training."

"Killed," Sofia said. "Because of what you did."

Asha couldn't meet Sofia's eyes.

Joseph spoke. "There are one-thousand-five-hundred-and-twenty-four of you remaining. If we had not saved you--"

"You could have *chosen* us and not given us the T-Fourteen," Sofia pointed out. "We'd be on the mothership right now. I'd be with my nana. We'd be safe."

Joseph agreed. "True. But we don't know where the mothership is or if it's safe or not. And Mrs. Parrish's plan to wipe the planet clean with the *Danse* was so terrible we had to find an alternative. Beyond that, the future of mankind was on the precipice even without the Swarm arriving."

Sofia closed her eyes and was still. Asha shifted uncomfortably while Joseph watched her, his face passive.

Both became aware that activity in the Facility had ceased. All the Metabols were still, eyes closed. This lasted a long minute.

Then they all opened their eyes and continued what they had been doing. Sofia faced the two adults. "We forgive you."

THE MILKY WAY GALAXY

The duty was designated by the simple fact that this particular Battle Core was the closest to the Earth solar system. The loss of a Battle Core was unprecedented and required examination.

A course was calculated by the Supreme Swarm on board. The Core initiated Faster Than Light Transit. At the same time, nine other Battle Cores also Transitioned, bound for the same destination.

ORION FLEET HEADQUARTERS, ARLIA EMPIRE

Military commanders are renowned for not studying the causes of defeats because they dread uncovering their own mistakes. Even worse, though, they avoid attributing the causes of victory to anything other than their own decisions and actions. Luck, or perhaps the unknown is rarely considered.

This was the case for the Admiral in charge of Orion Fleet. The system in which this Airlia Fleet made its home had been attacked by a Battle Core. A new tactic, the Teardrop program using humans as cannon fodder to counter-attack the Core while it was inbound. had apparently worked. Enough humans carrying nuclear warheads had gotten inside and detonated, causing the Battle Core to abruptly cease its attack and transition to FTLT. At least that's what appeared to have happened. It wasn't a total victory in that the Core hadn't been destroyed, but it was enough of a victory for the Admiral to feel very confident in the effectiveness of the Teardrop program.

The Admiral had no way of knowing, of course, that the Core's abrupt withdrawal had been the result of the loss of a Core in another solar system. Oddly, though, as fate often draws coincidences, in the desire to ramp up the Teardrop program, more humans were needed and in the catalogue of worlds the Airlia had rule over that also had humans, the one that had defeated the Swarm was there. Earth was in the records that communication had been lost with that outpost long ago and a Kortad mothership under the command of an Airlia named Artad had been sent to discover why. The loss of communications with Artad had also been noted and the planet written off as a loss in a program that had shown low potential.

It was now written back in.

Thus, a mothership was detailed to head to Earth and see what was what and whether there were humans that could be Tallied into the Teardrop Program.

WHIDBEY ISLAND, WASHINGTON

Nosferatu kept the helicopter low as he crossed the narrow strait between Everett and Whidbey Island. Nekhbet was in the co-pilot's seat and Tasha in the rear. The ash was swirling as the wind gusted. The water below was dark and turbulent. Eight-foot-high waves roiled with whitecaps.

They flew over a capsized ferry, the hull awash. As they approached the shoreline where the ferry had once docked at the town of Clinton, the effect of the tsunami from Poseidon's detonation was apparent. The pilings still remained along with the tarmac, but the toll booths were gone, along with the houses at water level. Cars that been crowded there from people desperate to get off the island had been swept to the base of the bluffs and tossed there like so many toys. The *Fynbar* had landed in the middle of the empty lot.

"My dear," Nekhbet said, an edge of anxiety immediately getting Nosferatu's attention.

He glanced over and saw what had caused her to stir. Water was swirling in a cone from the ocean as far up into the grey that one could see. The waterspout grew in width to a quarter mile wide in just the few seconds he watched and it was moving fast. Directly toward them.

Nosferatu banked the helicopter away from it. At that moment wind shear slammed into the blades and they dropped forty feet in a split second, Nosferatu battling with the controls and barely managing to keep them from striking the water.

He increased speed. They were one hundred yards away from shore when the waterspout enveloped the chopper. It jerked about wildly. Nosferatu was disoriented, unable to see more than a few feet. The force of the water hurricane was so great, the blades spun futilely.

"Hold on!" Nosferatu yelled, which Nekhbet took to mean reaching across and putting her hand on top of his that was controlling the cycle and squeezing incredibly hard.

They had a brief glimpse of something black and then they crashed, a scream from Tasha in the rear. The howl of the wind and the sound of rain hitting like bullets. The windshield shattered and water swirled inside.

Nekhbet still held on to Nosferatu's hand, which indicated she'd survived the crash. He turned in his seat and kicked his door open. He pulled Nekhbet with him and they tumbled onto the ferry parking lot.

Just as quickly as it had struck, the waterspout lifted and was gone, leaving them in the semi-dusk of steadily falling ash. Nosferatu lay on his back, soaked and bruised. "Nekhbet?" he gave her hand a squeeze and glanced at her.

She was next to him, a gash on her forehead already healing. She reached with her free hand and wiped the blood, then licked it off her fingers. She turned to him and smiled. "That was different."

Nosferatu looked about. Forty feet away, was the *Fynbar*. The hatch was closed and there was no sign of Turcotte. The pavement below the craft was cracked from the impact when the spaceship crashed.

He remembered Tasha. Letting go of Nekhbet he went to the wreckage. The Russian sailor was trapped in the back seat, impaled on a tube of metal. Her hands were wrapped around it, her eyes wide in fear and shock.

Nosferatu crawled into the crashed helicopter and grabbed the tube. He tried to withdraw it from her but to no avail other than a cry of pain from Tasha.

"She's almost dead," Nekhbet said. "You need the strength."

"Hush," Nosferatu said.

"Put her out of the pain," Nekhbet argued.

Nosferatu tried to free her once more.

"You're wasting blood," Nekhbet said.

Nosferatu leaned close to Tasha. "I'm sorry." He clamped down on her throat and quickly drained her, feeling the power of fresh blood. He sensed movement. Nekhbet was licking the blood on the tube and coming from the wound. It was over in a few moments.

The two Undead exited without speaking. Nosferatu led the way to the *Fynbar*. He climbed up the sloping side. Undid the hatch and entered.

Turcotte was in the fetal position in the pilot's compression, eyes closed. Nosferatu knelt next to him and shook his shoulder. No response. Checked for a pulse even though he could feel the heat of life coming from the body and smell the blood flowing in his veins.

"Is he alive?" Nekhbet called from above, her head framed in the hatch.

"Yes."

"What's wrong with him?"

Nosferatu checked the body. "Nothing obvious." He leaned close. "Turcotte! Turcotte!"

"Perhaps we need to check his blood?" Nekhbet said.

Nosferatu ignored her. He pulled Turcotte out of the depression and pondered what to do next.

"My dear," Nekhbet said from above.

"What?" Nosferatu snapped, tired of her constant desire for blood.

"A problem," Nekhbet was looking outward.

Nosferatu jumped up, grabbing the edge of the hatch and pulling himself up so he could see. The water had withdrawn from the land for two hundred yards, leaving fluffer mud exposed as far as could be seen both ways up and down the coast. The over-turned ferry was grounded in it.

"This is not good, is it?" Nekhbet said.

Nosferatu dropped back into the spaceship, grabbed Turcotte and tossed him over his shoulder. He climbed up the ladder to the hatch and shut it. "Run," he ordered Nekhbet. He slid down the side and dashed toward the road leading up from the ferry area between two bluffs. A battered sign depicting a ferry and a whale, with *Welcome To Whidbey Island* framed by two eagles facing each other was to their left.

A loud noise rumbled in the distance. They dodged parked cars, some with rotting bodies still inside, victims of the Danse Macabre who'd died before the Reaping. Boeing Field, just across the water, had been ground zero for the first release of the plague and the poor souls hadn't known they were headed in the wrong direction, not that it mattered, given how fast it had spread. Some of the cars were jammed in the gridlock heading toward the ferry, others caught trying to flee back onto the island, an indication of total confusion.

Nosferatu risked a glanced over his shoulder. A tsunami sixty feet high was roaring toward the shoreline. Nekhbet stumbled and Nosferatu reached out with his free hand, helping her to her feet. They sprinted uphill. The wave hit the ferry pier, washed over, struck the *Fynbar*, pushing it into the smashed pile of cars at the base of the slope.

Nosferatu and Nekhbet could hear the smashing, crunching of the approaching wall of water and debris behind them.

"Drop him!" Nekhbet shouted as she accelerated ahead of Nosferatu.

Nosferatu didn't reply. She was ten feet, fifteen in front of him, higher. A surge of water hit the rear of Nosferatu's knees, buckling them. He went down, still holding tight to Turcotte.

Nekhbet paused, turned. "Fool!" She ran back to him and helped him to his feet as water swirled about them, up to their waists. Together they pushed forward through the water and detritus, pulling Turcotte with them, one foot after another as the tsunami crested.

"Hold on," Nekhbet shouted as she grabbed onto the bumper of a large pick-up truck. The water was receding, trying to suck them back with it. Nosferatu clung to Turcotte over his shoulder with one hand and Nekhbet with his other.

Then they were free of the water. They watched as it slowly withdrew back to the Sound, taking flotsam with it.

"Why do I feel that the earth mother is angry with us?" Nekhbet asked as they staggered to the side of the road, clear of the vehicles.

Nosferatu laid Turcotte down and looked at her. "What?"

"The earth mother," Nekhbet said. She knelt and put both hands into the dirt. "Gaia *is* angry. Can't you feel it?"

"'Gaia'? That is just one of those foolish early religions. After the Airlia Gods of Egypt and before the Christians found their Jesus and the Muslims their Mohammed."

"Oh, my dear," Nekhbet said. "It is not foolish. All those years I lay in that coffin. When you were next to me in Egypt in the Roads of Rostau. And especially the centuries after you rescued me but could not bring me back to the living. Not dead, but not quite alive. I felt Gaia's presence because there was no other life around me. Particularly on the Skeleton Coast." She stood, looking out at the ash falling, the grey sky, and the debris floating in Puget Sound. "She has good reason to be angry."

MONS OLYMPUS, MARS

The form that had been Lisa Duncan sat up despite the fact her heart was not beating, nor her lungs breathing. She stood and walked about the compartment. Spotted a *ka* lying on the floor and picked it up. Stared at the device in its palm for a long time as the implant considered a conundrum.

Did it need the human part of her? The implant had all her memories; more than even the *ka* had loaded since Duncan had blocked some of her own history. The *ka* also didn't contain everything since her last backup and there had been a considerable amount of activity such as World War III, the defeat of the Airlia in which this crash played the last role, and the arrival of Battle Core.

But did it need the human part of her?

The implant made the decision. The hand closed around the *ka*, absorbing it and the data it contained. Not just Lisa Duncan's memories, but the essence of her as a person. Opened its hand and the *ka* was gone.

For the first time, the body drew its first long, shuddering breath. This initiated a sequence of events. Her lungs filled with air, supplying the blood that began circulating by a fluttering heart.

She had no immediate memory that she was Lisa Duncan as her brain, the most complex organ in the human body, was still forming and, for the moment, the implant was in total control, having done its first task of reconstituting the body.

In a way, Duncan, the human, was experiencing the opposite of the way memory evolves. When humans experience something, a long-term memory is not instantly formed. The sensory data from the nervous system about the event is encoded via a process of consolidation. How this worked, exactly, human scientists had not yet conclusively determined. In a way it's the epitome of not being able to be conscious of what we are not conscious of.

Regardless, significant memories are literally encoded in the brain. Explicit memory about events that happen in a person's life, along with general facts and information, are stored in three parts of the brain: the hippocampus, the neocortex and the amygdala. This is what is considered the conscious part of the brain. For Lisa Duncan, this part was, in essence, rebooting via what had been on the *ka* with assistance from the implant.

Implicit memories, which are what keep the body alive such as motor function, are in the basal ganglia and cerebellum and a part of being human. Babies don't have to learn how to breath once they exit the womb; it's implicit. This was functioning at a survival level; its activation had been the moment when the implant brought the human part 'alive' once more as a conscious entity.

Short term memory, more commonly known as working memory, generally resides in the pre-frontal cortex. This was also in the basic stages of development.

EARTH

The outer layer of the inner core locked into place laterally, rotating in concert with the center of the inner core. The two merged and connections were made between them that had been long dormant. Where the two had previously negated each other to a large extent, they were now one.

They contained a tremendous amount of energy, more than all the power mankind had managed to generate in its brief time on the planet which was over four and a half billion years old. Given that life above, as humans considered it, only came into existence four point one million years ago and the first mammals two hundred and twenty million years, the planet was ancient. Humans originally thought they developed two hundred thousand years ago, but recent discoveries pushed that number further and further back to perhaps four hundred thousand. Regardless, it was negligible in comparison to what had now just awakened.

The planet had been reacting so far.

Now it was time to act.

An Awakening.

LAST STAND OF IMPERIUM

TALIANT FLEET BASE.

MILLIONS OF YEARS AGO

Tai hurried to keep up with Librarian. She walked with purpose through old, musty corridors that dated back to the beginning of Taliant, when it was a single ring-band station, rotating around a central fusion power core. Slowly, over millennia, more rings were added. Then an outer shell had grown longitudinally toward both polar axis's until it became the artificial planet it currently was. To keep gravity relatively equal, dozens of rings inside the outer shell were rotating at their different angles and slightly different diameters and speeds to accommodate each other. Inside of the bands was space for the fleet to dock and power production from the fusion reactors.

There were also the low and zero-g laboratories and factories further inside the bands.

Tai and Librarian had to transition across seven, newer bands to get to this one, First Ring. Each one involving crossing an air lock that disconnected from the exit band, slid between the two moving rings before latching on to the new one and they could enter. The last transition they'd had the large airlock pod to themselves and the exit lock had been a model Tai hadn't seen since training at the Academy on the derelict and abandoned Saturn moon station for close quarters space battle.

There were few people about as they went farther into First Ring. Here and there they caught glimpses of squatters who quickly hid. They walked for over a quarter mile along a dimly lit corridor and encountered no one. Many of the doors were sealed, the rooms behind them abandoned in favor of more modern conveniences in newer rings. Tai didn't ask where they were going. He already knew the answer: *you'll know when we get there.*

Librarian paused and removed a platinum card from a pocket. She inserted it into a slot Tai hadn't spotted. A section of wall moved aside without a sound, a contradiction to the age of the gear.

"You won't find this on any schematics," Librarian said as they entered and the wall slid back behind them. "They built around this so long ago that anyone who remembered this section is long since dust. One advantage to this area, though.

It's heavily shielded and scanners can't penetrate. The old-timers built things to last."

"How do you know of it?" Tai asked as he followed her down a narrow service tunnel.

"Word of mouth from my predecessor. It has been a Librarian secret as long as can be remembered. After all, the Science Academy was originally founded in First Ring, while the Military and Political were still on Earth. Both spaced up long afterward. This section was the original Academy."

She halted, cables and pipes cluttering the ceiling and walls, some so old they had writing on them from ancient tongues before Imperium unified language into the Common. Tai recognized some as Old Earther. There were also Martian from that stretch of time Mars Colony was independent from Earth and other languages he didn't comprehend with strange symbols.

"Push the door open," Librarian ordered, indicating a narrow, vertical slit.

Tai couldn't recall ever having to physically open an interior door except in combat training. Then they normally used breaching charges. He looked at the faded grey metal. He gripped the narrow seam with the tips of his fingers. Pulled.

"It takes muscle, boy," Librarian said.

Tai pulled with all his might. He was rewarded as the door grunted open a few inches, allowing him a better grip. He shifted and pushed, using his legs, the prosthetic one providing more power than his natural one.

"Enough," Librarian said when the opening was wide enough for them to slip through. She led the way into the darkness beyond.

Tai followed but halted when his skin tingled.

"Biometric scanner," Librarian informed him. "If you weren't on the approved list, you'd be lasered to tiny little pieces. Shut the door."

Tai did so and they were in utter darkness. "Why the manual door?"

"Oh, it's not manual," Librarian said. "I can use the card to open it. But I wanted to see if you could."

The air had an odor he couldn't identify. It was also still and he wondered if the circulator worked in this section. If it didn't . . .

A light flickered, then grew stronger. Green tubes spaced around the area provided illumination. They were in a room that was quite large, over a hundred meters long and wide, with a ceiling twenty meters above them.

"An old maintenance bay," Librarian said. "As you may have guessed, this was built before our distant ancestors had mastered FTLT and were sending sub-light probes into the cosmos. They were launching transports with colonists in deep sleep." She shook her head at the irony of sub-light interstellar travel. "The first FTLT recons passed those ships. Then the FTLT landing ships also went past them. Established colonies greeted those sub-light passengers when they came out of deep sleep and arrived at what they thought would be wild worlds they had to tame. What a shock that must have been."

"What a disappointment," Tai muttered.

Librarian shot him a sharp glance. "How so?"

"Anyone who volunteered for such a dangerous and long mission must have longed for the adventure. To leave civilization and arrive at the same must have been hard. The challenge had already been overcome. The danger they had anticipated had been erased without their knowledge."

Librarian nodded. "I chose you wisely."

Tai focused on the dull red pyramid in the center of the cargo bay. It was 20 feet tall and the same across each side of the base. In front of it were dozens of rows of tables with smaller two-foot-tall black pyramids.

He indicated the pyramids. "What is this?"

"Ah yes. You've never seen the actual Compendium." Librarian pointed at the red pyramid. "That is an exact copy. The backup. The smaller pyramids are Guardians. Portable compendia, with some adjustments."

In front of each Guardian were two small black spheres, a quarter inch in diameter, set in cradles of silver metal. Tai walked up to a set. "What are these?"

"The future," Librarian said. "We call them Tesla's."

"'We', Librarian?"

"The Compendium has a duty larger than just accumulating knowledge. We are the lubricant between the military, political and science. We see the larger picture. Mankind stands on a knife's edge, Tai. How many intelligent alien species have humans met that still exist?"

"None, Librarian. That we know of. There might be remnants of some that escaped."

"There is always war upon contact," Librarian said. "Who fired first? No one knows. In fact, three of those alien races never fought us and were limited to their own solar system and didn't possess FTLT. They were obliterated by Fleet as a matter of course even though they posed no threat. We occupied their planets for their resources, even though there were many who protested such action. The military insisted it was our manifest destiny as a species.

"Other species, FTLT capable, were easily conquered given that their level of technology was far inferior to ours. We all know the history of the brutal and long wars with the real threats, other empires. Eventually we prevailed and they no longer exist or if any do, it is in the far reaches beyond the Boundary where the survivors escaped." She fell silent and they remained that way for a minute. When she spoke again, the usual edge was gone from her voice. "Does that make us right?" she asked. "Our manifest destiny?"

Tai knew what she meant. "It means we are more powerful. Beyond that, it's a question for the philosophers."

"Answered like a Marine," Librarian said. "But it's a question for all of us. I've been pondering what the Awakening means. If a planet can become sentient, or always has been sentient, what are we? Are we not like ants scuttling about?"

"'Ants'?"

Librarian shook her head. "You never visited Earth. Tiny little creatures living in the dirt that no one notices. A dozen could fit on your fingertip. Humans stepped on them without even noticing." She fell silent.

"You want to avoid us getting stepped on, Librarian," Tai said.

"It might be too late for that," Librarian said.

Tai waited, then indicated the Compendium, Guardians and Tesla. "What is the purpose of this?"

"You are really asking why have I brought you here," Librarian said. "This is the future, Captain Tai. And you are going to be part of it. My office oversees research in all three Academies. We knew it was inevitable that Imperium would collapse. All Empires do. It is the very nature of things. The cycle of life and death and rebirth. And not necessarily a bad thing."

Tai shot her a sharp look, but didn't say anything.

"Are we good, Tai? Were those alien species we destroyed bad or evil?"

"Again, those are questions for the philosophers," Tai said. "I didn't have that luxury when infiltrating a combat zone."

"Fair enough," Librarian said. "But you're not in a combat zone right now. Don't you think it's interesting that we don't have a philosopher Academy? It is a minor taught to a handful at Science Academy. There aren't courses in it at Military and Political. Considered frivolous and unimportant. I asked you earlier in my office where did we all come from? Have we always existed?" She waved a hand, dismissing it. "We are entering a combat zone. The entire species. The time for theory is over. Long before the Awakening and the war with Unity, my predecessor, by seven generations, foresaw the inevitable collapse of Imperium. After all, there were empires before us that reached great heights and collapsed and were lost in the dust of unknown history. So, she decided to do something about it."

"To prevent the collapse?" Tai asked, trying to follow.

Librarian smiled sadly and shook her head. "Did you not hear me say inevitable? It was too late for that even in her time. The projections all pointed toward an inevitable collapse from any number of reasons: encountering a superior alien race, rebellion, a cosmic event—" she paused—"even the discovery of a radically different type of life form or power. Such as a sentient planet. Who knows? There may be sentient galaxies?"

"A god?" Tai asked.

"Ah, the originator of the Chaos?" Librarian shrugged. "That is not the purpose of the program. It is to look to the future. To ensure everything isn't lost when Imperium falls. That we can do better next time."

"The Guardians I understand," Tai said. "The knowledge. But what are the black spheres?"

"Implants," Librarian said. "They go at the stem of the brain."

"That's illegal, Librarian," Tai automatically said. "From the time of the AI Wars. Brain implants are—"

Librarian cut him off. "I know the law, Tai. We all know the law and the danger. I'm curious, Captain. Why did you accept a prosthetic instead of having your leg regrown?"

"The technology for regrowth would have required I be evacuated and taken off the battle line for too long," Tai said. "They had the prosthesis available on the front line and I could adapt in a few days."

"But since?"

Tai shrugged. "Regrowth never is the same. With a prothesis I could remain on active duty."

"Until I plucked you," Librarian said.

"I do my duty, Librarian," Tai said.

"And it is appreciated. The truth, though, is that you kept the prothesis because it's stronger than your original leg. Correct? An unenhanced human couldn't have opened that door."

"I'm not enhanced," Tai said vehemently. "You tested me with the door."

"I showed you your own truth," Librarian said. "You can do things others can't. The AI Wars happened because humans invented the AI and programmed it. So, the AI had all our flaws."

"It killed millions before we pulled the plug," Tai said.

"But what about a different kind of—" Librarian paused, trying to figure out how to explain something she'd never explained before. "Not a machine or a computer like Compendium, Captain Tai. There are times I lie awake and fear we made a mistake. My predecessors." She pointed at the implants. "The truth is that these were discovered by a science recon party hundreds of years ago. We did find a radically different type of life form. Except they were dormant."

"How did they know it was a life form, then?" Tai asked.

"We didn't. Not right away. We thought they were artifacts left behind by some long-lost civilization. We've come across those on occasion. But there was a message in the structure in which they were found. Hieroglyphics. It took a while to decode. The man who did that was named Teslan. When he realized what they were and what they were designed to do, he went to Librarian. They knew they were sitting on a potential disaster. Or the best hope for mankind." She shook her head. "I know it's confusing. But the reason I sometimes think I made a mistake is that the Tesla, which is what they were named for obvious reasons, is a different kind of life form. A bridge between carbon based and silicon based."

"How do you know that?" Tai demanded. He pointed at the small spheres. "Those are intelligent?"

"The message said so," Librarian said.

Tai spread his hands in confusion. "I don't understand. They look like metal. If they're alive, why aren't they doing anything?"

"They've been waiting."

"For?"

"For someone like us to find them. It seems the Tesla's were a species that evolved to a point where some of them became, the best term to use is facilitators. Apparently, there has been conflict between the two types of life forms before: carbon and silicon. That's why I didn't doubt when Unity reported the Awakening. But since we never let Fleet know we'd found the Tesla's, we were in a bind. And there was also the problem of the man who'd translated the hieroglyphics."

Tai waited.

"Teslan had translated the instructions," Librarian said. "He followed them. He merged with the Tesla."

Tai shook his head. "The surgery to put one of those inside a person . . ." Tai shook his head. "You say the base of the skull, but there isn't room."

"Nanotechnology," Librarian said. "It dissolves and passes through the skin, through bone, through the membrane surrounding the brain and then reassembles. Teslan did this without permission. The good news is we know it works. It didn't kill him."

"The bad news?" Tai asked.

"Teslan became something that was no longer human, although he looked the same. He began speaking in the plural:

we. As if he, the man, were still in there, in his mind, but the implant was also alive. Teslan then told Librarian that he, they, had done calculations, and that Imperium was doomed. It was irreversible. In a way he predicted the Awakening, saying we would run into a lifeform we could not conquer. And that we were obviously incapable of making peace. Our history proved that. Our first reaction is always based on fear. He said that we'd have to, essentially, reboot. And the Tesla's could help us do that. They, it, whatever you want call what he was now, made all of these guardians. He laid out a plan for Librarian. One that has been passed down to me."

"What exactly do the Tesla's do?" Tai asked. "Can they become active on their own?"

"I don't know," Librarian admitted.

Tai looked at her.

She tried to explain. "Like FTLT, we know it works because it worked on Teslan. We're not sure how. It will change the user. Make them stronger, smarter, live longer. But they aren't human anymore."

"What is this plan?" he pressed. "Why are you showing me this, Librarian?"

"It is not yet time for me to reveal that," Librarian said. "I want you to know this exists and that if anything happens to me, you should come here and put your hands on the Compendium. It has been programmed to impart the plan to you." She reached into a pocket and retrieved a card key and handed it to him. "We must be very careful, Tai. There are enemies within and without." She headed for the door.

"Wait a minute, Librarian," Tai said. "What happened to Teslan?"

Librarian took a deep breath. "He, it, disappeared after building the guardians and imparting the plan. Took an FTLT scout ship and was gone. That was hundreds of years ago."

"Where did Teslan go?"

Librarian turned and faced Tai. "We didn't know. We searched, covertly, of course. But we could find no trace of where he went. But now? I believe I know."

"Where?"

"Teslan went to Light-Union-Twelve."

THE PRESENT

EXPLORATION

PACIFIC OCEAN

The Swarm kraken floated listlessly in that depth where sunlight is almost, but not quite, gone. It's two longest arms, drooped slightly. The other, shorter arms were curled back, as if exhausted. The entire creature, from tip of longest tentacles to the head with its sack for storing Scale, was seventy-five meters long, almost a football field. A deep chunk along one side of the body had been torn away, the result of a torpedo fired by a Chinese submarine before it was crushed and sent to a watery grave by a cluster of kraken. The others had made it back to the Swarm warship and been recovered, taken back up to the Core, only to perish into the sun. This one had not returned in time and been left behind. There was no Swarm in vicinity to issue it orders and no Scale life had been detected so it had adapted a hibernation mode, waiting for either orders or something to Reap to come within range. It drifted with the Pacific current.

However, there was other life.

The existence of genus Architeuthis had finally been admitted by scientists based on remains found in the stomachs of whales, but the giant squid was still mostly a creature of legend and myth with almost no live sightings as it inhabited the absolute darkness of the deep ocean. Only after undersea earthquakes or other rare events, did it unwillingly rise up. But those ancient encounters are the stuff of tales sailors told in dingy bars in sea ports all over the world for generations.

There had been a couple of videos made by deep sea explorers, quick glimpses of the beast, and speculation had been made that they grew to thirteen meters in length for females and ten for males. These were, of course, extrapolations from scant evidence. And, like many such, wrong.

Directly below the kraken, one of those creatures of legend, a giant squid, just a few meters shorter than the kraken, but much, much larger than scientific estimates, silently rose up from the depths. It was not alone. Circling the kraken was a pod of sperm whales, the giant squid's natural predator.

Yet they did not battle each other.

Only partly alert, the kraken reacted slowly to the giant squid's presence, trying to escape. But the two long tentacles from the squid wrapped around the kraken, just behind the large, saucer eyes. The kraken responded, lashing out at the squid. Which opened it up to the sperm whales, a predator whose normal meal was squid. A large, sixty-foot-long male whale, weighing over forty-five short tons, accelerated, jaw wide open, revealing a very unique mouth, with teeth on the lower jaw and open sockets on the top gum into which those teeth fit when the mouth closed. Those teeth ripped into the side of the kraken, gouging out a chunk of flesh. Grey blood flowed into the ocean from the wound.

In response, the other whales let out a series of high frequency clicks, projecting outward for miles, drawing more whales. They charged in to take their pounds of flesh.

The giant squid, its job done, slowly sank back down into the depths. The whales focused on the kraken, ripping it to shreds.

ASTEROID BELT, SOLAR SYSTEM

The Swarm scout ships gathered in pieces of debris. They were few and far between. Many humans had falsely envisioned the Asteroid Belt as this rock laden expanse with large asteroids that would be difficult to dodge if a ship tried to transit it, but the reality was anything but that. Over half the mass contained in the entire Belt was in the form of the four largest asteroids: Ceres, Vesta, Pallas and Hygiea. That sounds impressive until one realizes the entire mass of all the material in the Belt, if it were pulled together, would be about four percent of Earth's moon.

In essence the Asteroid Belt is empty space with the odds of a transiting spaceship hitting an asteroid around one in a billion. Thus, the scout ships had been forced to search with great diligence to recover what they did. Not just because the objects were few, but because they weren't looking for asteroids. They were searching for artifacts which were even rarer.

However, the scout ships had excellent scanners and picked up bits and pieces, the largest almost two inches long. As good as their long-range scanners were, the labs on board the warship had data accumulated over millennium by Battle Cores across the galaxies that they could access while examining the specimens.

The pieces and parts were analyzed and the results sent to the Command Swarm.

The most common element was a metal that was familiar to the Swarm. What the Airlia called *b'ja*. The stuff from which their motherships and warships were built. Extremely strong; but this was better that the version the Airlia currently used. It was also a silvery color rather than the black the Airlia used. And this metal predated the emergence of the Airlia Empire. There was no sign of pure Airlia material in the debris.

Metal like this was in the Swarm genetic memory. Uncovered in other debris fields across the galaxies. Signs of a massive empire. The most startling find though, was remnants of the hardened biological material that made up the outer hull of a Swarm Battle Core. An analysis of the material dated it. There was no current Swarm memory that went back that far.

What species had been here so long ago, during the previous cycle of civilization in this solar system? How had the Swarm been somewhere and somewhen that seemed to predate what they knew of themselves? And what had happened?

If a brain could shrug, the Command Swarm did the equivalent. Long ago was not a problem. The mission was here and now. Whoever had built that empire was long gone.

With the infinite patience the Swarm possessed, it focused on the sensors oriented toward the third, and dying, planet.

GLACIER NATIONAL PARK, MONTANA

Hands gently slid over T.J. Waterman's shoulders. The fingers were long, elegant and crowned with brilliant red fingernails. Lips came close to his ear and a tongue licked lightly in the spot he particularly enjoyed just behind the lobe.

"I'm working," he said, reading the computer's analysis of the weather, cloud cover, climate change, and radiation levels.

"I know," Portia said. A slight pout edged her next words. "You're always working. I miss you."

"I'm ensuring our future." He was encouraged by the radiation readings. It was dropping precipitously. Which meant that the nuclear conflagration had mostly been limited to the other side of the world and that the Big Three, the United States, China and Russia, had not launched their massive arsenals. That was good, very good. He felt the first stirrings of arousal reading the positive numbers.

"What can I do to help?" Portia asked as her hands slid lower, over his rock-hard stomach. They deftly unbuckled his pants and her right hand slipped inside. "Oh! I love when you go commando."

The big problem was the ash. That was going to take a while to clear. He remembered something one of the climate scientists had briefed him on. The largest volcanic eruption in recorded history had been Mount Tambora in 1815. He accessed that file and scanned the summary. One page, because he insisted on the key information always be summarized in one page. If a man or woman couldn't keep it to one page, they weren't concise and incisive.

Mount Tambora Eruption. 10 April 1815.

The eruption column of ash reached 141,000 feet. Heavier particles settled out after two weeks. Finer particles stayed airborne up to three years afterward. Longitudinal winds spread the ash around the globe. The ash contained carbon dioxide, water, hydrogen, sulfur dioxide, hydrogen chloride, hydrogen fluoride and others elements. CO2 and water are greenhouse gasses. During the summer of 1815, a strange fog was noticed in the Northeast United States. It was not dispersed by wind and sunrises and sunsets had an unusual red glow. It was not until the next summer, though, that Tambora's effect on the climate was truly felt. 1816 was dubbed 'The Year Without Summer'. Average global temperatures decreased by a range of 0.7 to 1.3 Fahrenheit. This is enough to cause agricultural disruption. Canada experienced extreme cold during the summer. Crops failed across the northern hemisphere. It was the second coldest year in the northern hemisphere since records began being kept in 1400. The 1810s are still the coldest decade on record.

Portia was stroking him, but he barely noticed. Her tongue was gentle on the back of his ear, but she knew better than to speak while he was reading.

The results extended beyond famine. Typhus epidemics struck Europe and the eastern Mediterranean. The India monsoon was interrupted, initiating three failed harvests. A new strain of cholera erupted in Bengal. Crops failed across the world initiating the worst famine of the 19th Century. There were devastating floods in China. It is not known how many died directly or indirectly from the Tambora eruption, but the numbers were in the hundreds of thousands if not millions.

T.J. ran the current data against the extrapolations of the Tambora numbers. This was worse. He initiated the program to calculate how long it would be before the atmosphere returned to normal, or at least livable normal on the outside. He leaned back in the chair as the computer went to work.

Portia took this as an invitation and got on her knees. She scooted under the edge of the desk. Her mouth joined her hands.

T.J. briefly closed his eyes, allowing himself to feel the pleasure, but only for a moment, before returning his attention to the screen. The answer appeared. The estimate was four years of nuclear winter, followed by slowly rising temperatures. He thought it ironic that the scientist who'd briefed him on Tambora and other climate matters had been so concerned about global warming. That problem seemed to have been human-engineered away.

Of course, T.J. didn't remember that the same man had committed suicide, lying in the pile of cash he'd been paid, when he'd realized he'd just been used and the T.J. Waterman had no intention of changing his business empire's practices to avoid climate change. In fact, T.J. used the data as an impetus to double-down on fracking.

He closed his eyes once more, giving himself the momentary pleasure of finishing in Portia's mouth. He opened his eyes and looked down to make sure that his pants weren't stained. Then he pushed the chair back. "I'm going to bed. Make sure the suit is cleaned." The last was unnecessary but some habits are hard to break.

Of course, Portia would do that. It was programmed into her by one the world's best robotics programmers, aided by data from the Airlia archives. The programmer moldered underneath the poured concrete in the death shaft.

THE FACILITY

"Have you figured out what happened with the Fade and the Cthulhu?" Joseph asked Sofia. "And the dragon," he added. "You said they merged. But who is in charge? It seemed the Cthulhu protected us."

Sofia shook her head. "I don't know. The Fade was still there in a way. But also, not there."

"What about the other Fades?" Asha asked. "You said you know where they are."

Sofia spread her hands. "Moving outward. Others have merged."

"With Swarm creatures?" Asha asked.

Sofia frowned. "It's hard to tell. They are . . ." she shook her head. "It's strange and—" she paused as the cavern floor shook and the earth grumbled. The shaking lasted for twenty seconds, then disappeared.

Asha glanced at Joseph. "Earthquake?"

"We're not in a zone," Joseph said, knowing she knew that.

"An attack?" Asha said. "More nukes going off?"

Joseph shook his head. "It came from below. The spirits of the underworld are unhappy."

Sofia had her eyes closed. "It is more than that. The planet is not happy. There is something much larger happening."

"What?" Asha asked.

"I'm hearing echoes," Sofia said.

"Of?" Asha prompted.

Sofia pointed down. "Out of the ground. From deep, deep inside. As if a voice, a primal one that has no words, is trying to communicate."

"What do you think it is?" Joseph asked.

Sofia's forehead crinkled in concentration. She whispered: "Earth Mother. She is becoming aware."

WHIDBEY ISLAND, WASHINGTON

Nekhbet was staring at Turcotte with a look that Nosferatu recognized. The former special operations soldier was curled in the fetal position, eyes closed. The only sign of life was his chest moving slowly. And the warm glow of his blood pulsing in his veins that both of the Undead could sense.

"He is a friend," Nosferatu chided her out of her constant, simmering blood lust.

"A girl can wonder," Nekhbet said. "He is quite the specimen of a man."

"Am I not enough for you, my love?" Nosferatu asked.

"You know what I mean," Nekhbet said. "Humans are meals."

"He is a friend," Nosferatu repeated. He was looking at the pile of smashed cars pressed up against the bluff where the ferry landing had once stood. There were just pilings poking up through the dark, angry water. The *Fynbar* was lying on top of the cars, angled, but intact.

"What is wrong with him?" Nekhbet asked.

"I am not a doctor," Nosferatu muttered. The helicopter was somewhere in that mess. "But we need him if we're going anywhere." He knelt next to Turcotte, felt the pulse on his throat. Steady and strong. Pulled an eyelid back. The pupil was wide and unfocused. He waved his hand in front of it. No reaction. Nosferatu frowned. Around the edges of the eye was an extremely narrow ring of black he'd never noticed before.

"Our ride is crushed," Nekhbet commented. She looked up the road, inland. "Is there another way off this island?"

"I don't know," Nosferatu said. "How far do you want to walk?"

"Not at all," Nekhbet said.

He looked north, up the road between lines of tall conifers. "There has to be an airfield on the island. We can find a plane."

There had been a long line of cars waiting for the ferry along the road above the parking lot. Even in the face of disaster, they were all on the right side of the road, parked in the waiting lane. Several were tossed aside or ripped open, the result of Naga or Cthulhu or dragons snatching the humans out of them to be Reaped.

He walked to them, choosing a four-wheel drive truck. The keys were in the ignition. The doors were open with no sign of violence. He slid inside and cranked the engine. The battery was weak and clicked several times. It started on the fourth attempt. He drove to Nekhbet and Turcotte. Together they put Turcotte in the back seat.

"Should we put his seat belt on?" Nekhbet asked, a hint of sarcasm in her voice.

"I don't plan on crashing," Nosferatu said as he slid behind the wheel.

"No one ever plans on crashing." Nekhbet claimed the passenger seat. "Yet they occur."

"See if there's a map in the glove compartment," Nosferatu asked, knowing that the truck's GPS would be worthless as the Battle Core had wiped out almost all satellites simply by going into orbit with its massive bulk and destroying everything in its path.

*****

Behind them, Turcotte's brain was undergoing a fundamental change as the implant exuded nanotechnology via the wires that spread out from it among the over one hundred billion cells inside his cranium. The most obvious transformation was the merging of the two cerebral hemispheres across the longitudinal fissure in the center of his brain.

Human scientists knew as much about how the brain functioned as they did about what lay underneath the oceans or inside the Earth. For a long time, it had been thought that certain functions of the brain were lateralized; located on one side or the other, such as creativity residing in the right side and practicality in the left. However, that was in the process of being rethought by the very brains that thought of it when the Swarm arrived and put an end to speculation.

However, there *are* differences to the hemispheres. The right is usually larger than the left. There is more norepinephrine, a neurotransmitter, on the right side while the left contained higher levels of a neurotransmitter, dopamine, which signals motivational prominence, that essentially means either wanting something or being averse to it. There are more longer axons on the right and more grey cells on the left. Turcotte's brain was merging and leveling between hemispheres.

How and why Turcotte's brain was now merging hemispheres was as much a mystery as how and why the implant had been placed inside his head. By who? Why was it active now?

But there was much, much more going on than that simple process of the brain. The implant wasn't mechanical. It was alive, but in a way that would defy any biologist to explain. Like the planet, it was silicon based.

As the tendrils wound through the brain, they also began extending into Turcotte's body, intertwining with his carbon base.

The pain, even though Turcotte was technically unconscious, was beyond anything he'd ever experienced. He had a mouth, yet he could not scream.

*****

"Here," Nekhbet said after rummaging through the glove compartment and producing a folding map.

"Airfield?"

Nekhbet opened it up as they drove north on Route 525, up the center of Whidbey Island, which was the fourth longest island in the United States, running north-south, but it was also narrow, sometimes less a mile wide.

"There's one not far ahead," Nekhbet said. "The Whidbey Air Park. Tiny. It doesn't look very promising."

"There will be a plane," Nosferatu said.

"I've always envied you that unfounded confidence," Nekhbet murmured as she looked at the map. "Hmm. Interesting."

"What?" Nosferatu asked, glancing away from the road for a moment.

"There's a military base at the north end. A Naval Air Station."

"Even better," Nosferatu said.

"If it survived the Swarm."

"Always gloom and doom," Nosferatu said as he drove around a tractor trailer truck that had been tipped on its side. As they cleared it, he stopped the truck. A barrier blocked the road a hundred meters ahead. It consisted of concrete partitions, trucks, logs and a hodgepodge of other building material. It stretched from the forest on one side to the other. It showed signs of explosions in several places but was impassable.

"What now?" Nekhbet asked.

Before Nosferatu could answer, a moan from the back seat caught their attention. They both looked over their shoulders.

Turcotte was stirring and his legs and arms were thrashing.

The windshield splintered, followed by the sound of guns firing.

"Down!" Nosferatu yelled, dragging Nekhbet below the dash. "Did you see who shot at us?"

"No. I assume humans."

There were pings as bullets struck the car.

"Survivors," Nosferatu said. "There had to be some."

"They're shooting at us," Nekhbet pointed out. "That means whoever it is, isn't our friend, correct? I can dine?"

The window imploded, sprinkling both of them with glass.

"This is getting irritating," Nekhbet said, wiping glass from her hair.

A man's voice called out. "Get out of the truck!"

"We don't want trouble," Nosferatu shouted, which earned a scoff from Nekhbet.

"Get out of the truck," the man repeated. "We've got a dozen guns aimed at you."

"That's not an inducement to get out," Nekhbet said to Nosferatu.

"Don't make us come and get you," the man yelled.

"Still no upside," Nekhbet said. "Do you have a plan, dear?"

"I'm working on one," Nosferatu said.

They were both startled by Turcotte's voice. "What's going on?"

"There are humans—" Nosferatu paused as Turcotte was sitting up, looking past them, exposing himself to the fire— "*shooting* at us. Get down!"

A bullet blew a chunk out of the headrest above Nekhbet and narrowly missed Turcotte, but spraying him with the stuffing from the interior of the headrest.

"There are six people at the barricade," Turcotte said, as he opened the side door and stepped out.

Given Turcotte wasn't armed, the firing dwindled to a halt.

The voice yelled: "Everyone out! We saw two people in the front."

"What are you doing?" Nosferatu demanded.

"We are peaceful," Turcotte yelled.

"Great," Nekhbet muttered. "Not."

Several men stood up behind the barrier, weapons at the ready.

"Who are you?" one of them demanded.

"Not an enemy," Turcotte said.

"Get the others out or we'll kill you."

"You won't," Turcotte said. "You can't."

One of the men fired on automatic, sending a spray of bullets into the truck, barely missing Nosferatu and Nekhbet.

The two Undead reluctantly got out, hands held up.

"This is not a plan," Nosferatu complained.

"We'll go back and take the *Fynbar*," Turcotte said to him and Nekhbet. He called out to the men at the barricade. "We're leaving."

"You aint going nowhere," one of the men yelled, climbing up on top and aiming his rifle. "We want the woman," he added, indicating Nekhbet.

"Oh, no," Turcotte said, "We don't think you do."

"Ditto," Nosferatu muttered.

Turcotte remained still for several seconds. He turned. "Come Nosferatu and Nekhbet." Turcotte began walking back the way they'd come.

"Hold on!"

A shot rang out and a bullet hit Turcotte in the back. He didn't stagger under the impact. Nor did the bullet penetrate.

"The land beneath this island isn't very stable," Turcotte commented to an astonished Nosferatu and Nekhbet. "Humans who live here should know that. They are foolish to make their homes on such ground."

The ground rumbled and then split, directly under the barricade. There were screams, more rumbling, then silence. A gash in the road thirty feet wide was all that remained.

"Did you do that?" Nosferatu asked.

"We did not," Turcotte said. "Gaia did it. She wants to speak to us. We must go to the *Fynbar*." Turcotte strode down the road, Nosferatu and Nekhbet hurrying to keep up with him.

"What do you know of Gaia?" Nekhbet asked.

"She is alive," Turcotte said. "And not very happy."

"How did you stop the bullet?" Nosferatu asked.

"In due time," Turcotte said. "First there are things to be done. A plan is being made. It is being implemented." He paused, head turning to and fro. "We wonder where she is?"

"Who?" Nosferatu said. "Lisa Duncan?"

"You know her as Leahy."

"She left on the mothership with Yakov," Nosferatu said.

"Odd," Turcotte said. "This is our assignment."

Nosferatu was trying to follow. "What is?"

"Earth," Turcotte said. He cocked his head in thought and his voice shifted slightly. "My human memory is slow to recover. It will come."

MONS OLYMPUS, MARS

Lisa Duncan, the flesh shell that had housed Lisa Duncan, opened its eyes. She immediately shut them as the images exploded in the newly formed brain, making no connections because it had fragmented memory. The body was the basest form of a human. A newborn in adult form, coming into a world all alone.

Except for the Tesla implant.

Eyes opened once again. The cockpit of the mothership was intact. The only light was a small red, emergency symbol in High Rune.

She looked at her hands, perfect, untouched. Her instinctual thought was that she had been reborn via a clone and the *ka*. But there was no regeneration tube in here. She had her memories of the crash up to an abrupt darkness. And memories before that, stretching back in time to her home world and the revolt against the Airlia.

She shuddered in sudden pain as she remembered leaving her son behind on a doomed world as she set forth on the mission to spread freedom to other human colonies. The emotional pain brought her to her knees.

Something that would not have happened to the implant.

This is why it had brought her back. To feel.

The humanness of Lisa Duncan, originally known as Donnchadh, began spreading not just through the flesh and blood and bones of her body, but into the parts that were purely implant and that was as painful as if it had gone the other way.

She screamed from the exquisite agony.

THE PRESENT

AWAKENING

THE CASCADIA SUBDUCTION ZONE.
PACIFIC NORTHWEST

In the Cascadia Subduction Zone, a massive cavern had been hollowed out by Poseidon's detonation. While it had vaporized the hadesarchaea, it had also salted the walls of the cavern with Cobalt-60. The bottom of the cavern had breached the crust and slivered into the mantle. A scratch in the surface of the planet, that had actually breached the skin and drawn 'blood'.

Pressing up from below, in response, a steady flow of molten metal was pushing into the cavern, not just filling it, but pressuring through cracks in the wall and actually surrounding the walls, pushing them inward, crumbling the cavern smaller and smaller.

The metal was lead; an effective shield for the deadly radiation.

Gaia, disturbed from her slumber, becoming aware, was healing her deepest wound.

The surface was another matter altogether. Humans, the dominant species, had been savaging the land, sea and air for generations. Killing off other species, destroying forests, wetlands and vegetation at a prodigious rate. The melting of the ice caps was so severe, the gravitational effect could be felt throughout the planet. The life of the ocean had been harvested at an unsustainable pace and pollution was killing off the coral and other underwater life.

In the cycle of life, Scale species almost invariably consumed themselves, which makes one wonder at the definition of 'intelligence'. World War III had been the epitome of that. There had been several nuclear exchanges between countries even as humans became aware that they were not alone in the universe: South Korea had deployed and detonated its nuclear mines to slow the attack from the North; Israel had used its nuclear arsenal against traditional enemies including wiping Tehran off the map; several other nukes had gone off in attempts to stop the Reaping. But it was the Asian subcontinent that had seen the epitome of man's folly as India and Pakistan dove deep into all out mutually assured destruction.

Even though the last nuclear weapon had detonated several days earlier, the cities of India and Pakistan, still burned. With buildings constructed mostly of wood, the inferno would have made Dante envious. Not just structures, but the surrounding countryside was being consumed. Firestorms raged, spreading, linking up, burning. Almost everything south of the Himalayas was on fire. It was spreading to the west, toward the lush jungles of Southeast Asia. The deserts of Southwest Asia had little to offer the firestorm.

It was destroying so much more life than just humans. The forests and the animals and the birds were consumed on an unprecedented scale.

There was, of course, a reaction to this blight on the surface of the planet in progress, now that the most immediate and deepest damage had been dealt with.

ASTEROID BELT

The Command Swarm was puzzled by the data coming in from Earth. The planet had shifted very slightly on its axis. Not enough to be felt on the surface, but sufficient to register on the Swarm's instruments in the Asteroid Belt. It was slight, but it was sudden. It would have an effect on the planet's climate.

Once more the Swarm memory was tapped and nothing resembling this had been recorded.

The anomaly was noted.

Of more immediate interest were the distress calls coming from the planet by a handful of warships and scout ships that had gone down and been damaged during the Reaping and been left behind by the abrupt departure of the Battle Core.

There were also calls coming in from mining ships left among the asteroids and in the Kuiper Belt, which extended outward from Neptune, the farthest planet in the solar system. That belt was much more extensive than this one. On its way in, the Battle Core had dropped off ships to gather raw materials, the plan being to pick them up on the way out of the system.

While the Supreme Swarm had ordered those warships and scouts still capable of flight to disperse, it had neglected to issue instructions regarding the mining craft since in the larger picture they were relatively unimportant and had only thrust speed, not even system interplanetary.

The Swarm never concerned itself with individuals. They were part of a larger entity, so there was never any consideration of whether rescuing these outliers was a moral or ethical issue. It was all about practicality. The mining ships were ordered to report what their cargoes were from their work. As far as the Swarm on Earth, the Command Swarm instructed those that could still communicate to send constant status reports to complement that which the warship's sensors were accumulating.

It also awaited a report from the scout ship sent to investigate what had happened to the hadesarchaea.

DAVIS MOUNTAINS, TEXAS

Asha and Joseph studied the data in the command center of the Facility.

"We thought we'd get more energy from solar," Asha said to Joseph, noting the dismal numbers. "The cloud and ash cover, combined with the ash on top of the panels, has us at fifteen percent solar. We never expected to go below fifty." She indicated another read out. "Wind is at eighty percent, which is about as good as can be expected."

Joseph pointed to a monitor. "Ash is piling up in the Inrotor turbines. If we don't clear it out, they'll eventually seize up. The good news is the Tesla batteries are holding a solid charge."

"Without the lights," Asha said, "we're going to eventually have crop failure. We don't have enough power to run them for a proper daylight."

"We need to clean off the panels and the Inrotor blades," Joseph said.

"But the sunlight is still blocked," Asha pointed out.

They both turned as Sofia entered the command center. "I sense a problem."

Asha and Joseph exchanged a glance.

"You're worried," Sofia said. She glanced at the displays and monitors. "The system is degrading, isn't it? Power is down further."

"Slowly," Asha allowed. "It's not catastrophic. We've got plenty of time."

"Time for what?" Sofia asked. "Mrs. Parrish's strategy was to wipe out most of mankind and have the Chosen reclaim the surface world. Half of that has been accomplished—" she

paused and cocked her head and amended her comment—
"mostly. There are still people outside. All over the world. Very
few. They avoided the Reaping and the *Danse*. But the surface
isn't tenable because of the ash cloud. Temperatures have
already dropped slightly."

"We just need more power," Asha said. "We have to keep
the crop cycle viable. Not only for food, but to replenish the
oxygen. We've got the scrubbers but they require power, so
that's not viable long term."

"I told you," Sofia said. "The air outside is safe. We can allow
it in. The Danse burned out. What do your radiation monitors
indicate?" she asked Asha.

"Levels have been dropping," Asha said. "You're right. Soon
we can exchange air with the outside world, so that will save
power by shutting down the scrubbers."

"What else can be done?" Joseph asked.

"I think we should restart the nuclear reactor," Asha said.

Sofia shook her head. "That's not's viable."

"Why not?" Joseph asked.

"Gaia will not allow it," Sofia said.

"'Gaia'?" Asha repeated. "What do you mean?"

Sofia smiled at Joseph. "As you call it: the Earth Mother.
She's very angry with humans. Too much damage has been done.
She will not allow more."

Asha was trying to understand. "You're talking as if the
planet is alive."

"It is," Sofia said. "It's always been alive. But now . . ." She paused, trying to explain what she could only feel. "Now it is taking action. It will take action if we restart the reactor. Too many nuclear weapons have gone off."

Joseph faced the young girl. "What do you suggest, Sofia?"

"We wait," Sofia said. "And we pray as we have always prayed under your guidance, Joseph."

WHIDBEY ISLAND, WASHINGTON STATE

The trek back to the south end of the island was made in silence, Nosferatu and Nekhbet lost in contemplation of this strange twist and Turcotte was whoever he was now, which obviously was as talkative as the Turcotte whom they had known previously, which is to say, not at all.

They arrived at the bluff overlooking where the ferry dock had been. The *Fynbar* lay on top of the pile of cars that had been swept to the base of the hill. Turcotte led the way down. He scrambled over the debris to the spacecraft. Opened the hatch and disappeared inside without a word.

"Are you going with him?" Nekhbet asked.

"Are you staying here?" Nosferatu asked her.

She sighed. "He was shot, dear. The bullet didn't penetrate. Either he's wearing a vest which he magically procured in the backseat of that truck or . . ."

"He's not wearing a vest," Nosferatu said. "He's not who he was."

"Deep insight as always."

They both backed off as the *Fynbar* lifted off the pile of cars and leveled. It edged forward, the front slope less than a foot from where they stood. Turcotte popped his head out of the hatch. "Do you wish to come? Or do you want us to drop you off somewhere?" He shook his head. "We think it's best you come with us. It won't be safe for you if you're not with us."

"He's referring to himself in multiple third person," Nekhbet muttered. "That's worse than singular third person."

Nosferatu ignored her. "Where are you going, my friend?"

Turcotte held his hands up, looking at them in the gathering dusk. "We are not complete."

"He answers as clearly as you do," Nekhbet complained to Nosferatu.

"What would make you complete?" Nosferatu asked Turcotte.

"We'll know by the time we arrive." Turcotte stared at them, unblinking.

"Great," Nekhbet said, but Nosferatu took her elbow. "We will be honored to join you."

They stepped across the narrow void onto the deck of the *Fynbar* and walked up to the hatch. Nekhbet went inside, Nosferatu following.

"Make sure the hatch is secure," Turcotte said from the pilot's depression.

"Any particular reason?" Nosferatu asked as he did so.

"We're going to get wet."

VICNITY GIZA PLATEUA, EGYPT

The Swarm warship had been struck by multiple surface to air missiles while descending over Cairo to deposit the Metamorphosis for Reaping. It had returned fire at the launch site automatically, obliterating it.

Initially, the damage had not been deemed significant by the Command Swarm in charge of the ship. The various creatures had been dispersed while the warship remained in place, with one of the arms touching the ground. As the first of the Reaped marched back under thrall of the parasites, they'd been loaded.

Once capacity had been reached and the Metamorphosis brought back on board, the warship had lifted to rendezvous with the Core. It had been less than a half mile up when an Egyptian pilot had flown his fighter jet armed with the country's lone nuclear warhead, long secreted away and reserved for Israel but never used, directly at the Swarm craft. He detonated it just before slamming into the large warship.

The explosion had blown off two of the eight arms and opened a hole two hundred meters wide into the side of the craft. Despite that, the Command Swarm tried to make the rendezvous, only to lose all power. The warship had arced over, slamming into the deep desert miles from Giza.

Those thralled humans and Swarm not killed in the crash, had succumbed to the *Danse Macabre*. Except for a handful of Swarm who'd been in positions on board the warship and not been in contact with the humans.

The surviving Swarm had crawled out of the pods and the wreckage of the warship and gathered together. They'd felt the Battle Core destroy itself, as had the Swarm across the far reaches of space. They gathered together with the wreckage of the warship, still under the control of the Command Swarm, which had lived through the crash, but was trapped deep inside.

Then, without guidance from the Supreme Swarm, it had to decide on a course of action. The warship was damaged beyond repair. There was no way off this planet. While this cluster of Swarm was in the midst of contemplating an unprecedented future, the ground beneath them began to shift. Imperceptibly at first, then at a faster pace. The sand dropped in a circle five miles wide, well over twice the circumference of the warship. The ship, and the Swarm were sliding into the Earth. The Command Swarm ordered the survivors to scatter, but their thin arms, better adapted to moving in low or zero gravity, could get little purchase in the sand as they tried to battle their way up out of the sinkhole.

It took less than thirty seconds for the wreckage, and the Swarm, to be swallowed by the deep sands. Two minutes later, there was no sign there had been anything here but desert.

The Great Sphinx and the Pyramids of Giza remained, stone untouched, as they had for centuries.

GLASTONBURY TOR, ENGLAND

Across Southwest England, the Druids came out of the hidden caves that had sheltered them since the earliest days of their existence. There weren't many, because the ancient ways had melted away over the centuries and Christianity had done its best to stamp them out, often in ways that were diametrically opposed to the dogma of the faith, a contradiction few stopped to ponder as they tortured and murdered those who did not convert. In the modern world being a Druid was considered some sort of fad associated with gaming, but the true ones didn't play games and dedicated their life to their beliefs. They didn't go out in public dressed in their robes and they hid their tattoos from view.

They accept that their name had been corrupted and taken by other groups that did not follow the true and straight path. It had become a fad with ebbs and flows in popularity, but the true believers of the old ways kept their silence. The prayers and the teachings were passed from generation to generation, but that too led to a diminishment of their numbers. Where once they had been spread across England and into France in the tens of thousands, now there were barely a hundred. It had been years since they'd all gathered, but when the world unraveled with the revelations of the Airlia, World War III and the approach and arrival of the Swarm Battle Core, that remnant had done as their ancestors had in time of peril: retreated to the caves in the hills not far from the center of their beliefs. Those caves had sheltered them from the Romans, the Vikings, the Christians and more. Now that refuge had done the same with the Swarm and the latest World War.

They knew of the Watchers and the *Myrddin*, another secret they had kept for centuries. After all, the Watchers had often been confused with the Druids. This was not simply coincidence.

Lost in the fog of pre-history, after the fall of Atlantis, and before the First Age of Egypt, the Druids had been founded by a second son of the Watcher of Avalon. That is the place where the Watchers had been founded by Lisa Duncan and her mate, Gwalcmai to keep track of the Airlia since the time of the destruction of Atlantis and their founding. The first son of a Watcher took his father's place. Subsequent sons went off to find other occupations, but kept in contact in case their elder sibling did not produce an heir.

One such second son saw the wisdom in an order dedicated to a cause, but he took it in a different direction. A group focused on healing and wisdom. The Druids reached their peak just before the Roman invasion of England.

The grey skies, fallen ash, and lack of people had finally drawn the modern Druids forth from their refuge. They marched from the hills onto the Salisbury Plain, passing empty towns, abandoned cars, and signs of violence everywhere.

And death. Those who had succumbed to the Danse were well into decomposition. Fortunately, unknown to the Druids, the virus had burned out as designed. It took hours to reach their destination on foot.

The Druids assembled at the base of Avalon, which in ancient days had been an island surrounded by a lake of water. It was across that water that Arthur, Artad's Shadow, had been rowed by Percival in an attempt to find a Druid to heal him. And at Arthur's request who knew it wasn't healing that was needed. Getting his *ka* recovered by his followers was the goal.

Renamed Glastonbury Tor, St. Michael's Abbey had been built on top. And destroyed. And rebuilt over the ages. But what lay underneath, the headquarters of the Watchers, was known only to those with ties to the Watchers and a handful of Druids and *Myrddin*.

The Tor rises over five hundred feet above the surrounding terrain, terraced in a way that did not appear natural, but science had not been able to explain. Carrying torches against the dark night, the Druids marched single file, led by their current High Priest, up the tourist path that zig-zagged to the top. The ruin of

St. Michaels stands forlornly, roof collapsed. It is surrounded by scattered stones from that ruin and earlier ones.

The High Priest went to a specific stone as he'd been taught by his predecessor. He removed the Medallion from his pocket and placed it on the long, grey stone. The stone slid down and to the side, revealing a set of stairs. Leaving his followers outside, the High Priest adopted more modern lighting, turning on a halogen flashlight. He descended into the underground labyrinth. Once he was clear of the opening, the stone slid back into place, giving him pause. He assumed that was the way it worked, since he'd never been inside before. He was simply following the orders he'd received from his predecessor along with the medallion.

It was damp and chilly in the smoothly cut tunnel. He had the way memorized. Took a ninety degree turn to the right when he reached a landing deep inside the Tor. Used the medallion to open another hidden door. He gasped when the light from his hand-torch was reflected by the crystals in the cave that appeared as the door slid aside. The large cavern, two hundred meters long, by one hundred wide was full of them.

"Merlin's cave," the High Priest whispered. He hesitated, feeling the weight of history as much as that of the rock of the Tor above his head. There was a smooth path through the crystals and he set out on it, going to a door set between two stone pillars. This one opened with just a touch, no need for the medallion now that he was this far in. A kilometer-long tunnel lay ahead. He realized he'd lost his sense of direction and didn't know in which azimuth he was headed or if he were still under the Tor.

The High Priest saw light ahead, which had not been in the briefing. He hurried down the tunnel, surprisingly eager to return to a devastated surface. He didn't have to keep pace count to find the next key spot, given the light spilling out of the open doorway to his destination.

He entered a chamber lit by a Tesla bulb. Ten meters by five, it was the archives of the Watchers. The walls were lined with wood racks holding scrolls, many written in original Airlia hieroglyphics. What caught the High Priest's attention though was the mummified body on the floor, most of the head blown away. Dried blood and brains stained the racks behind the dead man. The gun he'd used to kill himself was by his hand.

The High Priest swallowed hard. The *wedjat* of Avalon had committed suicide. Of course, the High Priest had no way of knowing that the dead man had actually killed the Watcher and taken his place and committed suicide after being confronted by Nosferatu, but that didn't really matter.

This left only one last instruction. The High Priest looked at the racks, searching for the Druid symbol. He found it. The scroll was old, yellowing parchment. Gingerly, he retrieved it from the shelf. Tucked it inside his coat. Then he retraced his steps, leaving the body and the story of the world since before what had been known as recorded history, behind.

When he got back to the surface, and the stone door slid up and sealed, it was pitch black. The Druids were gathered in the ruins, their torches flickering off the old stone. He turned off his flashlight and joined. They circled as he carefully opened the scroll.

"The old tongue," someone said as the hieroglyphics were revealed.

The High Priest looked up as the group parted and a diminutive old woman came through. She fumbled in the pocket of her raincoat and withdrew a pair of reading glasses. Put them on, realized they were smudged, cleaned them off, and put them on once more. The High Priest held up the scroll so she could read. Her head slowly went back and forth and she read the symbols.

It took several minutes, while the Druids shifted uneasily in the darkness. It was strange to have no lights where the town was, no airplanes flying overhead. Just drifting ash and a night so dark with no stars visible.

Finally, the old woman turned away from the scroll. "We must go to Stonehenge."

The Druids murmured and nodded. This was to be expected. It was the epicenter of their faith.

"And then?" someone asked.

"There is something we must find," the old woman said. "Two things."

"And then?" The High Priest asked.

The old woman looked up. "And then we must sacrifice."

MPONENG GOLD MINE, SOUTH AFRICA

The species Halicephalobus Mephisto is named after Mephistopheles, the Lord of the Underworld in Faust. It had been discovered in 2011 because the roundworm lived deeper inside the planet than any other known animal. No other multicellular organism had ever been found deeper than a mile; but these existed over two miles below ground in veins of groundwater three to ten thousand years old. They feed on subterranean bacteria and reproduce asexually. The discoverers speculated that they had originally been like their surface cousins but had been driven deeper underground by rainwater and gradually adapted to the extreme temperatures and pressures.

The first miners who saw the tiny creatures were frightened because they had assumed nothing could be alive in these dark depths. Even with this discovery, though, few thought anything could live deeper inside the planet. At least nothing like what we knew as life.

The miners had never suspected that they, and their families, would end up living in these tunnels. But the approach of the Swarm Battle Core had led to desperate action all over the world and the miners had sought refuge in the safest place they knew.

They had originally hidden at the bottom of the mine, two and a half miles beneath the surface. It took over an hour via a series of elevators to get that deep. But when the power to the slurry ice pumper had gone out, the temperature had begun to rise without the artificial cooling. Since the unaltered temperature at the bottom was 151 degrees Fahrenheit, the miners and their families had begun a slow, but steady ascent, using the rungs on the sides of the shafts to climb given the elevators didn't work, but staying as deep as bearable. They were now a mile and a half below surface.

The miners were armed with shovels, picks and crowbars. The weapons they'd used to overwhelm and kill the guards at the entrance to the mine when the Battle Core came into orbit. They'd guided their families in, shutting gates and vault doors behind them. The latter designed specifically to keep people out of one of the world's most valuable gold mines. To protect riches that were no longer worth anything.

Besides the rising temperatures, they were low on supplies, especially water. The miners had tapped into some of the concrete barrier walls which contained pockets of water designed to cool the working areas, but those bled out quickly. It also increased the temperature by degrading the shielding.

The leaders of the two hundred South African natives were arguing about what to do, although the course of action was inevitable: they would eventually have to go back to the surface. The fact no one had come down after them given they'd killed the guards and were ensconced in one of the richest places in the world indicated things up there were not good. An apocalyptic Catch-22.

The arguments ceased when a woman screamed. She was joined by several others as the walls of the mine shaft secreted hundreds of thousands of Halicephalobus Mephisto. They were tiny, less than a quarter of an inch in length, but there were so many, they seemed a black ooze. The husbands reassured their wives as to what they were seeing, but were disconcerted because while they'd seen small pockets during their shifts, no group had been more than a couple of inches in size. Now, the walls were covered with them. Unknown to them, there was another creature among the Mephisto. Something that came from dozens of miles down and had never seen the light of day. So tiny, they were unseen, they oozed out of the rocks and formed an invisible coating that the miners and their family members touched without realizing it. They were part of Gaia, connected yet separate.

What was causing both them and the Mephisto to come out of the rock?

The answer wasn't long in arriving. A cracking sound echoed up from the deepest reaches, where they'd first hidden. A scout braved the heat in a special suit and hurriedly climbed back up the shaft to report that a fast-rising tide of molten gold was filling the mine. This was initially met with disbelief, but between the Battle Core days ago and the worms coming out of the walls, it was a time of beyond belief.

The largest reef of gold that had ever been found in the mind had been just a meter thick. This in a mine that went two and half miles down. How could that much gold be coming? What had melted it, because gold only changed form above 1,948 degrees Fahrenheit and the temperature in the lower levels while high, was nowhere close to that. This was impossible.

But it was happening.

A short argument ensued, but the heat where they were was rising faster than could be accounted for. Others looked down the vertical shaft and spotted the golden glow. The decision made for them; the miners began to assist their families upward. It was a time-consuming process as it took more time to ascend than descend.

Eventually, the flood of gold broached into a cross tunnel where the tail end of the column of refugees was waiting their turn. Oddly, though, it stopped just a few feet short of where three miners where desperately trying to pile rocks to stem it and gain time. Sweat poured off their bodies from the sweltering wave of heat emanating from the liquid gold. What made sense to none of them was why wasn't the gold solidifying?

The miners retreated and the gold advanced in a strange dance. The Earth wanted them out, but was giving them time to get to the surface.

INDIAN SUBCONTINENT

Firestorms were merging, the result of the hundreds of nuclear detonations in the cities of Pakistan and India. The fires were spreading beyond national borders because nature didn't recognize those arbitral man-made lines. While the deserts of southwest Asia and the frozen Himalayas to the north were barriers to the flames, the lush jungles of southwest Asia were a different matter. Bangladesh and Burma were ripe tinder awaiting destruction.

The firestorm was self-propagating in that the intense heat produced strong winds which fanned the flames, which spread the fire and pushed the heat wave farther out.

The entire Subcontinent area is a mixture of geology, ranging from the lush shorelines where the majority of the population lived, to the peaks of the Himalayas. It is a geologically active area, because the plate on which it rests is moving steadily north at a rate faster than two and a half inches per year, raising the peaks of the mountains a fifth an inch in altitude. Due to climate change, the seas have steadily been encroaching, creeping inward. It was estimated, before World War III, that most of the coastlines would either be under water or face severe flooding in the next century. The vast majority of the humans who'd been concerned about it no longer needed to be; because they were dead.

The Indian monsoon first began about eight million years ago as the Tibetan Plateau began to uplift as the Indian subcontinent slid underneath it. Despite being one of the most studied events in that area, due to the fact agriculture and water supplies relied on the yearly event, the monsoon was still little understood by humans. Prediction is spotty at best.

The word itself, monsoon, is derived from the Arabic *mausam*, which means season. It is caused by wind and temperature. The Indian monsoon is the result of winds changing direction, with the winds of the South China Sea reversing direction and intersecting with the wind coming from the Bay of Bengal. The rain occurs because of the water surrounding the subcontinent and the temperature changes as water evaporating from those oceans is carried over land and higher in altitude. Without the Himalayas to the north, the monsoon would most likely continue on their way northward into Asia. However, that massive barrier causes 'bursting' over the subcontinent where the skies unload their precipitation in torrents of rain.

It was not monsoon season in the subcontinent, yet the winds were shifting. There were no meteorologists observing as massive clouds full of precipitation formed over the oceans and began to blow ashore.

The heavens opened up and a deluge began, akin to the forty days and forty nights mythologized in the Bible.

Rain pounded the entire area and slowly, but surely, water began to win the battle over fire.

LAST STAND OF IMPERIUM

TALIANT FLEET BASE.
MILLIONS OF YEARS AGO

"I told you they were retreating," Fleet Admiral gloated. The map showed over a dozen red spots where Unity ships had gone FTLT.

"All are transiting to the L-U-Twelve system?" VicDep asked.

"Yes," Admiral said.

"Why?" Librarian asked. Captain Tai stood along the wall behind her with the other assistants.

Fleet Admiral hesitated and glanced at the row of his people, all of whom avoided his gaze. "We're not sure," he finally admitted.

"What about your stealth probe in the system?" Librarian pushed.

"It's gone dark," Admiral said.

"'Gone dark'," Librarian repeated. "Tell me something, Fleet Admiral. Your probe has been there since the start of this. Since the Awakening. Why was Compendium never informed? Why did you not share the data with us?"

"It was a security issue," Admiral said.

"Whose?" Librarian snapped. "Imperium or yours? You have data on the Awakening, don't you?"

"Garbage data," Admiral said. "The key is that Unity—" he paused as a half dozen assistants along the rear wall reacted to information being imparted to them through their earhears. It had to be significant to cause so many to break decorum.

"What is it?" VicDep demanded of his chief assistant.

"An FTL transmission from Unity, VicDep. The Speaker." The assistant stepped forward and waved his hands, wiping out the star map and revealing the image of the leader of Unity, a tall thin, hairless woman with alabaster skin, common to those born on her home world, near the fringes of deep space on the Boundary.

"Imperium," Speaker began. "You did not respond to our request for a truce, but it doesn't matter anymore. As you already know, we have pulled back from the zone of conflict. The war is over. Our war between humans." She paused and glanced away from the camera as there was a commotion off screen. Angry voices. She waved a dismissive hand in that direction, then focused back. "I entreat you to listen. I hope you will understand and agree."

She pointed at them. "You attacked us after your weapons test went wrong at Light Union Twelve. You blamed us and you didn't believe us about the Awakening. You did not believe L-U-Twelve had become sentient. Self-aware."

Voices shouted in the background and she leaned forward. "There's no time to get you up to speed on things you already know. We found your stealth probe in the L-U-Twelve system. You've known all along what happened to your ships. Why didn't you listen to us? Why did you attack us? After all, *you* started this. Your weapon test. You tried to blow up L-U-Twelve. Obviously, it didn't appreciate that." Her voice went up in anger. "L-U-Twelve didn't destroy your ships. It absorbed them. It absorbed our ship that was monitoring your incursion."

Admiral was startled. "What do you mean 'absorbed'?"

"It took them," Speaker said. "Drew them down to the planet. Even your ships of the line. It's got them now. The FTLT drives. The weapons. The crews, although stars know what it did with them."

"How do you know this?" Admiral demanded. "How can a planet take ships? Make them land?"

Speaker laughed bitterly. "Your people landed on L-U-Twelve to investigate why your great weapon didn't work. They were infected with something. They carried it back with them onto the ships. That's how."

"Infected with what?" Librarian asked.

"The planet," Speaker said. "Admiral, stop with the secrets. You heard the transmissions from your ships before they went down to the planet. The confusion. The reports of the crews being infected by some sort of parasite that the ground parties had brought back with them."

"Is this true?" Librarian demanded of Admiral, but he waved her off, his focus on Speaker.

"What about your ship?" he demanded.

"Before we understood what was going on, one of your ship's hailed our craft which was observing on the edge of the system for help. An SOS. I don't know if Fleet still goes by the Law of Space but all Unity ships do. Our people answered. And then went dark.

"After this, we left a squadron outside the system to monitor but not approach. To enact a quarantine of the system. We had our scientists trying to figure out a way to communicate with whatever was awake at Light Union Twelve. We never received a reply but we were never attacked. It was as if they knew we, Unity, weren't a threat." She took a deep breath. "We lost all contact with that squadron several days ago. But we did get one last image."

Speaker disappeared and Light-Union-Twelve appeared. The planet was dark, almost black, with grey swirls. It would not support human life and thus had never been colonized. None of the planets in the star system were habitable. It was a nothing solar system in a quadrant of the galaxy along the Border that had been ignored.

"This is the system as it was," Speaker said. "This is the image we received before our squadron went dark." The change was obvious. Light-Union-Twelve now had six small red moons.

"They are each four hundred miles in diameter," Speaker said. "They were not there four days ago. Which means they came from the planet. More are forming on the surface of L-U-Twelve."

"What are they?" Admiral asked.

"We don't know," Speaker replied. "But the last message was a video lasting sixteen seconds. In that short period of time, our analysis indicates these spheres are growing. A tiny fraction, but, again, it was only sixteen seconds."

The image of the system disappeared and Speaker was back. "We pulled four squadrons and had them relocate to the system. They came out of FTLT, confirmed arrival, then went black. We're rallying the rest of our ships to a staging position near the system but not in it. Something is happening. Something big. We're asking you to join us. We're afraid whatever is at L-U-Twelve is a threat to *all* mankind: Unity and Imperium and the Indies who've stayed out of this."

Admiral didn't reply. He glanced at VicDep, the first time he'd deferred.

Speaker pressed her point. "Here's something that *should* worry you. It knows where your squadron came from. From your ships' logs. It knows all about Imperium."

"That doesn't mean they can FTLT," Admiral said.

"It took your ships," Speaker said. "That means it has the FTLT drives. It took our ships too. How many drives is that total?" She spread her hands, part supplication, part frustration. "We don't know what's going on, but this is a threat to all humanity." She paused, muted the mike and yelled to someone to her right. She activated the mike. "We need more than a truce. We need help. We've tried for five years to understand what happened during the Awakening. To explain to you. To stop this useless war." More noise off screen. Speaker grimaced. "I'm heading there myself. We all are. All of Unity. Join us. Our survival depends on this."

The image disappeared. But the transmission was still open as a series of dots and dashes repeated on audio. The age-old spacefarer's signal of distress. A signal that had to be answered under the Law of Space.

"Cut audio," Fleet Admiral snapped.

The sound faded.

"What did you do?" Librarian demanded of the Admiral. "You lied about the recon. It was a weapons test. You lied about the loss of the squadron, instead blaming it on Unity. You started the Awakening. You started this war. What else have you done?"

"It was crazy talk," Admiral said. "Unity claiming that a planet had come alive and wiped out a squadron? Insanity. This is a ploy by Unity to draw what's left of Fleet into a trap."

"They built six moons to trap us?" Librarian was incredulous. "Those are each a third the size of this station which took millennia to construct. And they're still expanding."

"How can a planet be alive?" Admiral demanded. "This is craziness."

Librarian rubbed her forehead. "Admiral, every alien species we've encountered so far has been carbon based. We knew, theoretically, that life could be silicon based. What little data we had on Light-Union-Twelve indicates it is mineral heavy. It was actually listed for mining exploitation when needed.

"Now we know silicon-based life exists for certain. Just on a scale we didn't expect. Who knows what you woke up? And, on top of that, you attacked Unity. Killed billions in a war based on a mistake on your part." She turned to VicDep. "We must help Unity."

"Never!" Admiral swore. He glared at her. "You've kept *your* own secrets, haven't you, Librarian?"

Librarian didn't respond, but this piqued VicDep's interest; anything to avoid making a decision regarding Unity's request. "What are you speaking of?"

"Librarian has been conducting secret meetings in First Ring," Admiral said.

VicDep blinked. "'First Ring'? I haven't been there in years. I thought it was uninhabited."

Librarian glanced over her shoulder at Captain Tai. He gave the slightest shake of his head.

"With whom?" VicDep asked, directing the question to Librarian. "And for what reason?"

"Research," Librarian said. "I have volunteers who are helping with an experiment. From all walks of life. Science, politics, maintenance; even some from Fleet."

"Does this experiment have anything to do with Unity?" Admiral pressed. "With you supporting them about the Awakening rather than Imperium?"

"It has nothing to do with Unity," Librarian said.

"Why in First Ring, though?" Admiral asked. "What do you have there?"

"I'm using the grounds of the original Science Academy," Librarian said.

"To do what?" Admiral demanded.

"I've said," Librarian snapped.

Admiral shook his head. "If you were important, I'd be concerned. But you're nothing. You have no power." He shifted his gaze to VicDep. "And you? An incompetent politician who hamstrung us from the very beginning. We'd have won this war five years ago if it hadn't been for you and your comrades. No more."

Admiral gestured and his military assistants drew weapons. Everyone else was unarmed. Captain Tai twitched, hand moving toward his waist where his sidearm used to reside.

"We are at war," Admiral said. "Anyone who opposes us is a traitor." He glared at Librarian, then VicDep. "Is that clear?"

She stood. "Sir, I serve Imperium. The people of Imperium. I also serve humanity. It is part of my oath of office. Are you going to shoot me here, in the Star Chamber?" She pointed up at the embeds. "In front of Imperium?"

Fleet Admiral smiled coldly. "The embeds are off. This chamber is dark. And if you want to walk out of here alive, I suggest you go find some hole to crawl into and never come out of."

Librarian waited a few heartbeats, then nodded at Captain Tai and the two left Star Chamber.

Tai hurried to keep up with her.

As soon as they were far enough away, she spun and faced him.

"How did Admiral know about First Ring?"

"I didn't—"

"I know you didn't," Librarian snapped. "He tracked me."

"He tracked us," Tai said.

"Yes, yes," Librarian said, trying to figure it out.

"Come," Tai said.

"What?" Librarian was confused.

Tai led her down the corridor to her office. They entered. He went to a shelf and retrieved a handheld scanner. Ran it over his artificial leg. "They bugged me."

"How?" Librarian asked. "When?"

"The tracker was most likely in there from the beginning," Tai said. He looked at Librarian. "What do we do? Fleet Admiral just violated his oath of office to Magnus Charter. It cannot be allowed."

"We can't fight him," Librarian said. "Nor is there any point to it. Imperium is doomed. He is just accelerating the process. I feared this but was also prepared. It is time for you to meet the others."

THE PRESENT

"PART OF"

WHIDBEY ISLAND, WASHINGTON STATE

Turcotte lifted the *Fynbar*, gaining altitude above Puget Sound. Nosferatu was in the co-pilot's seat while Nekhbet had made herself as comfortable as possible where the regeneration tube had been that they'd removed and given to Mrs. Parrish at Area 51 for her vain hope to bring her husband back.

A light flashed on one of the panels and Turcotte brought the space craft to a hover. "Radar warning. There's a ship coming in from orbit."

"Swarm?" Nosferatu asked.

Turcotte closed his eyes briefly, then opened them. "Yes. A scout ship."

Nosferatu frowned. "How do you know?"

"We know."

Nosferatu glanced over his shoulder at Nekhbet who spread her hands, indicating WTF?

"Is it coming for us?" Nosferatu asked.

Turcotte shook his head as he stared flying east. "No. It's heading for the Cascadia subduction zone."

"Why?" Nekhbet asked as the *Fynbar* picked up speed.

"To learn what happened to the hadesarchaea," Turcotte said. Before Nosferatu could ask, he explained. "To discover why the weapon the Swarm left behind didn't split the planet apart."

Nekhbet spoke up. "Why didn't that bullet penetrate? What happened to you?"

"We're not sure," Turcotte said. "We're still trying to understand."

"Why are you using the plural?" Nekhbet demanded.

"We don't quite know yet," Turcotte said. "But we'll know soon." He looked over at Nosferatu. "I am still here." He pointed at his head. "But there is something else also. It's always been in my head, but now its awake. It's changed my body. It hasn't wiped me out, but I'm not exactly in charge either."

"What is it?" Nosferatu asked.

"Who we allowed myself to become for the greater good," Turcotte said. He frowned. "I was someone, a long, long time ago. Then, over the years, I was no one for long period of time. Then became other people. It's very confusing."

Nosferatu tried a new line of questioning. "Where are we going?"

"To touch the Earth," Turcotte said. "We must make peace."

"With Gaia," Nosferatu said.

"With Gaia," Turcotte confirmed.

THE CASCADIA SUBDUCTION ZONE, PACIFIC NORTHWEST

The scout ship didn't slow as it approached the ocean. It splashed in and descended. It began to decelerate as it approached the ocean floor, halting just above the heavy silt that filled the split between tectonic plates.

Sensors were activated and pulses sent into the planet to learn the fate of the hadesarchaea.

The response was immediate as the silt began to slide aside, revealing the split in the planet. The Swarm on the scout ship were puzzled at this unusual response to their probing. They descended into the gap to get better readings and to understand this development.

Five hundred meters in.

Deeper and deeper. Readings began to come in. Dead hadesarchaea that had been irradiated with no sign of the radiation that had killed it. There was also something else that was strange, but could explain the lack of radiation. Abnormally large amounts of lead. The scout ship stopped almost a kilometer into the subduction zone breach. The lead was massed just below it.

The Swarm was still puzzling over this when dozens of lava tubes opened in the sides of the breach above the ship and magma poured down onto the ship. Designed to travel in the extreme temperatures of space, the hull of the scout ship could handle the heat. What the ship couldn't counter was the weight flowing on top of it. The ship was pushed downward, buried under molten rock until it came to rest on the top of the lead encapsulating the Cobalt-60. Then the lead parted and the ship passed through into the chamber the Poseidon explosion had carved out. The lead sealed behind, imprisoning the Swarm scout ship with the Cobalt-60.

VICINITY DAVIS MOUNTAINS, TEXAS

Twelve Fades, the Cthulhu/Fade hybrid, and a Naga/Fade hybrid were gathered in the open, flat plain near the mountains. The latter was a massive, seven headed snake that had consumed a Fade, or been infected by a Fade depending on perspective, a few hours earlier. Darkness had fallen not long ago and the overcast sky allowed no light to pierce it. A brittle, cold wind blew ash about but the group was still, gathered in a circle.

Out of the darkness another creature approached. Similar to the Cthulhu in body, a Swarm orb rested on top, controlling the body. It was the commander of a Reaping party of dragons, Cthulhu, Naga and parasites that had been left behind during the hasty evacuation. The Naga and Cthulhu in the circle had drawn it in. However, the two creatures were not responding to the Swarm's orders.

The Swarm was startled as a dragon swooped down and landed next to the group. It too wouldn't respond to commands. Puzzled, the Swarm halted ten meters from the group, uncertain how to proceed.

One of the Fades walked forward, stopping just in front of it. Opened her mouth, not to speak, but in invitation. The Swarm carrier leaned forward. An arm detached from the Swarm orb and slithered into the Fade's mouth.

The two merged.

PACIFIC OCEAN

The *USS Pennsylvania* had held the record for the longest on-station patrol for a boomer, missile submarine, in Navy history at 140 days prior to World War III.

It had now been at sea for more than that and the Captain could sense the growing unease in the crew. He'd obeyed the last orders from command to dive as far down as the sub could go and run silent. Silent and deep were two maxims of submarine lore and they had done that.

They were used to being cut off from the world for periods of time but never in such unusual circumstances. The desperation of the order to *not* participate in the defense against the alien Battle Core had not only been surprised but deeply unsettling.

The Captain, and his officers, had a dilemma. How long should they maintain the last order? Should they see if there had been an update? What had happened? The order had not contained any instructions beyond hiding. It had left open the key question of: until when?

What had happened to the world? Of more particular concern, many in the crew were anxious about their families back at their home port. Were they safe? Was the country safe?

They'd been at max depth of twelve hundred feet; four hundred feet deeper than the publicly reported safety depth of the Ohio class submarine, for longer than anyone was comfortable with.

The Captain knew what was inevitable and decided it was time, before morale degraded further and there were discipline problems. He ordered the *Pennsylvania* roused from the silent and deep. Carefully and slowly.

The five-hundred and sixty-foot long submarine, carrying twenty-four Trident ballistic missile with eight nuclear warheads each, enough power to destroy most of the world, ascended. He wanted to get to a depth where he could disperse a buoy capable of receiving satellite transmissions.

"Multiple contacts," the sonar man announced as they were halfway to the surface.

"Composition?" the Captain asked.

"Whales?" the sonar man's answer was more a question, indicating the confusion. "But a bunch. Like twenty. Very big." He paused. "There's something coming up from below us also. Big. Not as solid as a whale."

Despite running the human equivalent of silent and deep, the ocean, and thus the Earth, knew where the submarine was located. It was an unnatural intrusion into the natural world. Fish, even the water around it, had sensed its presence.

As they had with the kraken, the giant squid struck the *Pennsylvania* first, wrapping its tentacles around the submarine.

Inside the sub, they felt the shock of the initial attack. Their ascent was halted. As the Captain ordered more power, he checked the CCTV mounted on the sail. They were just into the zone where daylight penetrated.

"Oh my God," someone muttered as the long arms of the giant squid wrapped around the hull were displayed.

"More power," the Captain repeated.

Something large came into view. A blue whale. Unlike the kraken, though, there was no tearing of flesh that wasn't there. The whale simply settled down on the forward deck of the sub. Another one did the same on the rear deck.

The *Pennsylvania* began to descend.

"Blow all tanks," the Captain ordered. "Emergency surface."

Pressurized air was pumped into the ballast tanks, filling them. Four more whales added their bulk to the ones already on top of the submarine. The pinnacle of man's engineering versus the largest mammals on the planet. Due to the uneven distribution of the whales on the sub, it rolled thirty degrees to starboard, causing the sailors inside to grab on to anything they could to prevent from tumbling against the sides of their compartments.

For several moments the equation hung in an even balance. But the ballast tanks were only so large and once they were full, there was nothing more. The Captain stared at the display, which showed only the skin of a blue whale just a few feet from the camera. He looked about the control room. Some of the crew were praying, others were staring at him, waiting for the instructions that would free them from this situation. The submarine was vibrating from the force of the engines running at full power, trying to push through.

The Captain glanced at the HD screen that indicated depth. It was steady at 514 feet. Then it began to click downward. 515. 517.

"Sir!" the Executive Officer broke through his commander's bewilderment. "What are your orders?"

520. 530. 545.

The Captain checked the helmsman's display. They were at full power with the plane's rotated so that they should be pushing forward and up. Except they weren't. There was no more buoyancy to be gained in the tanks. A solid thud resounded through the hull as a sperm whale slammed its large forehead into the side of the sub, sending those precariously perched in the angled interior stumbling.

600.

"Captain?" The XO said it with a hint of resignation, able to read the gauges. They all knew it in the command center.

The Captain thought of all the power resting in the warheads on top of the missiles in the silos. For what? He'd spent many restless nights contemplating whether he'd ever be able to turn the key and launch them. His immediate instinct, the first time he'd been handed the command, the key and the responsibility was of course he would. It was his duty. He'd spent over two decades in uniform, from a wide-eyed eighteen-year-old reporting at the Naval Academy up to achieving this plum assignment, commanding one of the eighteen Ohio Class boomers in the Navy. He'd spent all those years obsessed with getting chosen for this.

700.

But once the key was hanging on the thin chain around his neck and he took the *Pennsylvania* to sea for the first time, a sudden weight had settled on him. Almost physical. He'd nearly had a breakdown when he returned from that cruise, because unlike most of his fellow captains, he had an imagination.

800.

Distantly, as if from a great distance, he heard the XO saying something over the intercom to the crew that wasn't privy to the data in the control center, assuring them everything possible was being done to correct the current situation.

900.

The Captain finally acted. He took the mike from the XO's hand and keyed it. "Men. We're going down. Make your peace. May God have mercy on our souls."

1000.

The Captain handed the mike back to the stunned XO. "Relax, Jim," he told the man he'd served with for the last two years. "There are worse things that we could have done. We're getting off easy."

1100

A noise like a ping pong ball bouncing off of metal resonated through the ship. Everyone turned in the direction it came from. Where the whale had struck. Was the hull breached? If so, why hadn't they imploded?

1200

This was the max depth the Captain was authorized to take the Pennsylvania according to the classified briefing he'd received from the men who put it together at Groton shipyards. They'd been very proud of that.

1300

They'd be prouder if they knew the sub was 100 feet below that depth, except none of them were alive.

"Sir?" his XO said.

"Yes?"

"It's been an honor to have—" he never finished as the hull imploded at 1396 feet. It was over for everyone inside in an instant.

The whales spread away from the ship as its own weight now took it down to the depths. The giant squid escorted it, far into the darkness that was its natural habitat.

STONEHENGE, ENGLAND

Dawn was breaking as the Druids gathered around Stonehenge. They'd taken a bus most of the way, then had to abandon it when the road was blocked several miles from Stonehenge. Cars were in an eternal traffic jam heading toward the ancient site. But there was no sign of the people who'd been in them as this place had been thoroughly Reaped by the Swarm.

Even though Stonehenge had been weathered by time and many of the stones knocked over and then placed upright once more, the latest degradation had occurred when the *Fynbar*, parked underneath it, had taken flight at the hands of the Swarm who'd kidnapped Lisa Duncan. Only three stones remained upright. A number had tumbled into the sinkhole caused by the removal of the ship that had been under it since Duncan and her partner brought the original stones here to mark the site when they landed in pre-history to begin the campaign against the Airlia.

That had been the origin of Stonehenge: humans from another world. Certainly, something archeologists and scholars would have rejected up until recently. Subsequent stones had been brought here by generations of Druids; the purpose of which no one in the current group was quite sure of other than this place was the beginning.

The High Priest stood outside where the circle had been, trying to get oriented to this new arrangement. The old woman consulted the scroll.

"Which one?" the High Priest asked.

She pointed.

He took his medallion and went to the stone. Ran the emblem up and down. One side. Then the next. On the third side there was a slight shock, which ran up his arm. He pressed the emblem against the stone.

A section slid aside. Resting inside was a two-foot-high pyramid. Its silver surface was glowing. The High Priest wrapped his cloak around around it. He joined the others, where the old woman was checking the scroll and looking about.

"Where now?" the High Priest asked.

She pointed. "There."

The High Priest led the group away from Stonehenge toward a low ridge on the horizon. When they got there, Stonehenge was silhouetted against the rising sun.

The old woman checked the scroll against the azimuth. "This is it. There used to be an oak tree, but, of course, that's long gone. Whatever was buried here, happened in five-twenty-eight."

The High Priest set the pyramid down. "Does this date from the same time?"

"That was here at the beginning," the old woman said.

"Does it say what it is?" he wondered.

"No." She anticipated his next question. "And it doesn't tell us what we're looking for or how it will appear. We must prepare."

The High Priest shrugged off his backpack. Discarded his jacket and pulled out the robe of his office. The other Druids did the same. The High Priest gave orders. There were four distinct colors to the robes. He aligned the yellow Druids to the north, representing air. To the west, blue signifying water. The east was green for earth. And finally, to the south, red, representing fire.

He led them in a prayer in the ancient tongue, which only the old woman partially understood. For the rest it was like Catholics back when the mass was in Latin: words rehearsed and memorized but the exact translation unknown.

"Earth Mother. Source of All,

All-Fertile, All-Destroying Gaia,

Who Brings Forth Life

And Embraces Death

Who Connects The Eternal to the Now

Immortal and Blessed."

The High Priest began to turn in each cardinal direction as they continued.

"The Land,

The Air,

The Water

The Fire."

The High Priest was startled as he felt something on his leg. He looked down. Several tendrils of grass were sliding up his calves. He swallowed and continued with the rest of the Druids.

"Bountiful Mother. Source of All,

"Dark forests, nurturing fields, nurturing rain,

"Deep oceans, fast running streams."

The grass was to his waist now, curling around his body. Some of the surrounding Druids saw what was happening. A few faltered in their reciting, but the rest pressed on.

"Bright skies, surrounded by the stars,

Eternal and Divine."

The grass was entwining, the strands becoming like ropes, looping over his shoulders, around his chest. The ground at his feet began to shake.

"We are one with Gaia,

"Come bless, Mother

"And hear the prayers of Your Children."

The ground opened up beneath the high priest's feet and the vines pulled him down. The Earth closed up and he was gone.

WESTERN PACIFIC OCEAN, AIRSPACE

Nekhbet had joined Nosferatu in the co-pilot depression. They were slender enough that both fit. They'd slept for over an hour while Turcotte flew the *Fynbar*. They both started awake at the slight jolt of deceleration.

"Are we there?" Nosferatu asked. He glanced at the monitor and saw endless ocean. "Wherever there is?"

"We are close," Turcotte confirmed. He suddenly turned his head to the left.

"What?" Nosferatu asked.

"Something is happening."

"What you talking about?" Nekhbet grumbled.

"Stonehenge," Turcotte said.

"Oh, we've been there," Nekhbet said. "Close by at least. To that dreary cave."

"The Headquarters of the Watchers," Turcotte said.

"The last Watcher had been killed," Nosferatu said. "By one of the *Myrddin*. Unfortunately for him, he met me."

"And you didn't bring me back anything to drink," Nekhbet complained.

"Something's been uncovered at Stonehenge," Turcotte said. "Something that has been lost for a very long time. Something Duncan and her partner brought with them from their home world. We knew it had to be somewhere." He frowned. "This is very confusing." He placed his hands on either side of his face and pressed. Then moved a hand in front of his eyes and looked at it, as if it weren't his. "Tough having two sentient beings in our head." He looked over at Nosferatu. "Why did you allow the *Danse Macabre* to be unleashed when you could have stopped it?"

"Who else is in there with you?" Nekhbet wanted to know, but Nosferatu and Turcotte ignored the question.

"Humans deserved it," Nosferatu said. "I've been alive for thousands of years. Not conscious for most of it, true. But I've seen a lot. Too much. I would like to say I've experienced the best of humanity, but the truth is, I've mostly seen the worst. The very fact one of them came up with *Danse* damns them."

"But you're wrong, my dear," Nekhbet interjected.

Both Turcotte and Nosferatu looked over their shoulder at her.

"It was Vampyr who made the *Danse*," Nekhbet said. "One of us. And he was, you have to admit, the worst of the lot."

"He just combined what humans had already invented," Nosferatu argued. "It was Mrs. Parrish who came up with the plan to wipe out her species." He shook his head. "The massacres, the tortures, the hatred over the centuries. I was tired of it."

Nekhbet came forward and sat down next to him, cross-legged. She put a hand on his shoulder. "It *is* wearisome, being alive for so long, my dear. But really. Allowing the humans to kill themselves is a bit over the top. And who would we feed on then? Sometimes you go too far."

Nosferatu nodded very slightly. "I was tired and perhaps not thinking clearly."

Turcotte was looking forward. "The *Danse* infected the Swarm and caused them to fly into the sun."

"Luck," Nosferatu said.

"Perhaps," Turcotte replied as he moved the controls and the *Fynbar* began to descend. "Or fate."

Nekhbet stood and took her place behind both of them. "Are you going to commune with the ocean?" she asked.

Turcotte glanced over at her. "We told you. We're going to touch the Earth."

"That's ocean," Nekhbet said. "I don't—" she didn't finish as they splashed in and went down swiftly. They passed through the illuminated band of water quickly and were into pitch darkness. Turcotte didn't turn the outside lights on.

"Where are we?" Nosferatu asked.

"The Marianas Trench," Turcotte replied. "We are going to the Challenger Deep. The closest we can get."

"To the center of the planet," Nekhbet said.

"Correct." Turcotte had his eyes focused on the monitors even though they only showed darkness.

"How deep?" Nosferatu asked. He heard Nekhbet's irritated sigh. "I am just making conversation."

"It has been charted by humans at thirty-six thousand, seventy feet below sea level," Turcotte said. He was silent for a moment. "They are off by sixty-four feet."

"Right," Nekhbet muttered. "Let's sue the scientists, except they're all dead anyway."

"Humans have been down here before," Turcotte said. "Just not like this."

"You mean in a spaceship?" Nekhbet asked.

"No." Turcotte indicated the screen. "Like this."

A faint red glow was far below, growing brighter. "We are expected." He slowed the *Fynbar* as they approached the deepest point on the planet. Brought it to a halt above a bright red chasm.

Nosferatu and Nekhbet exchanged glances, but neither said anything. Turcotte closed his eyes.

Nekhbet started as a black tendril came up out of the magma. It rose up above the *Fynbar*, then began to fan out.

"What is that?" she asked.

"We know you are with us," Turcotte said. "We will keep you safe. We're going to have a conversation. We've already asked for help and gotten it."

The black spread wider, surrounding the spaceship until they were completely enclosed. Turcotte twitched the controls and the *Fynbar* settled down with a bump. The water outside began to go down, indicating it was being expelled from the enclosure. Within ten seconds the water was gone.

"There is oxygen," Turcotte said, as he got out of the pilot's seat.

"The pressure," Nosferatu argued, "will crush us."

"No." Turcotte went to the ladder. "We said we will keep you safe. But you can stay inside if you like." He threw open the hatch and exited.

Nosferatu followed; Nekhbet also, but with less alacrity.

Turcotte went down the side of the Fynbar onto the floor of the chamber. It was metal, the exact composition uncertain. He walked to the wall and raised his hands. Placed them on it. They sunk in to the wrists. Then he was slowly drawn in until he disappeared into the black.

He was part of.

BEYOND THE HELIOSPHERE

The sun emits a constant flow of charged particles, plasma, traveling at the speed of light. This is solar wind. It flows outward, beyond the Kuiper Belt and its dwarf planets, which Pluto has been relegated to. Indeed, the solar wind goes out three times farther than that. It is, in effect, a protective barrier from cosmic radiation and is called the heliosphere.

The Solar System is moving through space, rather fast, at 514,000 miles per hour. The heliosphere provides a shock wave of solar wind to protect it. That power loses energy and eventually ceases. Just outside of that, is interstellar space.

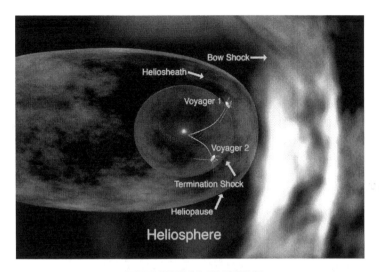

THE HELIOSPHERE

The Swarm Battle Core came out of FTLT, Faster Than Light Transit, in interstellar space as was the norm. There were dangers in either coming out of, or engaging FTLT inside a solar system. It was done, if necessary, but rarely. Add in the factor that this Core was facing a previously unknown event, the loss of another Core, it was prudent to transit outside the system.

This would give it time to deploy sensors. Also, there were other Battle Cores en route, and transit did take some time. Best to be safe. There was no rush. There rarely was for the Swarm.

The surface of a Core is black, fractured with red from within in random patterns due to the unique nature of its outer hull.

SWARM BATTLE CORE

The reason for the red is that the surface is under constant repair and is a combination of animate and inanimate material. The black inanimate is the dead exoskeleton. The red is where living cells much like coral grow outward regenerating the twenty-mile thick exoskeleton of the Battle Core.

The Airlia Sentinels that had been deployed around the heliosphere had been destroyed by the previous Battle Core as it came into system so this arrival wasn't noted. Not that there were any Airlia left in the system to read an alert if one had been issued. The last Airlia, Nyx, manning their base at Cydonia on Mars, had departed on board the mothership with Leahy, Yakov, the Chosen and others.

However, the Swarm war ship currently in the Asteroid Belt was immediately aware of the presence.

DAVIS MOUNTAINS, TEXAS

"Praying won't provide the light the crops need," Asha said to Joseph. They were sharing a pot of tea that Joseph had just brewed over a small stove.

"You worry too much," Joseph said. "The Tesla batteries will last a long time. Much will happen between now and then. The skies may clear and the solar will work. The radiation from the fallout will certainly dissipate and we can clean the InRotor turbines. As Sofia said, we don't have to worry about air."

The two were seated on a bench in the middle of the town. Metabols were moving about, doing various tasks. Others were resting.

"I think Leahy chose me because I worry," Asha said.

"She chose you because you make good decisions," Joseph said.

Asha shrugged. "I'm not in charge any more. I don't make the decisions."

"I will tell you a truth," Joseph said.

Asha waited, then finally prodded him. "And that is?"

"You were not chosen for your patience."

Asha laughed for the first time in many days.

Joseph indicated the Facility. "We are alive when most everyone is dead. We are with the future of mankind. We don't know what that will be, but I trust these children. They have good hearts."

"And Leahy?" Asha asked. "What did you sense about her? I always had the feeling that there was something off about her and I noticed you never warmed to her."

"She was a spirit," Joseph said. "Not an evil one, but not a benevolent one either. She wasn't human."

Asha was shocked. "What! Are you speaking allegorically? I know she was cold and distant."

"I am not a Metabol," Joseph said. "I am just an old man who has seen much. But I was raised in the old ways of my people. If I had not ended up here, and that is a long story for another day, I would have become what you would call a medicine man. Because I have the gift of sight. I can see the auras around people. Leahy had no aura. She is a skin-walker. Someone who resembles a human being on the outside, but is something else on the inside."

Asha sat still for a few seconds, processing that. "What do you think she was? Is?"

"I don't know."

"Was Mrs. Parrish a skin-walker?" Asha asked, trying to understand this startling disclosure.

"She had an aura," Joseph said. "Black as the evil in her heart." He smiled. "And before you ask, yours is yellow fringed with purple. A good heart with, as I have said, impatience, but not anger."

"Why didn't you tell me this about Leahy earlier?"

"You would have believed me?" Joseph asked. He didn't wait for an answer. "I trusted what she wanted to achieve: produce the Metabols out of the abomination of the Chosen program." He paused in thought. "And, to be honest, I was afraid of her. Of what she was."

A voice behind them caused both to start.

"What do you think she is?" Sofia asked.

"Ah, my dear," Joseph said. "Would you like some tea?"

"Yes, please." Sofia sat cross-legged on the other side of the stove.

Joseph poured her a cup and passed it to her before he answered. "She is something other than human. Perhaps one of the Undead we have heard of? A human-Airlia half-breed, but even then I think the human part would show something."

Sofia cradled the cup in her hand. "I never met her, so I cannot speculate. There are obviously other life forms in the universe. We know of the Airlia. The Swarm. Perhaps she is an alien?"

Asha was startled. "I'd never considered that."

Joseph smiled at Sofia. "Your mind is open. That is good."

"Everything has changed," Sofia said. "The world everyone was used to is gone." Sofia took a sip of tea. "The planet. It is alive."

"It has always been alive," Joseph said.

"Yes," Sofia agreed, "but it was sleeping. It is no longer sleeping."

"What does that mean?" Asha asked.

"She is angry," Sofia said. "Particularly at humans. We have been hurting her for many years."

"You say 'she'," Asha noted.

"Gaia," Sofia said. "The Earth Mother."

"What can we do?" Joseph asked. "Besides pray. I suspect she does not care for our prayers, but would prefer action."

"We must show her that we are her friend," Sofia said. She indicated the Facility. "This place is wonderful and has been our home. But it is human made. And an intrusion into the Earth. We must leave and go outside and start over."

Asha shook her head. "It's not livable out there. The radiation is low enough, but the ash cloud is bringing winter too soon and for too long. We won't be able to grow our crops. Our only chance is staying in here until the long winter passes. My calculations estimate at least three years."

"We will not be allowed to stay here three years," Sofia said.

"The Earth Mother is that angry?" Joseph asked.

"That is our sense," Sofia said.

Joseph stood. "Then we must go."

"Wait!" Asha protested. "We can't."

"We must," Sofia said. "We must trust that Gaia will take care of us." She handed the cup back to Joseph. "Thank you for the tea."

INDIAN SUBCONTINENT

The monsoon had put out all the fires and soaked the ground and debris so thoroughly that all lingering sparks were out. Streams and rivers were full. There was little left alive, but there was enough. Pockets of vegetation and animal life. Enough to begin spreading.

That wasn't good enough.

Plants and trees began growing at abnormal rates, many times their usual. Roots in burn zones that were close to death, were rejuvenated and began to propagate. What would take a normal day was happening in five minutes.

Animals began mating, but this wasn't as high a priority as getting the ecosystem back in balance.

Polar motion of the axis had always existed; in the past century it had moved about four inches per year. Some of that was due to the loss of mass on Greenland from melting ice sheets. Some was also due to glacial rebound as land that had been pressed down underneath glaciers rises back up without the weight.

Deep inside, Gaia once more adjusted the mantle flow to cause another shift in the polar axis. There was other movement going on underneath the planet's crust to achieve local changes. In a complicated series of calculations that would have overwhelmed mankind's best supercomputer ability to program, Gaia was using the shift as part of a series of maneuvers to help counteract man's depredations on the surface of the planet.

It was like a person adjusting the way they were sitting in a seat to get to a more optimal position. Except this was global.

GLACIER NATIONAL PARK, MONTANA

Thomas Jefferson Waterman double-checked the data. The change was tiny, almost imperceptible, but it was there. He had learned early in his career to note small changes because they led to big things.

The amount of ash being read by his sensors was slightly below the projected curve that had been calculated. That this could be positive news was beside the point. For the first time since sealing himself inside Heorot, T.J. experienced frustration. He had no contact with the outside world other than the sensors in the surrounding mountains directly linked to his control center. Things were happening beyond his field of vision and control and that was intolerable.

He felt the hands lightly touch his shoulders and he spun about, rising up, and his fist smashed into Portia's chin, his large ring tearing 'flesh'.

Portia staggered back under the blow, but not as far as a human would. She was six feet tall; T.J. had always liked women as tall as he, slender and blonde. On the surface. Her bosom was large, but not overly, as T.J. despised the artificiality of woman who augmented themselves.

"I am so sorry, Mister Waterman," Portia automatically replied, eyes downcast. She shifted into a seductive voice as she knelt. She looked up at him, a supplicant. "May I do something for you?"

For some reason T.J. would never be able to fathom, this infuriated him even more. He kicked Portia in the chest. She went with the blow, falling on her back. She remained there.

"I am so, so, sorry, Mister Waterman." Her head lifted up slightly so she could look at him. "May I do something for you?"

Waterman reached behind him and grabbed the chair. He swung it with all his might.

Portia didn't put up a hand to defend herself. The leg of the chair smashed into her head, bouncing it off the hard floor. T.J. lifted and struck again. And again. The outer layer was torn and there were audible cracks as things inside gave way.

It took over a dozen blows and half a minute before T.J. threw the chair to the side, breathing hard. He didn't bother to look down on what he had wrought. He walked out of the control room. "I'm going for a swim."

Behind him, Portia tried to get to her feet, but one of her knee joints was broken. As standing was impossible, she began to crawl toward the door she had come in from.

LAST STAND OF IMPERIUM

TALIANT FLEET BASE.

MILLIONS OF YEARS AGO

"Who are they?" Tai asked as they entered the chamber holding the Compendium, guardian computers, and Teslas. There were couples standing behind each table. They snapped to attention when they saw Librarian.

Tai was on crutches, having removed his prosthetic and giving it to one of Librarian's other assistants to take on a journey around the Military Academy. They'd taken a roundabout route here, Tai making sure they weren't being followed. First Ring was 'dark' and he'd taken a route he also knew to be dark from his Academy days when he and fellow cadets would travel about Taliant after taps avoiding detection on various personal missions of mischief.

"They are your comrades in the future," Librarian said. "Relax," she called out to the others. She indicated for Tai to take his place next to a young woman who had no partner. The woman twitched a brief smile of greeting at him, but focused on Librarian as she walked to the front of the room, just in front of the red pyramid.

There was a murmur among those gathered. They wore a variety of uniforms. Many were military of varying ranks. There were also scientists, a scattering of politicians and common folk who inhabited the warrens of Taliant, including a number who wore the dull brown of maintenance. Tai briefly wondered what traits they all shared for Librarian to have plucked them out of the millions on board Taliant and the billions in Imperium.

Librarian stood in front of the red pyramid, dwarfed by the Compendium. "There are times when a generation is called upon to make the ultimate sacrifice. It is regrettable that this duty falls to yours. I wish with all my heart I could take this burden from you. All of you have been specifically chosen. You were asked, without details, whether you would make that sacrifice. You all accepted. Now is the time for specifics as much as I know, which I will be honest, is not much."

Tai frowned because he'd caught a shift in Librarian's eyes, very slight, almost imperceptible but something he'd noted in the past.

Librarian continued. "As some of you are aware, the implants were named by the man who headed the project that invented them: Teslan. They are a form of life. Something to bridge the gap between carbon-based and silicon-based. We know the latter exists now, because of the Awakening at Light-Union-Twelve."

A rustle ran through those gathered.

"We know the Tesla can merge with humans because Teslan allowed one to enter him. Whatever he became put together the plan which you are about to implement. Events are moving quickly. Unity is massing its Militia near L-U-Twelve. The war is over. Between humans. What comes next will be the final chapter in Imperium."

Librarian indicated the large red pyramid behind her. "Teslan, the Tesla plan, was left in this Compendium."

"What is our mission?" Tai asked.

"You will help rebuild Imperium," Librarian said. As several voices were raised in question, she held up a hand, silencing them. "Not this Imperium. Something different. More inclusive. And containing more than just humans. Intelligent species must learn to not just co-exist but live together. Your mission will be to spread out among the habitable worlds. Both still in Imperium and in Unity. And the Indies. And wait."

"How long?" someone asked.

"As long as it takes," Librarian said. "Probably hundreds of thousands of years. Perhaps millions until the next Empire rises from the dust."

A rumble of confusion, surprise and denial arose.

Tai, used to taking command of a group, spoke in a command voice. "Silence! Let Librarian explain."

The group quieted.

"I wish I could," Librarian said. She indicated the Compendium. "It will show you what to do next when the time is right. There are ships in the next hanger. FTLT scout ships. Each can hold two people. A team. Each ship will also have a guardian. The one in front of you. It contains what to do once you get to your destination. The ultimate answer doesn't lie with me. It lies in the Teslas. You will be hosts for the Tesla in front of you. Vessels, so to speak."

As the selected ones turned to each other, Tai hobbled to Librarian. "What will you do?"

"I must go back," Librarian said. "Take my place, even though my word will mean nothing. This—" she gestured at the hangar—"is my legacy and I am content."

THE PRESENT

ARRIVAL

BEYOND THE HELIOSPHERE

The Airlia mothership transitioned out of FTLT farther from the edge of the heliosphere than the Swarm Battle Core had, but on the side, which meant it was actually much closer to the system and the planet that was its destination.

Besides the dangers of in system transit, the Airlia had a standing policy of keeping transition points away from the mothership's origin and final destination because the Swarm picked up on the event in some manner that the Airlia had never been able to decipher.

The mothership had already done four transitions on the way here, covering its trail as best as possible in order to not lead the Swarm back to its start point. Of course, given that the Swarm had just assaulted and retreated from Orion Fleet headquarters, this seemed unnecessary and redundant. However, the war with the Swarm had been going on so long, rules were followed, regardless of common sense.

Regardless, unknown to the Airlia on the mothership, their arrival was immediately noted by the Battle Core that had arrived just hours before it.

CASCADIA SUBDUCTION ZONE

The Swarm scout ship had a hull that could handle space travel, where radiation levels are often quite high. While the Cobalt 60 was powerful, the crew inside was safe. From the radiation at least. Not only was the ship shielded, Swarm could deal with radiation levels that would cook other Scale life.

A thick strand of black metal extended from the closest wall and wrapped around the scout ship. It spread outward, encapsulating the ship. The Swarm inside noted this event and logged it. They didn't panic, because Swarm don't panic. The Swarm wasn't even curious, because Swarm aren't curious. The black metal pulled away from the hull, leaving an opening just outside the ship's hatch, indicating intelligence and knowledge of the scout ship's design. The radiation level in the small pocket was negligible.

This was, obviously, an invitation. The Swarm in charge accepted the invitation because why would one not if the mission is reconnaissance?

It entered the airlock, made sure the inner one was sealed, and then exited. It crept close to the black metal. Then, as if it had no will of its own, reached out with one arm. The three fingers on the end touched and sank in.

The other arms stopped moving and the Swarm became still. It was part of.

PACIFIC OCEAN

The crushed remains of the *USS Pennsylvania* lay on the ocean bed, three miles down. There is life that deep in the ocean. Some of it recorded by scientists, much of it unknown. Existing at such extreme pressure, these creatures became part of the world around them, not fighting the external pressure, but imbibing it as part of their constitution. If brought up to sea level, they would explode.

The submarine was dead, along with all inside, except for one part. The nuclear reactor was still active and was in the last stages of meltdown. There were also multiple nuclear warheads in the Trident missiles.

This was noted. The ocean bed beneath the *Pennsylvania* opened up and the submarine fell into a newly formed cavern. It was lined with black metal. The roof closed and all on the ocean floor was as it had been.

When the reactor went critical, the event was so contained, the ground barely vibrated. Then black tendrils reached out to the ship and began to disassemble it down to its component elements, including the nuclear material, returning to Earth what had come out of Earth.

STONHENGE, ENGLAND

Twelve feet underneath where the priest had been pulled into the earth, there was a small, black sphere resting inside a human skull.

Gwalcmai's skull.

Duncan had taken his armor off before burying him. His bones showed the damage done by Excalibur, including the fatal blow that had pierced armor and cleaved his *ka* and chest. He rested where Lisa Duncan had buried him in 528 A.D. Time had added more dirt on top and the trees had been cleared off, but otherwise he'd been undisturbed for a millennium and a half.

The implant was untouched by time. But it had spread its microscopic tendrils into the surrounding terrain. It knew what Gaia was doing. It had been paying attention for thousands of years, awaiting this moment.

The earth around the bones opened and the High Priest arrived at his destination. He was in a catatonic state, thorns in the vines that were wrapped around him having injected a natural sedative. This was the role he had chosen without having any idea that it would come to this. His unconscious form ended up lying next to Gwalcmai's bones.

From the implant, more tendrils snaked out the open bottom of the skull and into the High Priest's mouth. Once they anchored, the implant was pulled out and across and then into man's mouth. Those feeds that had been in the earth were drawn back into the small orb as it pressed through the back of his mouth, by dissolving into microscopic nanotechnology and reassembling at the base of the brain. The tendrils spread into the brain. The implant took command.

Within moments the High Priest was no longer who he had been.

THE FACILITY

They carried backpacks full of as much food as they could bear along with all the canteens and water containers possible. Despite this, Asha estimated they could survive perhaps a week on the outside. She was the last one out of the Facility and she shut the door, full expecting to have to open it again at the end of that week.

She hurried to catch up with Joseph who was walking with Sofia at the head of the long column of one-thousand-five-hundred-and-twenty-four Metabols. It occurred to Asha that there had been no destination chosen, no plan made, other than leaving the facility. She was breathing hard when she reached the young girl and old Native American. They were coming to the end of the valley bordering the mountain range under which the Facility and Mrs. Parrish's headquarters had been built.

"Where are we going?" Asha asked after catching her breath.

Instead of answering, Sofia, and all the Metabols, turned to face back the way they'd come. The ground shook under their feet. Asha reached out and Joseph took her hand as both of them held Sofia. The terrain over the Facility crumbled. It took only twenty seconds.

"It's all gone," Asha whispered in shock as a wave of dust and debris floated toward them. It was also that moment when she realized the falling ash was much lighter than it had been the other day.

Sofia, and all the Metabols, knelt. Sofia bowed her head and whispered: "*Earth Mother, source of all. All-fertile, all-destroying Gaia. Who brings forth life and embraces death. Who connects the eternal to the now. Immortal and blessed. Thank you for allowing us the time to leave. Thank you for the warning.*"

The Metabols stood.

"Where did you learn that prayer?" Joseph asked.

"We just know it," Sofia said.

"Is the Earth, Gaia, speaking to you?" Joseph asked.

Sofia shrugged, for a moment looking like the young girl she was; and wasn't. "We just know."

"Where do we go now?" Asha said, knowing the Facility was destroyed and there was no returning.

Sofia frowned. Then she faced the east. "The land." She turned to the right and south. "The fire." West. "The water." North. "The air." Took a deep breath, closed her eyes. Remained still for a long minute. Opened her eyes. "Air."

She strode off in that direction. Joseph and Asha hurried to catch up as the long column of Metabols fell in behind.

Asha started as a dragon swooped overhead, banked and flew by once more before landing on a rocky promontory to the east, watching them.

Sofia reassured her. "It is the same one we met the other day." She pointed to the west. "See." The large bulk of Cthulhu was silhouetted on the top of a ridge line.

"Are they following us?" Joseph asked. He was limping slightly, the miles they'd covered through the desolate land of West Texas taking their toll.

"They are escorting us," Sofia said. "There are still Swarm and their creatures out here that are not part of. And because we are not part of, it might be a problem."

"Part of what?" Asha asked.

"Gaia."

"You mean that Cthulhu and dragon are part of Earth?" Asha said.

"The part of the Fade that is with them made them part of," Sofia said. She held up a hand and the column stopped, not accordion-like, as a normal line of fifteen hundred people would, but instantly. She turned to Joseph. "You are hurting."

"It is nothing," Joseph lied.

Sofia pointed. "We do not have to walk. There is a train line north. We can ride."

"How are we going to run a train?" Asha asked.

Sofia looked at her, slightly surprised. "You helped build and run the Facility, Asha. Certainly, you can get a train moving."

"To where?" Asha asked. "What is the destination?"

"We'll know when we're there."

ASTEROID BELT, SOLAR SYSTEM

The Swarm warship had lost contact with the scout ship sent to investigate what had happened with the hadesarchaea. The last message indicated it had arrived at the subduction zone; then nothing.

This indicated one of two things: an accident or an incident. The former happened, but rarely. The latter meant there was a force at work and it was most likely inimical to the Swarm since contact had been terminated. An enemy.

The Command Swarm sent a message to the Supreme Swarm on board the inbound Battle Core, alerting them to the possibility that whatever had caused the previous Core to suicide might still be present. The last transmission from that Core had indicated it was thoroughly infected with something deadly and it was destroying itself to keep this from spreading. This infection had been transmitted by the Reaped Scale after infecting themselves, an extraordinary method of defense. That did not, however, rule out that many of the Scale—humans still existed on the planet. In fact, one of the reasons the hadesarchaea had been deployed was to ensure the surface of the planet was wiped clean of Scale life.

Another factor was picked up by the sensors: the cloud cover of ash and debris from the nuclear warheads was lessening at a rate that could not be accounted for by natural means. Some other force was at play; on a planetary level.

A major threat given all that had happened so far.

The Command Swarm received a startling message, if Swarm could be startled, back from the Supreme: nine more Battle Cores were inbound.

MONS OLYMPUS, MARS

What had been Lisa Duncan was no longer. Or rather, the real entity that had invaded Lisa Duncan a long, long time ago, was here, now. The consciousness that had been in the implant was now fully formed. She was part of it in a way, but also part of something much more.

She stood in the center of mothership's control room and surveyed the contents. She was naked and the temperature was dropping, bit by bit, as the emergency batteries built into the compartment were weakening. The air was foul, but the oxygen sufficient. Freezing would claim her first if she were still human, except she wasn't.

The implant had always been alive but mostly dormant. It had been around far longer than Lisa Duncan or even Donnchadh had existed.

Bit by bit, the human part of her re-learned her life.

MPONENG GOLD MINE, SOUTH AFRICA

The miners and their families gathered on the surface, shocked at what they saw. Where there had been foul slurry mounds of the material pulled out of the mines and dumped after being sifted through for the precious gold, there were now grass covered hills.

There was no sign of the bodies of the guards; or the miners who'd died battling them to get access to save their families.

Just nature reclaiming land that had been savaged and scarred by man in his vain search for a mineral that was valuable because it was scarce and hard to get. Now they had a rich vein filling the mine. And the people could care less.

They were, of course, all infected by the Gaia virus.

GLACIER NATIONAL PARK. MONTANA

Hands gently slid over T.J. Waterman's shoulders. Formerly broken fingers were once more long, elegant and crowned with brilliant red fingernails. Lips that had been battered, split and bleeding, were now perfect. They came close to his ear and a tongue licked lightly in the perfect spot just behind the lobe.

"I'm working," he said, checking the computer's analysis of the weather, cloud cover, climate change, and radiation levels. It was changing much faster than the models had projected. It was good news but out of the norm and T.J. Waterman didn't like out of the norm. Something was at work out there, something he didn't control.

"I am grateful that you are working," Portia said. "You work to ensure our future."

T.J. frowned but she wasn't important.

"You deserve a reward for all your hard work," Portia said as she got on her knees and crawled under the console. "I love when you go commando."

T.J. frowned again even though he didn't consciously hear her. He knew that the computer models were just simulations. He'd bought his scientists unlimited time on the most powerful quantum computers available, but even their capabilities couldn't match up to the number of variables possible on a planetary scale.

He felt better as he read the numbers. They'd erred on the negative side, something that scientists were wont to do. He remembered all the scare tactics over the decades. His favorite had been Peak Oil. Tree-huggers scientists had been screaming that since his grandfather's time. The deadlines they'd set for the production of oil to start falling had come and passed too many times to count. The only science that counted was that which produced actual results, not the science that threw out fearful projections.

There had always been more oil. He knew that more than anyone as his subsidiaries extracted it with a vengeance from among the shale and under the oceans.

Portia had his pants open and her mouth and hands were doing what he'd had programmed. He'd felt no shame instructing the geek who'd written Portia's program about the specifics. After all, the geek was at the bottom of the shaft with the rest of them. How smart had she been?

He spared a glance. Her face was perfect, unmarked. "The hair color is off," he noted. "Lighter."

She nodded, unable to speak at the moment.

The previous estimate of four years of nuclear winter was now three point seven. An amazing change in just a few days. At this rate? He tapped the keys as Portia worked harder, since the mean time for normal ejaculation had passed, which looped on her system that she wasn't performing up to the standard.

"Stop!" T.J. shouted.

Portia froze.

"Slow down," T.J. said. He smiled. "You're enjoying this, aren't you?"

Portia murmured an assent, lifting her eyes to see his.

"Continue," T.J. ordered.

When he was done, she scooted back. He checked for stains, zipped his pants, and stood. "I feel like doing some laps. Make sure the suit is cleaned." He walked out of the control room.

Portia remained kneeling under the console. She stayed like that for five minutes, staring at the door T.J. had gone through. The face showed no emotion. The eyes were unblinking. Finally, she got to her feet and turned and looked at the monitors, one by one. Taking in their data.

Then she turned and walked out.

There was a suit to be cleaned.

THE CHALLENGER DEEP. PACIFIC OCEAN.

"I'm hungry," Nekhbet complained.

Nosferatu didn't bother to reply. They were sitting on the deck of the *Fynbar*.

"Do you have a plan, my dear?" Nekhbet asked. "In case our miracle man does not return?"

"He'll return."

"Your confidence has left me in the lurch once or twice over the years," Nekhbet noted.

Nosferatu turned toward her and lightly ran a finger along the side of her cheek. "But I've always come through in the end, haven't I?"

"You have such a way." Nekhbet leaned into him. "If we are fated to die in this, this, I don't even know what to call it, why don't we enjoy our last moments?" She lifted her head, thin, pale lips slightly parted, revealing her overly large canines.

At that moment a noise distracted them. A bulge in the wall, and then the image of a man. Turcotte reappeared, none the worse for his disappearance. He strode to the Fynbar and climbed up and entered without a word.

"Not very polite," Nekhbet said.

The two Undead followed. Turcotte was in the pilot's depression, looking over the control. Nosferatu loudly clanged the hatch shut and sealed it. He climbed down, past Nekhbet's glower, and slid into the co-pilot's sink.

"I don't know who the 'we' is, that I'm talking to," Nosferatu said, "but a little enlightenment would be appreciated. We have been patient."

Turcotte looked over. "We must leave."

The Fynbar rocked as the walls around them dissipated and sea water rushed in. As soon as the craft was clear, Turcotte adjusted the controls and they ascended.

"Leave to go where?" Nosferatu pressed.

Turcotte was focused on the ship. "We must leave."

"Yes," Nosferatu said, "but where are we going?"

As they ascended from the depths, Turcotte looked at Nosferatu. "Gaia says we must leave."

"Like, the planet?" Nekhbet said.

"Correct."

"Well. Okay," Nekhbet said. "To go where?"

"We don't know. But humans must leave."

"Got that part," Nekhbet said.

Light flickered on the forward-looking console, indicating they were in the upper reaches of the Pacific. They burst out of the water, heading straight up, and he angled the ship to the northwest.

"Are we leaving now?" Nekhbet asked.

"Not yet," Turcotte said. "There is someone we have to meet."

TALIANT FLEET BASE.
MILLIONS OF YEARS AGO

"By the time you get this message from our emergency comms buoy, we will be dead," Speaker said, her holographic image flickering in the center of the Star Chamber. "I hope we will be dead, because we are receiving reports that something else is happening to those that are captured. Something worse." Speaker was on the bridge of a ship of the line and there was smoke behind her, always a bad sign on a space ship. There were voices in the background, terse orders being issued.

"There's now sixteen of these Cores," Speaker said. "We have engaged them. And we are losing. They have taken the weapons from the ships they absorbed and mounted them on the surface of the Cores. Which aren't like anything we've encountered before. As best we can tell, the hull is some sort of organic material. It can repair itself. They are still growing, even as they battle us." She shook her head. "We've blown huge chunks out of them, yet it seems to have no effect. We're targeting the weapon systems on the surface of the Cores, but to little avail."

Librarian glanced over her shoulder, at the empty spot where Captain Tai should be standing, then focused back on Speaker.

"There are more of these Cores forming on Light-Union-Twelve's surface. We made a mistake coming here to fight them. We are simply supplying them with more FTLT and weapon systems. I've ordered the ships that can escape via FTLT to do and return to their home worlds. I am staying."

A man bleeding from a gash on the side of his head came into the projection, gripped her shoulder, and whispered something into her ear. She grimaced as he disappeared. "As I warned and feared. We have failed to stop it. One of the Cores has broken off from the battle and is accelerating out of system. I've sent two of my remaining ships in pursuit. It's going to transit if we don't stop it." She muted and yelled something to her right, then unmuted. "I wanted to get this message out along with the data we've accumulated so far. Not much, but it's more than we had than when we came into the system. We don't know if the Cores are the life we're fighting or if they're manned by someone, something, we haven't met yet. Something from L-U-Twelve. But once they launch the Cores that are forming on the surface we'll be swarmed under."

A voice exclaimed in the background.

"The escaping Core is slowing," Speaker said, looking up at something, most likely a monitor in the top front of the bridge. "No!" she shouted. "Order them to break off. Break off!"

Librarian glanced at Fleet Admiral. He was in his chair, hands gripping the arm rests.

Speaker's shoulders slumped and she returned her attention to the camera. "They impacted on the Core. Smashed into it, firing their weapons the entire way. They knew they couldn't avoid collision at their trajectory so our ships accelerated. Their sacrifice had no effect. The Core is moving outward again." She glanced to her right. "We've got incoming. I have to send this buoy while I still can. You should have—" she paused as something distracted her. "That Core just transitioned. There are more and—" she staggered as the sound of a heavy explosion echoed. "Damn it! Buoy away." Her image abruptly disappeared.

Silence reigned in the Star Chamber for several seconds. There was no chirp of a ship in distress.

Fleet Admiral stood. "We will attack. We can destroy those things. We'll use our planet buster."

"You'll use the device that woke L-U-Twelve up?" Librarian was incredulous. "Brilliant. Just brilliant." She turned to VicDep. "We must—" she never finished as the energy pulse hit her in the side.

Librarian collapsed to the clear floor under feet, face down.

"Dispense of her," Fleet Admiral order.

A pair of aides grabbed Librarian's body and dragged it out of the Star Chamber. They found the closest disposal chute and shoved her into it, before hurrying back.

THE PRESENT

MORE ARRIVALS

BEYOND THE HELIOSPHERE

Nine Battle Cores came out of FTLT within minutes of each other and not far apart on the Solar System scale, considering their massive size. As they slowed below light speed, they headed inward, toward the third planet.

SOLAR SYSTEM, KUIPER BELT

The mothership had arrived after the first Battle Core and thus had been unaware of its presence. But nine Cores coming out of FTLT was picked up. Alarms went off. The readings were unprecedented because the Airlia had never encountered more than one Battle Core at a time.

A warning buoy that could send an FTL transmission was jettisoned, speeding back out of the Solar System in order to fire off a warning message.

Were the Cores here because Teardrop had worked? Were they trying to destroy worlds with humans on them before the Airlia could tally the population into its weapon system?

Despite the overwhelming odds, the captain of the Mothership continued on course for Earth. They had orders, after all. And, more importantly, they were closer than the Cores to reaching the planet as they entered the Kuiper Belt at STL.

The eighteen talons, claw-shaped warships attached to the outside of the mothership, nine on each end, powered up and detached, spreading out in a defensive pattern around the larger ship.

AMAZON BASIN

South America had been relatively untouched by World War III with no nuclear powers. The Reaping had been effective, snatching almost all of the human population. The flora and fauna remained untouched; at least as much as had not already been devastated by mankind's encroachment.

Gaia seized the absence of humans as the opportunity it was. The Amazon rain forest, slashed and burned for decades, rapidly began to reclaim lost terrain at a rate that compressed years into hours. As destructive as man had been, Gaia was much more constructive.

HOUSTON, TEXAS

Oil refineries, no longer tended to, began to explode, setting off a chain reaction. Flames leapt high into the sky, while that which didn't burn spread outward.

Nearby chemical plants, lacking power and human oversight also failed. Some exploded, others were breached, spreading their own toxicity.

Gaia reacted. The ground beneath opened. Oil, chemicals, polluted water poured down into the Earth. This process was happening all over the planet where the lack of human control was leading to environmental catastrophe. The toxins were broken down into component elements and redistributed through the mantle.

Most nuclear power plants went into shutdown/safe mode, the cores safely retracted. However, a handful didn't and they too were absorbed.

Once inside the planet, they were drawn through the crust into the mantle. Those elements were also broken down and absorbed.

STONEHENGE, ENGLAND.

While many things were being drawn down into the Earth, the crowd of chanting Druids, weary, wet, exhausted, staying on duty in shifts, was startled when the ground rumbled under their feet. Those on duty paused in their chant, because something was emerging where their High Priest had been consumed.

A naked man arose, dirt sliding off his muscled body. He stood in the center of the Druids, eyes slowly focusing. He turned, looking at them, past them. Then upward at the grey sky.

"Where are we?" he whispered. He looked back at the Druids. "You will be part of." As he said it, his body morphed and the outer layer became the armor he had worn when his human form had been a member of King Arthur's court.

The Druids were snatched by the plants and pulled into the Earth.

Gwalcmai removed the cloth covering the two-foot-high guardian computer. He knelt and placed his hands on it. The black surface shimmered into silver. A glow flowed from the pyramid and around him. He remained like that for thirty seconds; not long to be updated on thousands of years of information.

He let go and the shield dissipated. Gwalcmai stood and looked upward at the dark grey sky, peering intently as if he could see through the ash and into the heavens.

"We will get you," he whispered.

MONS OLYMPUS, MARS

Lisa Duncan, now more appropriately Donnchadh, halted in her futile examination of the control pod of the mothership.

There was nothing usable and the few instruments that were working indicated that the battery powered life support was limited and failing. She, the flesh, would die.

The implant, on the other hand, would survive. But to do so would require reversing the transformation of bringing back the human part. Donnchadh raised a hand, looking at it almost curiously. The flesh rippled, became silver. She extended it into the closest console, merging with it.

There was no more pain because the human had already been subsumed by the implant. Her carbon form began to be transformed into a silicon one, to become a complete Tesla.

As this was occurring, her head cocked and she looked upward. "We are here. We will wait." The transformation paused.

AIRSPACE, SOUTHEAST ASIA

"We're just going to keep flying into space?" Nekhbet asked. "No destination in particular?"

Turcotte abruptly halted the *Fynbar*, caused Nekhbet to lose her grip and slide along the floor. Nosferatu reached out and grabbed her, saving her from slamming into the side.

"What the—" Nekhbet began but Turcotte made an abrupt movement with his hand and for once she was silent. He remained perfectly still for several moments.

"Interesting. There are two now. He was here all the time. Part of. And she is up there." He nodded toward the skies above. "We thought she was gone, but she is not."

Nekhbet and Nosferatu exchanged a look, but neither spoke.

"Who first?" Turcotte said. He frowned. "The Swarm are still here. There is a warship in the Asteroid Belt. They sent a scout ship down. The one we saw. It knows. It will go back with the message."

"What message?" Nosferatu dared to ask.

"The one the Swarm has been waiting for," Turcotte said, "even though it does not know it was waiting for it."

"Right," Nekhbet said. "Got it."

Turcotte looked at her. "You are a hybrid of two Scale species. But they came out of the same species to begin with so it is not so surprising that they should come back together."

"Which one came first?" Nosferatu asked. "Human or Airlia?"

"Neither were first," Turcotte said. "All came after. Does it matter? We are here now." He took the controls and the *Fynbar* headed straight up.

"Where are we going now?" Nekhbet asked.

"Mars."

"Why?" Nekhbet asked.

"We are all coming together."

"Right." Nekhbet moved forward and slid into the co-pilot's depression with Nosferatu. "Let me know when we get there."

VICINITY COLORADO SPRINGS, COLORADO

The Metabols left the steam powered locomotive and rail cars behind on a deserted spur of a north-south line just outside of Colorado Springs. Sofia was in the lead, flanked by Asha and Joseph. The rest of the Metabols were stretched out in a long column behind them as they pushed into the Rocky Mountains, going around the bulk of Cheyenne Mountain.

What had been Cheyenne Mountain. The Swarm Battle Core had blasted the mountain several times before dropping the metamorphosis for the Reaping. The command center inside, built to take a direct nuclear strike, didn't exist anymore.

They skirted around the rubble of the once massive mountain just south of Pikes Peak to the west side. Sofia led them on the narrow path to Tesla's hidden laboratory. They went up three switchbacks and reached a wooden door set in the side of the mountain.

"How did you know how to find this?" Joseph asked, breathing hard. The trip on the train had rested him, but the march into the mountains had been difficult.

"Darlene sent me an image before being absorbed into the Swarm," Sofia said. "Nikola Tesla worked out of Colorado Springs for several years and there were rumors he had a secret lab in the mountains." She indicated the door. "This was an abandoned mine when he got here in 1900."

"How do we get in?" Asha asked, indicating the slot of an old skeleton key.

"We open the door," Sofia said and she did just that, pulling it back on well-oiled hinges. "I don't think Leahy was worried about anyone coming in after she left it."

Tesla lights flickered on, illuminating a smooth tunnel sliced through the granite.

Sofia turned to the Metabols. "We camp here for now. Gather food and water."

The children spread out into the forest.

"Will they be safe?" Asha worried.

"I'll help them," Joseph said. "I've taught them how to live off the land but this is their first opportunity to actually do it." He limped off.

Sofia and Asha walked two hundred feet to a second wood door. That opened as easily. An open space beyond was crowded with benches and tables. There was equipment on most of them, some of which Asha recognized, other of which was foreign to her. There was a metal spiral staircase in the center which went up. Racks filled with weathered and aged scrolls lined one wall.

Asha pointed. "Look." A flat screen monitor was flickering, just static, but it was working. "Something's activated it."

"What?" Asha asked as she walked among the work benches, looking for anything that might be useful.

"There's a feed out there, somewhere," Sofia said, looking over the control console. There was an empty spot where something with a base two feet square had once resided. "Interesting."

"Here!" Asha said, holding up a *ka*. "This must be Darlene." She frowned. "But she still needs a body. An empty vessel to be downloaded into. And the technology which Turcotte has. We don't even know if he's alive. Or where he and the *Fynbar* are. He probably escaped on the mothership."

They were both startled when a male voice came out of the speaker built into the static-covered display. "He didn't. He's on the *Fynbar* right now. Flying to Mars."

"Who are you?" Asha demanded. "Where are you?"

"Our name is Gwalcmai. We're in England. Not far from Stonehenge. Something where you are is connected to my—"he paused—"computer. We can hear you but not see you. You are not one of us. Who are you?"

"I'm Asha. And this is Sofia."

"Interesting," Gwalcmai said. "There must have been a computer similar to mine hooked to the device we're speaking through. But the owner is gone. We searched for the Tesla's for many years after we arrived on this planet. But we never found them. They hid well. Waited well. Turcotte is on his way to Mars to get our other. But his other. I don't sense her in this star system."

Asha looked at Sofia, utterly confused, but Sofia had put some of the pieces together. "You're talking about Professor Leahy. She claims to be a granddaughter of Tesla."

"Tesla isn't a person," Gwalcmai said. "It is us."

"And what are you?" Sofia asked.

"We are the facilitators."

Sofia arched a dark eyebrow and glanced at Asha. "What are you facilitating?"

"The future."

There was silence for several seconds.

"What should we do?" Sofia asked. "We have the essence of a friend that we need Turcotte's help with and something on his ship to bring her back. How can we get hold of him?"

Gwalcmai said: "Here is what you must do and where you must go so it all comes together."

ASTEROID BELT

The Swarm scout ship rendezvoused with the warship not far from Mars orbit. The Command Swarm had been moving the craft closer to Earth as the Cores came in system. As soon as the scout docked, the Swarm who'd left the ship in the Cascadia Zone exited. It moved through zero-g swiftly inside the hangar bay. It had not 'transmitted' any of what it had learned because all the Swarm would then be aware. This was one of those rare occasions where the information was of a nature that it needed to be kept close.

It made its way into the depths of the warship until it was close to the center. Then it placed an arm into an opening on a wall that was made of red, organic material: the essence of the Swarm ships. Through it the three fingers touched one of the long arms of the Command Swarm.

This is what is happening.

After imparting what it had learned from Gaia, the Swarm withdrew its arm and headed back to the scout ship.

The warship changed course, heading directly toward the closest, incoming Core.

MPONENG GOLD MINE, SOUTH AFRICA

They'd gone back to the way that their ancestors had lived before being lured into the mines because of the need for money. Hunting, gathering, living as a village of equals. Even the handful of guards who'd thrown down their weapons and joined them in entering the mine, quickly became part of the rhythm of this new life.

The land was evolving, changing faster than any could believe but they accepted its bounty. Without choice, but adapting to what was, they were going to a way of life when humans had worked in concert with the land.

They all felt better than they could remember. Despite what had happened, there was a sense of optimism and contentment.

The Gaia infection meant that while they were still human, they were different. As the Metabols were different, these South Africans and the others who'd joined them, were in tune, but instead of which each other, which most had already possessed, they were working with the Earth.

THE MOFFAT TUNNEL, COLORADO

The steam locomotive had had a tough go of it, negotiating the switchbacks fifty miles west of Denver but it finally pulled the cars holding the Metabols to the entrance of the Moffat Tunnel, 9,239 feet above sea level. The sky was still grey and overcast, although not as much ash was falling.

Sofia was in the cab of the locomotive along with one of the Metabols who had helped Asha get the old locomotive running. Asha was there also, but Joseph was back in the cars with the Metabols, resting after the trek from Tesla's lab back to the train. Four other Metabols helped grab wood off the next car and throw it in the raging furnace that produced the steam in the engine.

They were following Gwalcmai's instructions to head west to Area 51. When Sofia had pressed him for a reason why, he'd simply repeated the suggestion, which sounded more like an order, and then had gone silent.

"I don't like the looks of that," Asha said as they approached the east portal to the tunnel.

"Are you claustrophobic?" Sofia asked.

Asha shook her head. "No. But the power is out in the tunnel. The lights and fans will be off. If we stall in there, we'll smother ourselves."

"We won't stall," the Metabol said. "We have enough wood to get through. Then we must gather more." He glanced at Sofia and smiled. "But only dead wood. No cutting of trees."

"No cutting of trees," Sofia agreed.

The train plunged into the darkness. They'd scavenged the train and cars from a tourist attraction not far from the Davis Mountains. Someone standing in the back could see where they'd come in, a sliver of light that became smaller and smaller. There was only black ahead. The tunnel is 6.2 miles long and the sound of the engine and the old wheels on the tracks reverberated off the stone walls. The smoke pouring out of the locomotive stack blew back on all the cars, where the windows were tightly closed. In the cab, Asha, Sofia and the Metabols dealt with it as best they could with wet clothes over their mouths. A Tesla lamp provided enough light that they could see the controls.

The traverse seemed to take hours, but it was only thirty minutes. Then the welcome sight of a speck of light ahead. It grew larger and then they exited on the west side of the Continental Divide.

The bigger surprise was that they exited the tunnel into bright sunlight. A hole in the ash cloud, not very large, but enough to bathe the train in its welcome glow. From the high vantage point of the West Portal, the snow-capped Rocky Mountains ahead shimmered with patches of sun.

"A sign," Sofia said.

"Of what?"

"Gaia favors us," Sofia said.

SOLAR SYSTEM

The Airlia Mothership was moving faster than regulations prescribed, but the presence of so many Battle Cores made such concern irrelevant. The talons were spread out around it, a feeble curtain of defense if it had to engage a Battle Core.

There were radiation hot spots indicating nuclear detonations. What was also disturbing was the first sensor readings of the third planet. That, combined with no sign of Airlia technology, including any sign of the Sentinel early warning platforms, was worrisome. More detailed imaging revealed no Airlia and scant indication of human life. Piled on top were the obvious indications that the planet had been Reaped, which explained the lack of Airlia and humans, but not why Battle Cores were heading toward the planet.

It was perplexing.

The Airlia commander was further confused when they picked up another ship coming out of FTLT on the far side of the Solar System. The signature indicated it was another mothership. A hail was sent, but there was no response and there was no transponder signal.

GLACIER NATIONAL PARK. MONTANA

T.J. couldn't believe what his cameras were displaying: sunlight. Patches of blue sky. It was impossible, but it was happening. He wasn't sure whether to be pissed at the scientist who'd given him the Mount Tambora and other environmental data, or glad that he could move his timetable up.

He double-checked the numbers, then triple-checked. This was not the time to make an error. Radiation levels were almost normal. Most of the ash was gone from the sky. Temperatures were roughly at their median for this time of year.

He distantly heard the doors slide open behind him, but he wasn't concerned. When Portia slid her hand over his shoulder, he shrugged it off. "Not now."

"I am so very grateful that you are working," Portia said. "You work to ensure our future."

For the first time, T.J. looked over his shoulder at her. "My future is a lot closer than I dreamed."

"You deserve a reward for all your hard work," Portia said as she got on her knees and crawled under the console.

T.J. kicked her away. "I'm serious. Not now. I'm implementing Resurrection." As Portia started to crawl back toward him, he held up a hand. "Program halt, command."

Portia froze, one hand halfway toward his crotch. T.J. moved around it as he scooted his chair to the console and typed in commands. Deep inside one of several vaults, lights came on and machines began to work. Frozen embryos were retrieved. The first wave. Eight androids, programmed to be nannies and configured on Mary Poppins and other famous mother figures from cinema were activated.

It had never occurred to T.J. to have one made in the image of his own mother, and if it had, he would have rejected it immediately. The AI programmer, who had quickly sized up and assessed T. J. (although not well enough, since she was now in the shaft) hadn't bothered to ask. Any mother that had produced such a man should not exist again.

Green lights lit up across the top of the panel and T.J. felt as much pride of parenthood as a man could who had just pushed some keys. He stroked more of them. The security requirements on this command were more stringent. He typed in a complicated 20 figure password he'd memorized and never written down. That allowed a scanner to pop up next to the keyboard and he leaned forward, allowing his retina to be scanned. The scanner retracted. He typed in the password again, except this time in reverse.

A distant explosion rumbled through the control room. A previously untouched side of the mountain beyond the exit vault door blew outward, exposing them to daylight for the first time.

T.J. launched a drone and directed it to take a look to make sure the heavy doors were clear of debris.

The explosives expert had been spot on: they were clear and ready to open.

T.J. shoved the chair back and strode out of the control room. He forgot all about Portia who remained frozen in place. He walked along long tunnels to a far wing of the complex. He had to open four heavy steel doors along the way, using a combination of the password and retina scans.

Then he arrived at the last door, two heavy doors, each twenty feet high and ten wide. He entered the core and did the scan.

For a moment nothing happened and T.J. experienced a moment of not quite panic, but anger that perhaps the engineer had screwed up, but then they cracked open. Fresh air circulated in and he was bathed in sunshine as they swung wide. He looked out over the Montana countryside. The land, as far as he could see, was his by deed.

But he was certain that even beyond the legal boundaries, which didn't exist anymore, he owned it all. He spread his arms wide, fingers extended as if he could grab it all and pull it in.

*****

In the control room, Portia was immobile as he had ordered. Forgotten.

But then, very slowly, millimeter by millimeter, she blinked.

MARS

Turcotte, in the form of the human with an inactive Tesla, had been to Mars before. The Tesla had traveled across galaxies. The human part felt like he was in a theater, sitting in the audience, watching himself on stage. He didn't have any control; that was the realm of the Tesla. How long had it been in his brain? He'd learned his past was a lie when he checked the paperwork Mrs. Parrish had given him about his father which indicated he'd had no children. Where had he come from?

Turcotte had been through a lot this past year, ever since being drafted into the security unit for Area 51 by Lisa Duncan, who had supposedly been the President's science advisor for Majestic-12, the mysterious organization that ran Area 51. She, of course, had not at all been who she pretended to be, and worse, who she'd thought she was. Turcotte had learned of the mothership and alien life. About the Airlia. Different versions of how humans came to be.

There were many characters and scenes on the Tesla stage. Truths, most of which blew away what he'd thought were truths, followed by deeper truths. Humans had not been made by the Airlia. In fact, they were branches of the same genetic tree, which made sense given the Undead like Nosferatu and Nekhbet who were in the *Fynbar* with him and had been uneasily quiet throughout the flight. He was aware of their discomfort but right now wasn't the time to explain.

The figures and images on the stage shifted and Turcotte realized that the Tesla was trying to arrange it to make sense to him. What he needed to know now.

Duncan/Tesla was alive. But she was actually the human before Duncan, Donnchadh. Her Tesla partner, Gwalcmai/Tesla was also alive and waiting at Stonehenge with their guardian computer. Turcotte/Tesla's partner was Leahy/Tesla who'd taken *their* guardian on the mothership along with the Chosen, Yakov and Nyx, the Airlia he'd rescued from her duty position at the Airlia base on Mars.

Full circle.

"Is something funny?" Nosferatu asked.

Turcotte hadn't realized he'd laughed. He still had some control; or more accurately he was still a partner with the Tesla. He wasn't entirely in the audience. This was a symbiotic partnership. He and the Tesla were one. Carbon and silicon-based life merged.

"Circles," Turcotte said. "Everything is looping. We were thinking about coming here and Duncan, actually we should probably call her Donnchadh now, taking out the Airlia FTL transmitter. And bringing Nyx back with us to Earth and now she's gone on the mothership. It's confusing until we start seeing the circle of chaos that actually makes sense."

"Right," Nekhbet muttered.

"Who exactly is 'us'?" Nosferatu asked.

Turcotte brought the Fynbar to a halt above the crater the mothership had created on Mons Olympus. He pointed at the back of his head. "The implant is a being. Millions of years old. Not like humans normally think of life. It's a bridge between silicon-based life and carbon-based. Actually, it was designed by a species that no longer exists; the Ancients. It's called a Tesla. They are Facilitators. That understand more about the universe than we could imagine. If you don't know the questions, you certainly can't ask the questions. Even if the answers are right in front of you, you can't see them. Humans, Airlia, are still too primitive. But there are sparks of hope." He pointed down. "Donnchadh is alive. She has a Tesla in her too. They've merged like we've merged."

"I'm enlightened," Nekhbet said. "What should we call you?"

"Turcotte will do." He dropped altitude toward the scar where the mile-long spaceship had crashed. It was but a scratch given the size of Mons Olympus. It grew larger as they got closer. The protective framing around the command capsule had given way at impact. It was thirty feet into the Martian soil. Turcotte landed next to the hole.

"How are we going to get her out?" Nosferatu asked as he got out of the co-pilot's depression. "We don't have a pressure suit. Or is she coming to us?"

Turcotte indicated where the regeneration tube had been that he gave to Mrs. Parrish. "There is still a line for oxygen." He grabbed a pair of masks. Hooked them into the line. "You will be cold, but you will live."

Turcotte went to the hatch and opened it. A blast of freezing Martian atmosphere greeted him as the air blew out. A hundred times thinner than Earth's atmosphere, the thin layer surrounding Mars consisted of ninety-five percent carbon dioxide. It didn't matter to Turcotte. He wasn't breathing it.

He exited and bounded to the hole. Looked down. Red soil covered the bottom. He jumped in and began pushing it aside with his hands until he reached black *b'ja* metal.

*****

Inside the command capsule, Donnchadh looked up. More accurately, to what had been the rear of the capsule. She climbed up the floor. Ripped the panel off that covered the manual crank for the hatch. Flipped the lever down. It was long enough for four Airlia to work it together as that was the strength required to open the bulkhead door.

She pulled to no avail for several seconds. Then her body reconfigured, warping from human shape into a form designed for leverage. Three points of contact on the floor and ceiling. One appendage to grip the handle. The form expanded and the lever turned. She cranked it and the door slid to the side. The little oxygen left puffed out and the temperature equalized to the minus twenty Fahrenheit outside.

Turcotte's figure was silhouetted against the Martian day. He knelt and reached down grabbing the appendage on the lever. As he pulled Donnchadh out, her body resumed form.

LAST STAND
OF IMPERIUM

In First Ring, Tai experienced a twinge of pride that he was the last to scream as the Tesla implant absorbed through the skin.

But he did scream from the excruciating pain as it dissolved and passed through and into the base of his skull and began reassembling. He was lying on his back in an acceleration couch in the cockpit of an S17 scout ship. The canopy was open and he'd heard the first person begin to yell twenty seconds ago. Now the sounds of dozens of humans in intense pain echoed off the walls of the hanger. His partner was next to him in the ship, the small compendia pyramid inserted in the console between them. They'd climbed in, following the instructions holo'd by the Compendium. The long line of S17's, top of the line Fleet craft that he'd thought were still in the experimental phase, were in cradles in the hanger next to the room containing the Compendium. The S17 held two people in the cockpit and was essentially a spacecraft built around an FTLT and power source. It was unarmed, built for speed and the ability to travel long distances.

Tai wanted to reach up and feel the back of his head, but his hands were encased in the gloves of his g-suit and he was nestled deep in the couch. He, and the others, had inserted the Tesla as directed into an empty slot in the back of the g-suit when they put them on. The cold metal had pressed against the base of their skulls until it activated and deconstructed in order to pass through and into their heads.

Tai could barely think through the pain, but he wondered if Librarian had had any idea how much this process would hurt? He noted through tears of agony that the cockpit was shutting, the canopy lowering to encase them. It was a clear bubble that gave an excellent view forward and up. It clicked shut just as the pain began to recede in the back of Tai's head.

The implant was reforming from the microscopic nano-particles into a small sphere at the base of his brain. The compendia pyramid began to glow silver. The pain was subsiding to a dull ache.

Tai turned his head as much as he could inside the helmet. He could see the outline of his partner's helmet, but that was it. "Radio check, over."

There was no reply.

"Radio check, over," Tai repeated.

"Yes?" his partner replied.

"Are you all right, over?" Tai asked.

"I feel like the back of my head was ripped apart."

It was, Tai thought but didn't say. He sensed, more than knew, that the hangar bay was depressurizing. It was a familiar feeling even though he was cocooned in the ship. Something one who'd done dozens of planet drops was familiar with. He was conscious of the lack of his prosthetic inside the empty leg of the suit. He looked up. A large door was moving aside above them, revealing a slice of the inner space of Taliant.

Tai felt inside his heavy gloves to the finger controls. Brought up the tactical overlay display on the interior of the cockpit.

"Did you do that?" his partner, whose name he just realized he did not know, asked.

"Yes. I'm Tai. Captain. Marines."

She laughed. "I saw the uniform. It's good to have a Marine for this, whatever this is going to be. I'm Donncan. Scientist, specialty electronics, although I'm not sure what good that's going to be. Librarian wasn't very forthcoming with the details."

"She rarely is." Tai frowned as he spotted a small blinking light on the tactical display. He twitched a finger and an alert flashed.

Librarian was dead. The plan was on autopilot under the control of the Compendium.

"Did you know her well?" Donncan asked.

"I worked for her," Tai said, compartmentalizing the information as he had in the past with the loss of comrades in combat.

"But did you know her?" Donncan asked.

Tai paused his scan of tactical to consider the question. "I was her primary aide for three point four years. But I would not say I knew her well."

"But you trusted her enough to volunteer for this?" Donncan asked.

"Didn't you?"

"I didn't know her at all until she contacted me. I just knew we have to act in the face of the insanity of this war."

The implants spread out their tendrils into the host bodies.

The screams reverberated inside the cockpits.

THE RECENT PAST

AFTERMATH OF THE ORION FLEET BASE BATTLE

SWARM BATTLE CORE.

SWARM ASSEMBLY POINT

The Battle Core holding the Reaped but not assimilated humans from the battle in the system containing Orion Fleet headquarters came out of FTLT in a remote part of the galaxy, between the two outermost arms, Cygnus and Perseus. There was no star system close, just the blankness of interstellar space. An apparently random spot in the midst of nothingness.

What awaited was a sight that would cause panic in any Scale species. There were forty-six full-sized, mature Battle Cores in varying stages of repair or disassembly. The Cores had been damaged either in battle and/or by the travails of time and distance. Each Core had been evaluated by the time it arrived. If regeneration could fix the damage, the Core was positioned in an area where it could be supplied with the materials needed.

If the Core was considered unredeemable, it became part of those raw materials, placed in another area. These were being broken apart by mining craft, the usable living, red material shifted to those being repaired. There were seven of those, orbs missing large slices as they were scavenged. Dead material from Cores that had been disassembled of everything useful floated in space not far away. A massive debris field hundreds of thousands of miles wide, indicative of how long this had been going on.

There were fourteen 'immature' red Cores clustered in another quadrant. These were of varying sizes, from the oldest, nearing operational Battle Core size, to the most recent, barely fifty miles in diameter. These were also being supplied with raw materials by incoming Cores and those being deconstructed. The hulls were expanding organically, while the interiors were being developed according to the master code. Weapons that had been taken from Scale life were positioned on the surface and FTLT drives ripped from Scale warships emplaced. The Swarm was a model of efficiency using everything from a Reaping, not just the organic material.

The newly arrived Core holding humans and other Scale species Reaped but not amalgamated, had been evaluated while en route. It had sustained over two hundred interior nuclear detonations from the Airlia Teardrop attack at Orion Fleet. That had been kamikaze attacks utilizing humans dropped onto the surface. One in every hundred humans had had a backpack nuclear weapon. The other ninety-nine had power weapons and their mission was to help the nuke carrier get inside. Given that millions had been 'tear-dropped', the fact so few had made it inside showed the difficulty of penetrating into a Core. There was also extensive surface damage accrued during the assault from Airlia motherships and talons of the fleet.

The decision wasn't difficult. The Core was past the point of effectively regenerating and would be positioned with the others being broken down. The Swarm on board would fly the scout and warships to the mature Cores that were being readied to venture back into interstellar space on their primary directive.

The Scale life imprisoned on board, of which the humans in one cargo bay were only a portion, was to be moved on. There were holds full of the selected from the humans, Airlia, Mercene and other Scale this Core had reaped over its millennia long journey through the stars. They were only a small percentage of those encountered. But they all shared the same trait: they had not fought.

Moved on did not mean transfer to another Battle Core.

It meant something rather different, because there was another type of Core in this assembly point.

*****

Two humans, Lina and Kray stood in a massive open space inside the damaged Battle Core. Lina had been Reaped years ago from her home world, while Kray had been in one of the

Teardrops that landed on the surface of this Core. He'd been one of those with a backpack nuke but he'd refused to detonate the warhead as he'd been programmed. Thus, he'd been spared being amalgamated into the organic soup that was the life blood of the Core. Above them, a Swarm warship floated into the bay.

Lina grasped Kray's hand tightly. "What now?" she whispered.

Kray watched it without fear. He was not a sociopath or psychopath, but came from a tribe on his home world, Earth15, that was renowned as healers and for their calm in extreme situations. They'd have made great warriors but they'd renounced violence many generations ago. They'd managed to survive among the warring tribes and kingdoms of their world because their medical talents were valued by all.

"It makes no sense that the Swarm will hurt us now after it has gone to so much trouble to assemble us all here," Kray said. "Why would they clothe us?"

"I believe you are right," Pitr agreed. He was from another world of humans; like them Reaped, but not amalgamated. Because he had not fought back.

"Then what do they want?" Lina asked.

"We will find out," Kray said. "Do not be afraid."

The warship rotated one of the weapons arms toward the floor and gently descended until the tip of the arm touched. The large bay door on the end of the arm, just like that through which most of the people had been brought aboard, under the thrall of a Swarm parasite from the surface of their reaped planet, slid open.

Now the humans had a choice with their own free will. There was little hesitation. Those closest to the arm entered until it was full. The floor lifted and they disappeared inside the ship. A minute later, the elevator returned, empty of people. The process was repeated. Finally, it was Kray and Lina and Pitr's turn. They went inside. The elevator went up, slowly at first, then faster and faster. The elevator slid along passages in the ship, before coming to a halt. A door slid open and an empty bay inside the warship beckoned. They exited and once they were all inside, the door slid shut behind them.

*****

Warships flew out of portals on the Battle Core, each carrying their cargo of various Scale life. They headed toward an entity that was different than all the others. It was much larger than any of the Cores, with a diameter of slightly over ten thousand miles, twenty-five percent larger than Earth.

The surface was perfectly smooth and black. It was rotating at a speed that produced centrifugal force on the interior of the outer shell.

Twenty equidistant portals led to the interior. As the warships entered their designated portal, they passed through a six-mile-thick, black exoskeleton, then red living material and a flexible airlock and then a two-kilometer-thick, hard inner frame. The interior was sectioned off, with narrow walls extending toward an inner power source that mimicked a sun.

This Core wasn't a Battle Core; it was a Life Core, designed to allow Scale to survive on the curvature on the inside the Core's hull.

It had once been known as Light-Union-Twelve.

THE PRESENT

COMING TOGETHER

ASTEROID BELT

The first Battle Core in the system met the warship at the far edge of the Asteroid Belt. The Command Swarm was too large to leave the warship. Instead, it docked inside the Core, one of the eight arms of the ship touching raw, red material. A tendril from the Command Swarm extending out of the end of the arm of its ship into that. Where it was met by a tendril from the Supreme Swarm of the Core.

The information learned on Earth was relayed.

The loss of the Core that had been Reaping Earth was only the surface of much deeper issues.

An FTL transmission was sent, not just to the other nine Cores in the system, but beyond.

EN ROUTE MARS TO EARTH

"I'm hungry," Nekhbet complained. Not for the first time. Nosferatu ignored her as did the other two in the *Fynbar*

Turcotte was in the pilot's depression and Donnchadh in the co-pilot's. The two held hands. Not out of affection but because they were updating each other on all that had happened; primarily information going from Turcotte to Donnchadh about what awaited them on Earth. When they were done, they let go.

"It is strange," Donnchadh said out loud.

"Pray tell," Nekhbet said. "What exactly is strange?"

Donnchadh pointed at her head. "I am still here, but it is as a we. A we that always existed except I wasn't aware."

"That makes sense," Nekhbet said.

"Hush," Nosferatu scolded.

"It *is* strange," Turcotte agreed. "Most of the time it is we. But for the moment, I can be." He sighed. "I am so tired."

Donnchadh nodded. "What little is left of me is exhausted. Humans weren't meant for this."

"We're just the vessels," Turcotte said. He looked at Donnchadh. "Gwalcmai has been resurrected."

"We know," Donnchadh said. "But, as you say, it is just the shell. The Tesla that was in him all the time. His memories, his essence as a human was lost when he was killed and his *ka* destroyed. He is gone forever. Unless the Tesla gives him back those memories. It hasn't yet. It has allowed me some of mine because it found my *ka*, but not all."

"I am sorry," Turcotte said.

"You didn't know your other half was Leahy?" Donnchadh asked.

Turcotte shook his head. "No. Her Tesla was active while ours was dormant. It did not let me know."

"We looked for you, Gwalcmai and I," Donnchadh said and she was back being the we. "The Teslas did although the human parts weren't consciously aware of it. We knew there was most likely a pair of Tesla's on Earth when we arrived. But there was no sign. No signal. However, we too stayed mostly dormant over the millennia. The Tesla part. It was not time to act."

Turcotte nodded. "We were mostly dormant. To the extent I did not know I was we. Leahy only became active a little over a hundred years ago."

"But we were drawn together," Donnchadh said. "Duncan picked you to infiltrate Area 51."

"That is true," Turcotte agreed.

Nekhbet looked at Nosferatu and rolled her eyes.

"It's strange how many lives we've gone through," Turcotte said. He indicated his body. "This is the latest of many. I am not the human who the Tesla started in."

"There were humans before me also," Donnchadh agreed, "but I regenerated many, many times as human while on Earth. And each time the Tesla found its way back in. Why were you dormant?"

"We were with Gaia," Turcotte said.

"Ah!" Donnchadh said, as if she/they understood. "And now Gaia is no longer dormant. Is that why your partner destroyed the Swarm scout ship? It is intriguing that in human form it took the name Tesla."

Turcotte nodded. "It was too soon for the Swarm to arrive in 1908. There was still hope that this species could pass the hurdles of self-destruction and evolve."

"We can hear you," Nekhbet said.

Turcotte glanced back at her and Nosferatu. "Some have evolved. The Metabols. We are going to meet them."

"But first," Donnchadh said, "we are going to get Gwalcmai."

"I'm still hungry," Nekhbet muttered.

SOLAR SYSTEM

The second mothership that had arrived just outside the Solar System was heading inward, just below light speed and slowing. In the bridge compartment was gathered an eclectic group. It had originally been Aspasia's mothership, arriving on Earth in pre-history to establish Atlantis. After the Airlia Civil War it had been hidden at Area 51. Finally it had been the lifeboat by which the Chosen had escaped and been deposited on Earth15.

Piloting the ship was the woman known as Professor Leahy to the others. They had believed her to be Nikola Tesla's granddaughter. But on Earth15 she had revealed that she was something entirely different, a creature made by what she called the Ancients. She'd shed no more light on what she was or who the Ancients were since they left Earth15 to return to Earth. Next to her on the console was a two-foot-high guardian computer. She was, of course, a Tesla. There was nothing left of human other than form.

In the co-pilot's seat was Yakov, a Russian, formerly of Section IV, the Russian equivalent of Majestic-12. A large, burly man, almost seven feet tall, with a dark beard, now greying, he'd spent much of the FTLT returning to the Solar System complaining about the lack of vodka on board the mothership. Mrs. Parrish and the Myrddin had thought of most everything so their Chosen could survive on another world, but vodka had not been among the supplies.

In the chief engineer's chair was Nyx, an Airlia scientist who'd been the lone survivor from their Cydonia base on Mars, where the FTL array was controlled. Before it was destroyed by Duncan/Donnhcadh crashing the mothership into it. She was tall, as Airlia were, six-fingered, with pale skin and short red hair. A dog lay behind them, George, who belonged to Maria, who had been Mrs. Parrish's personal assistant and was Sofia's grandmother. Maria sat in a chair off to the side, observing.

Completing the group that had left Earth15 was a human from that planet, Drusa. She'd volunteered to leave her home world and join them. She wore the blue cloak of her order, the healers of All-Life. She was a big woman, broad-shouldered, with dark hair gathered in a pony-tail extending midway down her back. Her face was weathered and creased with lines. Her skin was dark as night. As a young woman she had loved a man, Kray, who'd been taken by the Airlia in the Tally to become part of the Teardrop program many years ago.

The first sensor readings of Earth were coming up and they were both devastating and strange.

"It doesn't make sense," Nyx said from her position as she read the data. "We knew about the nuclear detonations before we went FTLT. Yet, the radiation readings are minimal. And the ash cloud is almost all dispersed."

"That is good news at least," Yakov said. "Let us hope our friends are alive." He turned to Leahy. "How long—" he stopped when he saw that her eyes were closed and her hand was on the small Tesla computer. A silver glow shimmered on the surface and was flowing over her hand, something it hadn't done before. The glow moved from her hand and up her arm. "Nyx," Yakov called out.

She came over from her station and was joined by Maria and Drusa. They hovered around Leahy, uncertain what to do.

"Should we pull her away from it?" Yakov asked as the glow spread to her head.

Drusa tapped Leahy on the shoulder not yet covered, opposite to the computer and stepped back in surprise. "She's hard."

"What do you mean?" Maria asked as the glow completely encapsulated Leahy.

"She is hard as stone," Drusa said. "She showed on my planet that she can change her body. I wonder what her real form would be?"

"It's doing something to her," Yakov said, partly a question.

"Or she is doing something to it," Nyx said.

*****

"They are back," Turcotte said.

"I feel them also," Donnchadh said.

Turcotte indicated the controls. "Take us to Gwalcmai," he said to Donnchadh.

Nosferatu was a bit behind on what was going on, but he picked up on that. "Is the mothership back?"

Turcotte closed his eyes. "Yes."

"Who is on it?" Nosferatu said.

"We will meet them at Area 51 and you will see."

SOUTHERN NEVADA

Area 51 is in the middle of nowhere on the way to nowhere, but one wouldn't know that based on the tens of thousands of abandoned vehicles clogging the one highway that led to it. Officially named Extraterrestrial Highway, Nevada 375 had more than earned that name when existence of the mothership and bouncers, atmospheric aircraft, hidden at Area 51 had become public. The occupants of the vehicles had fled toward the base when news of the Core became public and the mothership seemed like the only way to escape.

None of them had made it. The security forces protecting the base had held long enough for the mothership containing Yakov, Nyx, Leahy and the others, including the Chosen, to get away. The left behind had been Reaped.

Sofia had directed the train across western Colorado and into Utah. They'd angled south from Salt Lake City on the line to Las Vegas, a town which had grown mainly because it had been a stop on an east-west rail line during World War II and numerous troop trains had passed through the dusty cow-town. She'd had them turn onto an old, abandoned line that headed northwest out of Las Vegas, the Bullfrog Goldfield Railroad, which had been built to service mines in remote areas. Long abandoned, the steam engine rattled along rusted rails, some sections buried under sand. They'd paralleled the road full of abandoned vehicles then veered off to the west.

They were creeping along, at times uncertain if they still had track in front of them, when Sofia indicated for them to stop. The sun was beating down on the old locomotive and passenger cars. Sofia pointed north. "Area 51 is that way. We must walk." She knelt next to Joseph, who was sitting on a stool in the cabin. "Can you make it?"

Joseph nodded. "I can."

"How far?" Asha asked.

Sofia looked north as if she could see beyond the mountains. "We can walk in the dark. We'll wait for the sun to go down."

"That is a good idea," Joseph agreed.

STONEHENGE, ENGLAND

Gwalcmai stood in a warm rainstorm and waited as the *Fynbar* descended and landed next to what remained of Stonehenge. He picked up the guardian computer and carried it over as Donnchadh opened the hatch. The two met in the same place they'd landed so many years ago.

Donnchadh was a piece of data in Gwalcmai's Tesla. The human remnant of Donnchadh felt the pain of seeing her lover in his bright armor. She went to him and wrapped her arms around his stiff form. She let go. Then they entered the spaceship, Gwalcmai carrying the guardian.

Nosferatu extended his hand. "I am—"

"Nosferatu," Gwalcmai said. "And Nekhbet. And you are one of us," he added, nodding at Turcotte who had remained in the pilot's depression. "We are up to date."

"Good to know," Nekhbet muttered. "We're not."

"All will be made clear soon," Turcotte vaguely promised. He looked at the two. "You are together. Finally." He slid into the pilot's depression.

They nodded in sync. "We are." They faced each other and hugged.

"Sweet," Nekhbet said, but then took a step back as their forms began to dissolve in a bright glow that was blinding. This lasted for several seconds and then the light was gone. A single figure, smooth silver skin, mostly humanoid.

Turcotte glanced over his shoulder, didn't seem surprised, then took off. The figure slid into the co-pilot's seat without a word.

"Deeper into the rabbit hole," Nekhbet said to Nosferatu.

INSIDE MARS ORBIT

The silver glow snapped out of existence from around Leahy. She remained still for several seconds.

Drusa touched her shoulder. "Are you all right?"

Leahy looked at her. "We're fine."

"Who is we?" Yakov demanded. "You and the Tesla?"

"Turcotte is alive," Leahy said. "The other binary are now one."

"'Other binary'?" Yakov said.

"Donnchadh and Gwalcmai, the humans, are no longer. Their Teslas merged into one."

"Okay," Yakov said tentatively. "Donnchadh?"

"Who you knew as Lisa Duncan," Leahy said. "Her Tesla reconstructed her on Mars and Turcotte recovered her. Brought her back to Earth where her companion was also resurrected. But his essence was gone long ago. She had no will to live longer.

She was tired and had lived too long and died too many times. We understand that. It is better." She nodded toward Maria. "Sofia and the other Metabols are fine. As are Asha and Joseph."

"How do you know this?" Yakov asked.

"We conversed with Turcotte."

"Through that?" Yakov indicated the guardian.

"It helped," Leahy said. "There is an Airlia mothership going into orbit around Earth. From Orion Fleet. Like the one we met on Earth15, they want to tally humans for the Teardrop program, thinking it worked. By now this ship knows the situation is radically different. They are trying to find out what happened. There is a Swarm Battle Core in the Asteroid Belt also heading toward Earth."

"Another one!" Yakov exclaimed.

"Yes. And there are nine more Cores in the solar system," Leahy continued, as if her news were a weather report of no import. "All are coming together."

"For what?" Maria asked.

"We will know when we all meet," Leahy said.

"Even the Swarm?" Nyx asked. "Do you know what they are?"

"We know what they are," Leahy said. "And what their mission has always been."

"Do you care to enlighten?" Yakov asked.

"There are things to do first," Leahy said. She pointed at Nyx. "You must talk to your people. Get them to understand what Arcturus told the Airlia who landed on Earth-Fifteen. That the Teardrop program doesn't work. There are bigger issues you need to tell them about. That they must be part of or they will be no longer. The captain of the mothership is named Atram."

*****

The Orion Fleet mothership settled into a high orbit above the planet. The talons were deployed farther out, between it and the approaching Battle Core which had just cleared Mars orbit. A cluster of scout ships, which had been called Bouncers by the humans who'd recovered similar craft on the planet and learned to fly them, dropped out of hangar bays to conduct a detailed reconnaissance of the planet. These were disc-shaped craft thirty feet in diameter with silver metal hulls. The bottoms were flat and like one-way glass, could be seen through by the crew. There was a bulge on top eight feet around where the hatch was.

They sped through the atmosphere at high altitude, crisscrossing the planet, gathering information.

On the bridge of the mothership, the command crew puzzled over the data. Nuclear detonations, handfuls of Swarm/metamorphosis wandering about and tiny clusters of humans. It made no sense.

Then the communications officer announced that there was an incoming hail from the unidentified mothership.

*****

Nyx sat in the commander's chair. The others were to the side, out of sight as the screen in front of her glowed with the image of the Airlia commander of the mothership in orbit around Earth. Nyx glanced to the side, where Leahy stood, arms folded, then focused on the commander.

"Identification!" The Airlia commander demanded in the high-pitched language of their species. She was female, her red hair striated with grey, her alabaster skin mottled with scars on the right side of her face from some battle in the past. "Your transponder is off."

"Captain Atram. I am Nyx. Astrobiologist."

"I am Captain of Seven-Six-Two. Of the Orion Fleet. Where is your Captain?"

"I am the only one left."

"Where are you inbound from?" The Airlia muted the mike and said something to someone on the bridge to her right.

"Earth Fifteen," Nyx said.

Her previous sentence seemed to have sunk in to Atram. "You are the only one on your ship?"

"No, I am not," Nyx said. "I am the only Airlia on board."

"Who else is on board?"

"Others," Nyx said.

"Who?" Atram demanded. "What species? Scale or Swarm?" She muted the mike and shouted orders to her bridge crew.

Nyx didn't answer directly. "I met your fellow captain of Seven-One-Four at Earth-Fifteen. There to complete the Talley as you are here. But we learned that the Teardrop program did not work."

"It worked!" Atram snapped. "I was there. I saw the Core retreat, badly damaged."

"It withdrew because the Core attacking here, in this system," Nyx said, "flew into the star to destroy itself after becoming infected. *All* Battle Cores withdrew from where they were in all systems. As you know, there are now ten in this system. That is unprecedented. You must listen to me or all will be lost."

Atram processed that for a few moments. "Proceed."

LAST STAND OF IMPERIUM

As Tai regained his senses, he realized the hangar door to the outside of First Ring was completely open. The tactical overlay was a cluster of red warnings. He was disoriented and tried to understand what they meant. The last time he'd seen this was in the midst of battle.

Then he realized the ship was moving. They were sliding along a launch cable into position. The S17 ahead of them locked into place, then catapulted forward, an archaic, but effective way of clearing the ring. It was headed directly toward one of the openings in the outer skin of Taliant.

He rocked slightly inside the g-suit as the S17 was latched onto the launch cable.

"What is going on?" Donncan's voice was slurred, groggy.

Tai was about to respond when he was slammed back as the S17 was slung out of First Ring into the interior space of Taliant heading toward the opening. It took only a few seconds to traverse the distance and then they were through to the outside.

The flares of weapons firing caught Tai's attention. There were ships of the line in battle and for a moment he thought they were attacking the scout ships, but then he saw the massive sphere of a Swarm Core, half the size of Taliant, several thousand miles away. Its surface was bright red with slashes of black. The blinking of pulse weapons firing dotted the surface. He squinted as he could have sworn there were several more of the large Cores in the distance behind it, all approaching the space station.

"What the—" Tai began but then he felt that momentary tingle and all went dark as the S17 transited into FTLT.

THE RECENT PAST

AFTERMATH OF THE ORION FLEET BASE BATTLE

LIGHT UNION TWELVE.
SWARM ASSEMBLY POINT

Kray was the first to step out of the warship, his knees buckling as he adjusted to full gravity for the first time in a while. He paused in wonder as he was in the midst of a field of grass. Not far away was a forest. Except it curved upward, the opposite of a planet. This section of the Life Core stretched over one hundred and fifty kilometers wide and went north and south to each end, which were out of sight in the hazy distance. Far away, warships were doing the same, emptying their living cargo.

"What is this?" Lina wondered.

Kray knelt and ran a blade of the tall grass through his fingers. A deer startled out of the field and raced into the woods. There were thousands of humans being deposited here, marveling at the world around them as the warship returned to the portal and departed.

"It's our new home," Kray said.

"But why?" Lina voiced to question on everyone's mind.

Kray stood and looked about. "Perhaps this is a larger zoo? So, the Swarm can study us? Perhaps it is something else."

"How can we see up?" Lina asked. "This doesn't make sense. This world is curved in the wrong direction. I feel dizzy."

Kray nodded. "It is odd. As if we are on the inside of the world instead of the outside, which is likely what has happened. Remember the cargo bays? It is as if we are in one but on the roof." He pointed at a bright shining orb above them. "And that sun, whatever it is, I don't think it moves. There are clouds, though. Do you see? But they seem to be going in slow circles. This is very strange."

"It scares me," Lina said.

"As much as the cage?"

"No. Not as much as the cage."

Kray picked up a handful of dirt and showed it to Lina. "This is good soil. There are plants I recognize we can harvest." He pointed at a ribbon of blue, slightly above them on the curvature. "There is water." He turned to Lina and put his hands on her shoulders. "We can live. That is all that is important. Come. Let us pick a spot and make it home."

*****

As they set about to do that, there was a flurry of activity at Swarm Assembly. Battle Cores that were deployment ready moved outward. Light Union Twelve, which had not transitioned in millennia, brought its FTLT engines on line.

In a flash, seven Battle Cores and Light Union Twelve transitioned into FTLT.

THE PRESENT

AREA 51

AREA 51, NEVADA

The place was covered in bones, picked clean by weather, vultures and the predators of the desert. The remains of those who tried to storm Area 51 and were killed in those last desperate moments as the mothership rose into the sky and escaped just before the Reaping. Those who'd survived but been stranded, had been Reaped. Some had tried to escape to the west, only to either be Reaped or killed by the lingering radiation of the Nevada Test Site.

The Metabols came from the south, arriving in the chill dawn as the sun rose in the east in a sky clear of ash. Four were pulling a cart with Joseph in it. The retinue had rotated through the night, switching out every half hour. Joseph had protested initially, but given in to the reality of the condition of his old body and arthritis. They steered the cart through the field of bones, occasionally halting out of respect and moving some aside so as to not run over them. They arrived at the blasted and twisted doors that led into Hangar One, where Sofia called a halt.

She directed that the Metabols gather in the shade of Hanger One.

"What now?" Asha asked as she sat down, just inside the entrance to the hangar that had housed the bouncers.

"We wait," Sofia said.

"For?" Asha asked.

Sofia spread her hands. "I don't think we can imagine what is coming. Thus, it is fruitless to speculate."

"We will need water," Joseph said.

"We will," Sofia agreed.

The earth rumbled and dust came down from the rock roof above. Asha jumped up, startled and headed for the open air but Sofia stopped her. "We have water."

"What?" Asha was confused.

Sofia pointed. A trickle of water was coming from a new crack in the wall of the hangar. As they watched, the trickle expanded to a steady flow. The Metabols lined up with their canteens to fill them.

"It seems Gaia approves of us being here," Joseph said.

"For the moment," Sofia agreed. "Who knows what the future holds?"

EARTH

Around the planet, surviving Swarm and the monsters of the metamorphosis: Cthulhu, kraken, dragons, Naga and others paused in whatever they'd been doing; or, in the case of the majority of the beasts, roused out of a motionless hibernation. There was a Supreme Swarm in the solar system. They could feel its presence and receive its orders.

That these were strange didn't matter, nor were they considered odd as the Swarm and its creatures didn't understand the concept. They were orders. The monsters simply melted away. Their organic essence drained into the ground beneath. The kraken dissolved and became part of ocean, lake, river or whatever body of water they were in.

The surviving Swarm began to gather together in clusters for recovery.

*****

Some Fades who had spread out from the Facility had either merged with metamorphosis or Swarm. But most were still in human form. Regardless, all moved, either in human form or along with the beast or Swarm they were part of, to the Swarm assembly points. Because they were now going to be part of something different.

*****

Humans who had survived World War III, the *Danse Macabre* and the Reaping were few and far between. Nevertheless, out of

7.8 billion people, there were those who'd managed to avoid the trifecta of death. Unfortunately for the vast majority, Gaia had decimated the survivors in its wakening throes, unable to distinguish among the scattered individuals and groups. Gina Tarrenti had been among the first. There were now only a few thousand people alive around the world. With clear skies and the worst seeming to be over, they were emerging from wherever they'd hidden. For most, they could live off of scavenging what remained of civilization.

Of course, they were unaware of events developing at Area 51 that would determine their fate.

AREA 51

The *Fynbar* landed at Area 51 just outside the open doors of Hangar Two, a distance away from Hangar One. Inside the massive chamber was the cradle in which the mothership had been hidden that had been at the root of the beginning of the revolt against the Airlia.

Turcotte led the way out of the hatch, followed by Tesla, then Nosferatu and Nekhbet. The last two had wrapped cloth around their eyes to protect them from the glaring sunlight.

"I miss the ash," Nekhbet said. She looked around the desolate landscape, noting the bones. "It doesn't look like getting the Mothership away was easy."

"It wasn't," Turcotte said. He was peering toward the long runway on the Groom Lake basin. "The Metabols are on the way from Hangar One. The Airlia and Swarm are also coming."

"And then?" Nosferatu asked.

"There are others coming," Turcotte said.

"The mothership is returning," Nosferatu said. "Who else? Are we all going to sit around a camp fire and sing songs together?"

"There are others," Turcotte said. "You will see."

"Great," Nekhbet muttered.

"Incoming," Nosferatu warned.

A Swarm scout ship was approaching fast.

"They are expected," Turcotte said.

EARTH ORBIT

Commander Atram watched the Swarm Battle Core take up a much higher orbit from her mothership. It was going polar, while her ship was circling equatorially. The crew was on edge, given the fact they were heavily outgunned and nine more Cores were inbound. That wasn't helped when sensors detected seven more Cores coming out of FTLT inside the solar system, just outside of the Asteroid Belt. Along with something twice the size of the standard Battle Core.

It got worse as hundreds of warships spewed forth from the orbiting Core. They descended to the planet below. The Airlia tracked them, half-expecting a Reaping, even though the data indicated the planet was barely populated by human Scale. However, the first warships touched down and began on-loading the Swarm left behind.

That and the fact that the Core had not attacked her ship gave her some confidence in the instructions Nyx had relayed. Leaving her executive officer in command, Atram boarded a bouncer by herself and departed the mothership, descending toward the planet.

*****

Leahy was at the controls as she flew the mothership past the Swarm Battle Core and the Airlia motherships and into the atmosphere. They were flying fast and dropping precipitously through the atmosphere. The brown desert of Nevada was directly below. The slash indicating the Groom Lake runway came into sight before Leahy slowed the massive ship. They came to a hover and then she edged it forward, into the hangar and setting it down in the cradle.

"Home," Yakov said.

*****

"Nana is here," Sofia said as she led the Metabols toward Hangar Two along the base of Groom Mountain. She lengthened her stride, but then looked over at Joseph and slowed down. "I'm sorry."

Joseph waved a hand. "Go ahead. I'll be there eventually."

*****

"Ugly," Nekhbet said as the single Swarm slowly made its way on narrow tentacles from the scout ship toward them.

"They are not used to gravity," Turcotte said. "It is representing the Swarm."

"What are they?" Nosferatu asked. "You said you knew."

Turcotte glanced at the Tesla. "Let us wait until all are gathered together."

They were standing in the late morning shade of Groom Mountain. The mothership had passed overhead and landed in the cradle moments ago. A door at the base of the cradle swung open but no one appeared.

An Airlia bouncer landed to the right and the hatch on top opened. A single Airlia exited and walked toward them, giving a worrisome look at the Swarm also approaching.

Leahy emerged from the bottom of the strut in the cradle holding the mothership. She was flanked by Yakov and Nyx and Maria, with George, the black Labrador retriever at her side.

Sofia sprinted ahead of the long column of Metabols and threw herself into Maria's arms. George ran around them, tail wagging.

Turcotte and the Tesla watched the reunion of granddaughter and grandmother as Atram and the Swarm stopped on opposite sides of them. Nosferatu and Nekhbet stood off to the side, observers of the meeting of different life forms.

Leahy walked up to Turcotte. "Are you ready to move on?"

Turcotte nodded. "I am very tired."

"It is hard to sustain," Leahy agreed. "What the Tesla needs to do now is beyond us."

"I am already pushed aside," Turcotte acknowledged.

"I was pushed aside long ago," Leahy said, acknowledging that she had once been human.

The two wrapped their arms around each and merged, as Donnchadh and Gwalcmai had done. But the Tesla weren't done as that one turned to the other that had been Donnchadh and Gwalcmai and what had been four became one. A silver, smooth-skinned humanoid over eight feet tall.

It was perfectly still, but then pointed at Asha. "You have something?"

Asha was hesitant, but Sofia walked up next to her. "Give it the *ka*." When Asha didn't move, Sofia gently took it from her. She walked up to the Tesla and extended it. "This is Darlene. She was the first Metabol. Can you—"

Tesla replied before she completed the request. "Yes." It took the *ka* and went into the *Fynbar*. There was one black tube next to the console in the rear of the compartment; the other one had been given to Mrs. Parrish who'd hoped to resurrect her husband via a *ka*, only to have Maria destroy the small device as the mothership fled the solar system.

A body was in the tube. A young, virile man; a blank slate waiting to be inscribed upon with a consciousness. There was a skullcap on its head with wires running to a command console. Its eyes were open, but there was no intelligence or awareness.

Sofia had climbed in behind Tesla. It put the *ka* into a slot on the side of the console. A light turned green.

"Darlene was a woman," Sofia noted.

"Would she not prefer to live?" Tesla didn't wait for an answer, tapping commands on the hexagonal display. A machine arm extended from the side of the tube and reached the side of the head. A nanoprobe spread thin wires through the brain. Tesla typed in more commands. The probe withdrew, the orange light turned red. Flickered for thirty seconds, then turned green.

"When the body becomes conscious," Tesla said, "it will be Darlene. Up until the moment Leahy uploaded her essence. She will know nothing of what happened after that. Nothing of her death. That is a blessing."

"How long?" Sofia asked.

Tesla turned the console off and removed the *ka*. "Not long."

Sofia climbed out. She went to Nekhbet and Nosferatu. "You are hungry?"

For once Nekhbet was taken aback and didn't respond.

Nosferatu nodded. "We are, but it can—"

Sofia cut him off with a smile. "You may drink on us. Enough to sustain you. But not to darkness."

"We would never do that," Nosferatu protested.

"Drink or to darkness?" Sofia responded.

"Children, it's . . ." Nosferatu joined Nekhbet in wordlessness.

"You've done worse," Sofia said. "But we can change, can't we?" She tapped her neck. "A little from me. A little from the others. We all survive together and we all thrive together."

Overlooking all of them, Tesla appeared on top of the *Fynbar*. Sunlight reflecting off the silver figure.

GLACIER NATIONAL PARK. MONTANA

After closing the out doors, T.J. Waterman walked through his bunker with the assured stride of a man in charge of everything. His mother had once remarked, before his father sent her off to pre-nup hell and replaced her with a younger and firmer wife, that T.J. had crawled in the same manner.

He entered the nursery. Fifteen eggs, were now inseminated, the lights on top changed to green. They were suspended in amniotic fluid inside large, clear tubes. Small speakers on the side were already whispering words of knowledge, interspersed with classical music. T.J. wasn't sure he bought into the theory, but it couldn't hurt. A digital clock on each tube was counting down to birth.

He checked every tube, making sure all systems were functioning correctly.

Set into the wall were the robots, similar to Portia in construction but very different in appearance. They were matronly, designed to appear comforting and loving to the newborns when they slid out of the tube. They'd been programmed with all the best data on child-rearing tactics and techniques.

This was the first wave of the future, of the Resurrection.

He went to the control center for a final systems check.

Less than a minute after he sat down, hands gently slid over T.J. Waterman's shoulders.

"I'm working," he said, making sure all was ready for the first wave.

"I am grateful that you are working," Portia said. "You work to ensure our future."

"I do," T.J. agreed.

"You deserve a reward for all your hard work," Portia said.

T.J. frowned as her hands went up his shoulders to his neck. The hands slid around his neck.

"What are you—" T.J. began, then the perfectly manicured nails pressed on the carotid arteries, cutting the supply of blood to his brain. He had ten seconds of consciousness left and twenty-five of life.

"Program halt. Command."

"Not today," Portia whispered.

Strangely, T.J. smiled. "I love you," he managed to get out.

The fingers released pressure and the hands dropped.

T.J. turned around. Portia was inert. He stared at her for several seconds, then went behind her. Pressed a spot at the top of her spine and her CPU popped out. He took it to another computer, leaving the body standing there like a statue. Pushed the CPU in a slot and ran diagnostics, using a program he'd had developed for just this contingency from a different computer expert than the one who had used Airlia technology to make Portia.

It took a long time, almost a minute but there it was. A backdoor inserted. The android programmer hadn't been completely naïve. She'd planned a revenge just in case. It would have worked except T.J. had had the second programmer add a new deactivation phrase post-production.

T.J. shook his head as he read the code: react to abuse? Really? How can you abuse something that wasn't alive?

He scrubbed the backdoor giving Portia autonomy under certain circumstances. Took the CPU and replaced it.

"I'm going to sleep," T.J. said. "For a while."

He went down a long corridor, into the depths of his bunker. Opened a vault. An Airlia deep sleep tube awaited him. He climbed in. Did one last check, then closed the lid on himself.

When he awoke, the world would be his.

AREA 51

The Swarm Battle Core caused an eclipse as it passed overhead, north to south. Farther out, like moons, were the other nine Cores that had followed it into the Solar System.

Tesla raised its arms skyward and the ground beneath them rumbled with Gaia's acknowledgement. When the Tesla spoke, its voice was inside the brain of all those gathered round: human, Metabols, Undead, Swarm, and Airlia, speaking in their native tongue.

"Humans failed. Airlia failed. Hybrids of the species failed. Even facing an outside threat, humans fought each other. They could not unite. Airlia have used humans in their fighting and also fought humans."

Nosferatu hushed Nekhbet as she opened her mouth to say something.

Tesla went on. "We helped with the Metabols. They may stay. There are others who have joined with Gaia. They may stay. There are others coming here who have succeeded. They will stay."

Sofia stepped forward. "What of the humans who have survived?"

Tesla lowered its arms. "Those left alive have been made like Metabols by Gaia. It is unfortunate that Gaia was not completely aware earlier, but the damage was severe which brought an equally severe reaction.

Atram stepped up next to Sofia. "Who are you?" She demanded of Tesla. "Why do you believe you can order us about?"

"We are of the Ancients," Tesla said. "The Airlia have legends of the Ancients. The humans used to. Most think these aren't true. They are. The Ancient's domain spanned galaxies. But some among the Ancients could see into the future. They could see they had sown the seeds of their own doom in the very essence of what gave them great success. Some among them planned for a resurrection of intelligence life but in a wiser way. We are the Facilitators of that plan. The intelligent life on this planet has failed. It was Reaped because of that. But in failing, in that Reaping, was shown a spark of something more. A sacrifice on an unprecedented level to negate the Reaping. Also, one of us exceeded our mandate, but it was because throughout human history there have been sparks of something more."

Yakov's deep voice cut in. "You control the Swarm?"

"The Swarm are part of the Facilitation," Tesla said. "They have kept the virus of empires contained, as long as those empires used violence as their means to expand."

Sofia understood. "You're saying intelligent life is a virus and the Swarm have been the antibody."

"Correct," Tesla said, the flat, emotionless words not reflective of the billions upon billions of Reaped Scale life.

"These were worlds at war with themselves or with other Scale life. They brought it upon themselves. Realization should have come that killing was not the path of wisdom. Realization should have come that resistance brought destruction, but it did not. Realization should have come that the Swarm never concentrated and wiped out an entire Scale life, as Scale life has done to itself and each other. Swarm attacks were random. But realization never came."

"Has now," Nekhbet muttered, but without her normal edge and low so only Nosferatu could hear. Or so she thought.

"Yes, it has now," Tesla said. "But realization is not change. Action is change."

"What action?" Atram demanded.

Tesla responded. "Captain Atram. You will depart this system, never to return. This world, this star system will be off limits to all other life forms. There will be nine of what you call Battle Cores ringing this system to ensure that is so. Wipe it from your star maps. Erase it from all your records so no one will be tempted to do so in the future. Remember this: we know where your home world is. You have believed it safe from Swarm attack. It is not. You are getting a second chance."

Sofia spoke up. "What about my Nana? And Joseph? And Asha? And Darlene when she is complete? And Yakov? Nosferatu and Nekhbet?"

"A choice," Tesla said. "They may remain here or they may depart on the mothership. Either the craft is taken out of this system or it must be destroyed by flying it into the system's star. We can program it to do that."

"If we leave," Yakov said, "where will we take it?"

"That is not our concern. There—" Tesla paused as a figure climbed out of the hatch of the Fynbar. A strapping young man, well-muscled, smooth skin.

"Darlene!" Sofia cried out.

Darlene held her hands up in front of her face and looked from them, down her new body. "This is certainly different." She looked about, pausing to stare at Tesla. "Far out."

"Captain Atram," Tesla said. "Depart."

Atram turned on her heel and almost ran to the bouncer. It took off, quickly disappearing into the sky. The Swarm didn't need verbal orders. It went back to the scout ship and headed back to the Battle Core.

Tesla addressed those who remained. "You will wait here six days." It pointed to the stream coming out of Hanger Two. "There is water. There will be food." The arm swept out, covering the desolate land extending from Groom Mountain into the desert. "Stay in the Hangar. Do not wander into the desert. Not yet. Decide what you want to do with the mothership. Those who want to leave will be free to."

Then Tesla sank slowly into the Earth until there was no sign of it.

*****

Gaia was erasing mankind's mark. The Swarm had already devastated military bases around the planet. Warships had landed on top of cities, crushing buildings and structures below them, such as the Eiffel Tower. But now the planet was pulling what remained downward.

The Empire State Building, where the bones of the Assassin lay on the observation deck, sank into the bedrock on which it was built, the steel and concrete and other elements absorbed. Within hours, the epic skyline of the great city was gone.

The Brooklyn Bridge collapsed into the East River and the metal dissipated into the water. Around the world, dams crumbled and gave way, allowing water to once more flow freely. Hoover Dam, with the cement deep inside still cooling from when it was originally finished in 1936, crumbled. The Colorado River surged through and inundated the countryside down river taking out two more dams downstream.

Ancient artifacts weren't spared. The Giza Pyramids, built so long ago in a desperate attempt to signal the Airlia Empire crumbled, along with the Sphinx that had guarded the Roads of Rostau and the Ark of the Covenant which had held the Grail.

The Great Wall of China, which had stretched across the landscape for hundreds of years was not spared, rebuilt sections crumbling to dust and scattered stone.

What the Swarm hadn't already destroyed, Gaia was finishing off. The great achievements of humanity, some taking generations to construct were being wiped off the face of the planet in minutes and hours. Not just destroyed, but in most cases broken down to their fundamental elements and reabsorbed in the planet from which they been extracted.

*****

There was change at Area 51. Water bubbled up from the desert. Trees and plants sprang up at wildly accelerated rates. From the entrance to Hangar Two, Yakov, Nyx, Drusa, Maria, the Undead, Sofia, Asha, Joseph and the Metabols watched in amazement.

This went on for days.

On the sixth day, a daytime star appeared in the sky behind the Battle Cores. It was Light-Union-Twelve, the Life Core, halting outside the moon's orbit to minimize the gravitational effect on Earth. Late on the sixth day, Tesla reappeared. No one saw it come back, it was just there, standing in the entrance to Hanger Two, backdropped against the pocket of lush vegetation that was now fifteen miles in diameter and still expanding.

Sofia led the survivors to meet it. "Who is coming?"

"The people who will join you here," Tesla responded.

A warship descended. One of the arms touched the ground between the oasis of life and Groom Mountain. Thousands of humans exited in large groups. Most went into the verdant land.

But one came forward toward those gathered in front of Hangar Two.

"Kray!" Drusa cried out.

The two lovers, separated long ago by an Airlia Tally embraced.

"What have you decided?" Tesla asked the group.

"You know the Metabols are staying," Sofia said. "You made us."

The silver head bobbed ever so slightly in acknowledgement. "Yes."

"My nana, Asha, Darlene and Joseph are staying with us," Sofia said. "I cannot speak for the others."

Tesla turned slightly to face them.

Yakov stepped forward. "I will take the mothership. Not to fly it into the sun, but to travel. I am of old Earth. This--" he indicated the land outside the Hangar—"Is new Earth. It is not for me."

"Good," Tesla said.

"I will go with him," Nyx said. "I do not belong here. Besides," she added, "he will need help flying the ship."

"We will also take flight," Nosferatu said. "We have walked this planet for hundreds of years. It is time for change."

"That isn't change?" Nekhbet asked, indicating the fertile land.

"Hush," Nosferatu said.

"You don't want me to feed on—"

"Hush!" Nosferatu said.

Nekhbet sulked but quieted.

"The decisions are made," Tesla said.

"What will you do?" Sofia asked the being.

"We have facilitated as much as we can."

"Who were the Ancients?" Sofia pressed. "Where they Gods?"

Tesla didn't respond. It melted into the ground.

LAST STAND
OF IMPERIUM

The first Battle Core had blasted Taliant thoroughly with the scavenged weapons that dotted its surface. But that wasn't sufficient. It accelerated toward the fleet base. The handful of surviving human ships that tried to fight back splatted into the surface of the Battle Core like bugs on a windshield.

There were still scout ships to launch from First Ring when the Battle Core collided with the space station. The epitome of man's engineering genius crumpled from the impact. The last fourteen scouts didn't make it. However, a large spaceship, an old cargo hauler, dating back to the days of asteroid mining, STLed away through an opening on the far side of Taliant. While it appeared antiquated, the interior had been totally rebuilt. A top of the line FTL drive was already powered up and as it cleared the massive collision of Core and Taliant, the drive engaged.

There was no human crew. A single Tesla in human form was at the controls.

The Librarian.

Inside the cargo bay, battened down securely, was the Compendium.

As the last of Taliant was destroyed, the ship transitioned.

*****

The Battle Core continued toward Earth, as scavenger mechs gathered usable debris from Taliant that littered the surface. Behind it was a trail of wreckage. Other Battle Cores flanked it as it approached Mars.

The terra-forming that had been going on for thousands of years and was eighty-six percent complete was wiped out in less than five minutes. The Swarm fleet continued inward. Bracketed Earth. And the first Reaping of Earth began.

THE PRESENT

THE BEGINNING AND THE END

WORMEHILL TOWER, EARTH15

Arcturus opened his eyes. Pushed open the front of the vertical tube and stepped out. He dropped the shield wall around Wormehill Tower. He climbed the circular stairs on the outer wall of the tower. From the depths, through surface level, then up to the abbreviated top, where a powerful weapon had long ago blasted away the rest of the tower.

He looked up to the heavens. He knew what had awakened him.

"This is not the end," he whispered. "Nor is it the beginning of the end. But it is the end of the beginning and the start of a new path."

AREA 51, NEVADA

Thousand gathered in a large clearing in the center of the verdant valley that had once been Area 51. The vegetation was still expanding, but at a slower rate. The shift in the tilt of Earth's axis had changed the climate and what was desert was no longer. This would be sustainable.

Sofia stood among the group, holding hands with those next to her, as did everyone. They began to sing, with one voice, five thousand strong:

"Live your life that the fear of death can never enter your heart.

"Live your life that the fear of death can never enter your heart.

"Trouble no one about his religion.

"Respect others in their views and demand that they respect yours.

"Love your life, perfect your life, beautify all things in your life.

"Seek to make your life long and of service to your people.

"And to the planet we live upon.

"Earth Mother. Source of All,

"All-Fertile, All-Destroying Gaia,

"Who Brings Forth Life

"And Embraces Death

"Who Connects The Eternal to the Now

"Immortal and Blessed."

"Bountiful Mother. Source of All,

"Dark forests, nurturing fields, nurturing rain,

"Deep oceans, fast running streams."

"Bright skies, surrounded by the stars,

"Eternal and Divine."

"We are one with Gaia,

"Come bless, Mother

"And hear the prayers of Your Children."

As the sound of the voices faded, the humans began to scatter, to begin their new lives.

Joseph lay under a towering tree. Sofia went to him and knelt at his side. "How are you feeling?"

"I do not fear death," Joseph said with a tired smile. "Soon, I will be part of."

"We will remember you."

Joseph nodded. "What will you call this place?"

Sofia smiled. "Eden."

THE END

The Area 51 saga in order:

Area 51

Area 51: Reply

Area 51: Mission

Area 51: Sphinx

Area 51: Grail

Area 51: Excalibur

Area 51: Truth

For the story of Lisa Duncan and her mate, Gwalcmai,

read *Area 51: Legend.*

For the story of Nosferatu, Nekhbet, Vampyr and the

other half-breeds from the First Age of Egypt,

read *Area 51: Nosferatu.*

Area 51: Redemption

Area 51: Invasion

Area 51: Interstellar

Area 51: Earth Abides

This book is also available in audiobook at Audible
An Excerpt from *Lawyers, Guns and Money* follows author
and book information.

About the Author

Thanks for the read!
If you enjoyed the book, please leave a review. Cool Gus
likes them as much as he likes squirrels!

My newest series, part of the 2 million copy selling Green
Beret series is set in New York City in the late 1970s.
Dave Riley, hero of the Green Beret series makes an
appearance in the book as a young 17-year-old, which
features his older cousin, Will Kane, West Point class of
1966, ex-Special Forces and Vietnam Vet, who works for a
fixer in New York City.
The books are
New York Minute
Lawyers, Guns and Money
Walk on the Wild Side
Hell of a Town
Consider the novels as *Jack Reacher meets The Equalizer.*

.

Bob is a NY Times Bestselling author, graduate of West Point, former Green Beret and the feeder of Cool Gus. He's had over 80 books published including the #1 series Area 51, Atlantis, Time Patrol and The Green Berets. Born in the Bronx, having traveled the world he now lives peacefully with his wife and dogs.

For information on all his books, please get a free copy of the **Reader's Guide**. You can download it in mobi (Amazon) ePub (iBooks, Nook, Kobo) or PDF, from his home page at www.bobmayer.com

For free eBooks, short stories and audio short stories, please go to http://bobmayer.com/freebies/
The page includes free and discounted book constantly updated.
There are also free shorts stories and free audiobook stories.

There are over 220 free, downloadable Powerpoint presentations via Slideshare on a wide range of topics from history, to survival, to writing, to book trailers. This page and slideshows are constantly updated at:
http://bobmayer.com/workshops/

For free survival checklists, go to
http://bobmayer.com/3d-flip-book/survival-flipbook/

Questions, comments, suggestions: Bob@BobMayer.com
Subscribe to his newsletter for the latest news, free
eBooks, audio, etc.

ALL BOOKS

THE GREEN BERETS WILL KANE SERIES
New York Minute (June 2019)
Lawyers, Guns and Money (Sept 2019)
Walk on the Wild Side (early 2020)
Hell of a Town (June 2020)

THE GREEN BERETS
Eyes of the Hammer   Dragon Sim-13   Cut Out
Synbat   Eternity Base   Z: The Final Option
Chasing the Ghost   Chasing the Lost   Chasing the
Son
Old Soldiers (9 December 2019)

THE DUTY, HONOR, COUNTRY SERIES
Duty   Honor   Country

AREA 51
Area 51   Area 51 The Reply   Area 51 The Mission
Area 51 The Sphinx   Area 51 The Grail   Area 51
Excalibur
Area 51 The Truth   Area 51 Nosferatu   Area 51 Legend
Area 51 Redemption   Area 51 Invasion   Area 51
Interstellar

ATLANTIS

Atlantis   Atlantis Bermuda Triangle   Atlantis Devils Sea
Atlantis Gate   Assault on Atlantis   Battle for Atlantis

THE CELLAR
Bodyguard of Lies   Lost Girls

NIGHSTALKERS
Nightstalkers   Book of Truths   The Rift
Time Patrol
This fourth book in the Nightstalker book is the team
becoming the Time Patrol, thus it's labeled book 4 in that
series but it's actually book 1 in the Time Patrol series.

TIME PATROL
Black Tuesday   Ides of March   D-Day   Independence
Day
Fifth Floor   Nine-Eleven   Valentines Day   Hallows Eve

SHADOW WARRIORS
(these books are all stand-alone and don't need to be read
in order)
The Line   The Gate   Omega Missile   Omega Sanction
Section Eight

PRESIDENTIAL SERIES
The Jefferson Allegiance   The Kennedy Endeavor

BURNERS SERIES
Burners   Prime

PSYCHIC WARRIOR SERIES
Psychic Warrior   Psychic Warrior: Project Aura

STAND ALONE BOOKS:
THE ROCK   I, JUDAS THE 5TH GOSPEL

BUNDLES (Discounted 2 for 1 and 3 for 1):

Check web site, books, fiction and nonfiction.

COLLABORATIONS WITH JENNIFER CRUSIE
Don't Look Down   Agnes and The Hitman   Wild Ride

NON-FICTION:
The Procrastinator's Survival Guide: A Common Sense, Step-by-Step Handbook to Prepare for and Survive Any Emergency.
Survive Now-Thrive Later. The Pocket-Sized Survival Manual You Must Have
Stuff Doesn't Just Happen I: The Gift of Failure
Stuff Doesn't Just Happen II: The Gift of Failure
The Novel Writers Toolkit
Write It Forward: From Writer to Bestselling Author
Who Dares Wins: Special Operations Tactics for Success

All fiction is here: **Bob Mayer's Fiction**
All nonfiction is here: **Bob Mayer's Nonfiction**

Thank you!

Excerpt from

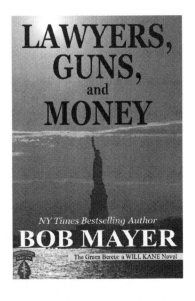

Thursday Night, 4 August 1977

UPPER BAY, NEW YORK HARBOR

The Statue of Liberty's torch, flickering in the dark and shrouded by rain, could be an invitation or, more realistically, a warning. Since he was piloting a boat, William Kane, who was fond of maps, likened Lady Liberty these days to those sea serpents drawn on the blank spaces of ancient charts with the dire warning: *Here there be monsters! Stay away!*

Three weeks earlier the city had been savaged by massive rioting during the nightlong Blackout on the 13th of July, an explosion on top of a decade of a slowly filling cesspool of blight and decay. There were many who felt New York would never recover and that the Blackout had been the death knell. They compared it to the fond memories of the '66 Blackout as proof the city had gone to hell.

Kane, who was also a student of history, was rather ambivalent about the memories and the projections. New York City had survived many trepidations and would plod into the future in one form or another. Being practical, he used glimpses of Lady Liberty's torch to the southwest to fix the boat's position in the rotten weather, drawing a mental line from it to the muted glow of the Twin Towers of the World Trade Center to the northeast. He twitched the dual throttles to keep the forty-two-footer in position, the eastern point in a triangle with Liberty and Ellis Island equidistant to the west.

"That's the subway," Kane nodded his head, indicating a barely visible dark mass in the harbor.

"Excuse me?" The man Kane had labeled Money, since he wasn't big on remembering names, had been a pain ever since boarding, ordering him about as if Kane were a servant, which technically was true, given he was on the job.

Money was seated in the plush chair to Kane's left rear. The Actress was in the chair next to him. Money was from Texas, a point he'd made within the first minute. He wore tailored jeans, a starched white shirt under an expensive sports jacket, alligator hide boots and a black Stetson crowning silver hair.

Kane's attire wasn't in the same income bracket, or fashion consciousness, with his dyed black jungle fatigue pants, grey t-shirt and unbuttoned blue denim shirt, sleeves rolled. He wore scuffed jungle boots, bloused inside the cuff of the pants with boot bands. A forty-five-caliber pistol rested in a supple leather holster under the denim shirt on his left hip, two spare magazines behind it on the belt, a commando knife in the small of his back and other assorted weapons secreted here and there.

"Ellis Island," Kane explained the comment as he released one of the throttles and pointed. "Most of it's built with fill from subway excavation. Originally, it was only three acres, but landfill expanded that to over twenty-seven. On top of old oyster beds. The island wouldn't exist without the subway and vice versa."

"Doesn't look like much of anything," Money said. "My waste yard on the ranch has more acreage. My people were in the States long before Ellis Island let in the riff-raff." He checked his watch as if he had an important date, beyond the beautiful woman seated next to him who'd been vaguely pitching him a movie concept since they pulled away from the Battery on the southwest shore of Manhattan. "This is bullshit," he muttered.

The Actress reached out and put a hand on the Money's arm. "See? History. That interests people. That's our film's motif and—"

Money cut her off. "You know what the blackout did to *Superman*? How far over-budget that is?"

"That's because of Brando, not the city," the Actress countered. "And that's not a New York movie. They only shot a couple of weeks at the Daily News as a stand in for the Daily

Planet. The rest was filmed elsewhere. *Saturday Night Fever* is under budget."

Money wasn't impressed. "A dancing movie with that disco bongo drum crap. It's buying a stud-bull that can't get it up. It'll disappear without anyone noticing it was ever made. Along with that *Welcome Back Kotter* kid they cast." He waved a dismissive hand. "The city's a pigsty." He indicated Kane. "We need a man with a gun just to go out on a boat. Are there pirates out here?"

Kane wasn't sure if the question was addressed to him, the Actress or rhetorical. His default mode was silence although he found the concept of pirates in New York Harbor intriguing. He remembered Brother Benedict mentioning pirates being part of the city's history. Captain William Kidd had used the harbor as his base for a while and had something to do with Trinity Church, which still overlooked Wall Street. Given the reaction to the Ellis Island/subway reference, he doubted Money would be interested in exploring history any further.

"And there's that loony, Son of Sam, shooting people," Money continued his New York City tirade, interrupting Kane's musings on Captain Kidd. "You know how much securing a set for three months at all the locations in that script would cost?"

The Actress, a voluptuous blonde wearing a low-cut dress that displayed her assets, and whose name Kane also couldn't remember although it rhymed with something, which he also couldn't remember, made a tactical shift in her pitch. "Perhaps if I show you the storyboards? They're below in the bedroom."

Money showed more interest in the possibilities below than above deck. The two descended via the hatch to Kane's left, Money leading. The Actress gave Kane a wan smile and rolled her eyes which earned her some points with the former Green Beret. She slid shut the teak door.

Kane peeled back the stained Velcro covering the glowing face and checked his watch. Adjusted the engines and wheel, pointing the yacht north into the outgoing tide combined with the flow of the Hudson River. He considered dropping anchor, since he had no idea how long 'going over the storyboards' would take and he was to the west of the shipping channel.

Kane focused on the faint silhouette of the Statue of Liberty to the port side, dredging up all sorts of history about it and the island upon which it was perched.

Kane cocked his head when he heard a muffled yelp for help. He sighed and headed below. Turned at the bottom of the steps toward the aft cabin. He passed through the Actress's scream as he slid open the door to the cabin. The Actress was on her back on the bed, scrambling to free herself, obviously panicked, naked from the waist up. Money lay on top of her, also with his shirt removed.

"Okay, sir, leave the lady—" Kane began, but sensed movement to his right and brought that arm up in a reflexive high block, partly deflecting the sap aimed at his head. The lead-filled leather weapon struck him a glancing blow and he staggered back.

Kane dropped to the deck, sweeping the attacker's legs with his left leg. As the man went down, Kane was on top of him, repeatedly smashing his elbow into the attacker's face at close range. The man scrambled to get away from the furious assault.

Kane let him, getting to one knee and drawing the forty-five, thumbing off the ambidextrous safety as he brought it level.

A muzzle flashed in the open aft sliding door and a bullet snapped by Kane's head accompanied by the sound of the gun firing. The shooter was behind and below the Sap Man, standing in a boat bobbing behind the narrow dive deck, which helped explain the miss. Kane fired, but the escaping sap-man was in the way and the round hit him in the shoulder, punch-spinning him out of the door and into the rubber boat.

An outboard engine roared to life.

Two flashes and the crack of shots from the boat. Bullets hit the ceiling above Kane. Crouching, he sidled left, weapon at the ready.

The engine accelerated.

Kane approached the door on an angle. Peered around, muzzle leading. The zodiac accelerated to the west, a dark figure at the driver's console, a wounded man in the back, and a third figure kneeling and aiming a gun this way, but not firing.

Kane brought the forty-five up, but spun about as he sensed someone behind him.

His finger twitched but he didn't fire at the Actress. He turned back, but the boat disappeared between the Statue of Liberty and Ellis Island in the rain and dark smudge of the Jersey shoreline.

"Fucking New Jersey," Kane muttered.

"Help him," the Actress said. She'd pulled her top up but that seemed to be the extent of her recovery.

"What happened?" Kane checked Money. It was obvious that Sap Man had hit him. Kane also noted the not inconsiderable pile of white powder on the small table next to the oval bed.

"I saw that guy coming up from behind and tried to warn Mister Crawford," the Actress said. "Did you shoot him?"

She was several lines behind in the script, but at least Crawford was stirring.

"I shot one of them." Kane felt along the wound on the older man's head. "His skull isn't busted. He's lucky."

"You really shot someone?" the Actress asked. "That was *really* loud! Really, really loud!"

Kane pulled off his denim shirt and used it to staunch the blood from the wound. "There's a first aid kit in the cockpit. Get it."

"Did you kill them?"

"First aid kit. Now!" Head wounds could be bad bleeders, a fact Kane had first-hand knowledge of given the old scar just above his right temple and extending underneath his thick, dark hair.

Crawford's eyelids flickered. "What the tarnation? Who slugged me?" He tried to sit.

Kane noted an old wicked scar on Crawford's abdomen, just below the rib cage. There was a faded eagle, globe and anchor tattoo on the older man's right shoulder.

"Easy," Kane said. "Stay down for a minute."

The Actress returned holding the kit. "Here."

Kane ripped open a gauze pack.

"I think I'm going to be sick," the Actress said.

"Head's over there," Kane said.

"What?"

"Bathroom," Kane amplified. He turned to the older man and replaced the shirt with gauze. The blood was mostly staunched, the laceration minimal. "You have a thick skull, Mister Crawford. You'll be okay. What day of the week is it?"

"Huh?"

"Day of the week," Kane repeated.

"Friday."

"Date?"

"Four August.

"Year?"

"Nineteen-seventy-seven. What in tarnation is going on?"

Kane didn't stop him from sitting up. "You don't have a concussion. You're probably gonna have a bad headache for a bit." Kane checked the carpeted floor. Wet spots where the intruder had been. Kane walked to the sliding door leading to the dive deck. Some blood spatter on the deck. The attackers must have rowed up in the dark from directly behind since he hadn't heard the engine. "You got enemies?" he asked Crawford.

"Sure, I have enemies. No one worth their salt doesn't have enemies." Crawford tried to retrieve his shirt from the deck, but couldn't make it. "A man who doesn't have enemies isn't a man."

Kane handed the shirt to the older man. "Enemy enough to want to kill you?"

"What happened?" Crawford demanded as he buttoned.

"I've got to radio the NYPD harbor patrol," Kane said.

"Whoa, buckaroo, hold your horses!" Crawford tried to stand, leaned right, and fell onto the bed. He held up a hand. "Just give me a sec, hombre." He slowly sat up, one hand on the bulkhead. "*What happened?*" he demanded in a voice used to being obeyed.

Kane gave a brief summary of recent events.

Crawford didn't interrupt. It took Kane under twenty seconds.

"No body?" Crawford asked.

"One of them is wounded," Kane said. "There's three bullet holes in here."

"The holes can be patched," Crawford said.

"Get to the point, please," Kane said to Crawford.

"I'm not going to get stuck in this hell's half acre over a little blood on a boat and some bullet holes," Crawford said. "I've got important business to attend to in the morning before I fly home."

"I just shot someone," Kane said.

"Not well enough. He's still breathing."

Kane didn't respond.

"They came at us," Crawford pointed out. "I doubt they'll be going to the police. Let sleeping doggies lie." He reached down and was able to pick up his Stetson without falling over. "Besides, you want to get the police involved in this, William Kane?"

Kane remained still, waiting for the inevitable.

Crawford felt his head, grimaced in pain. His hand came away sticky with blood. "Guess I won't be wearing my hat for a bit." He smiled crookedly at Kane. "Oh yeah, cowboy, we're all in this together."   •

"You were a Marine," Kane said.

"And you were Army," Crawford said. "Green Beret, right?"

"Your scar?"

"Jap bayonet on Makin Island."

"You were a Raider," Kane said.

For the first time Crawford seemed impressed. "You know a bit of history, eh?" He pointed at Kane with the hat in hand. "You got at least one scar I can see, compadre. And some fresh ones on your wrists and neck. I don't know what you got into recently but it wasn't pretty." Crawford shook his head, but stopped and winced. "Let it go. There'll be a tidy bonus in this for you. Take the boat back to the marina."

"You know who it was," Kane said.

"I don't have a blessed clue who it was," Crawford said. "But don't worry. My people will find out. Let them take care of it. New York cops couldn't find their behinds with both hands. Plus, all they're worried about right now is that Son of Sam bastard."

The Actress came out of the head and stood close to Crawford. "Are you all right?" she asked him, putting a hand on his shoulder.

"Fine, darling."

Kane indicated the cocaine. "Is that why?"

"It doesn't put a pretty shine on things," Crawford admitted. "But there's nothing to prove you didn't supply it."

"Please," the Actress pleaded. "I can't get in trouble."

"I shot someone," Kane said, but as he spoke the words, he knew they meant nothing and he was the one behind the script now.

"It's a done deed, cowboy," Crawford said. "And remember. We're the witnesses. We can remember it one way or the other." He looked at the Actress. "You're with me on this, darling, aren't you?" It was more a threat than a question.

She gave Kane an apologetic look and nodded assent.

"Right," Kane said. "The marina." He headed for the bridge.

*****

It was still a dark and stormy night, which was a cliché, but clichés are truisms and Kane didn't have many of those in his life so he took it at face value. The rain made the current job easier as he scrubbed blood off the dive deck. Another positive was that the drizzle was warm.

He'd docked at the pier from which they'd departed and where Crawford's limousine had been waiting the entire time. Crawford had thrust five thousand in crisp, new hundreds, still bank banded, into Kane's hands without comment, before heading to the limo. The Actress, whose name he still couldn't recall, had scurried after him, barely getting inside before the door was slammed shut and rubber burned as it peeled away.

He considered calling Toni, his boss for this job, and telling her about the evening's events, but he wasn't certain what to make of it, so tomorrow would be soon enough. He pulled out a flashlight and shined it on the deck to check his work. Clean of blood.

There were scuffmarks in the decking that no amount of scrubbing was going to fix, although some of them were old. The boat was a rental, via Toni, and he figured he'd gone above and beyond this evening. She could deal with the owner and the bullet holes and the marks. It was likely the boat had seen worse damage from partiers.

He sat down, feet dangling over the edge, just above the polluted water of the Hudson River, not exactly feeling like Huckleberry Finn on the Mississippi. Unconsciously, he ran his hand along the scar on the side of his head.

It didn't make sense. One of the intruders had a gun, but the one who'd come in had used a sap to attack Crawford. If the goal had been killing, the gun should have been first. Or both should have had guns. Unless a kidnapping? Crawford? The Actress? Or had the sap guy been in the cabin first, the gun man providing cover from the boat, and Crawford and the Actress interrupted something?

Kane glanced over his shoulder. Went to where the initial attacker had come from the side. There was a hatch there which led to the ladder descending to the engine room. It was unlatched. Kane pushed it open and flipped on the light.

The bomb was just inside, on the edge at the top of the ladder. A red light was flickering on top of the bundle of C-4, then it turned green.

Wednesday,
19 November 1967

HILL 875, DAK TO, VIETNAM

"Benedicat vos omnipotens Deus, Pater, et Filius, et Spiritus Sanctus."

"Amen," Kane whispers under his breath while he studies the topographic map spread on top of his rucksack with his platoon sergeant.

"Finding God in the foxhole, L.T.?" Sergeant Carter asks.

"He's omnipotent," Kane says. "He can find me if He wants to. Even here."

Forty feet away, Father Watters winds up the abbreviated service, holding his hands over the cluster of paratroopers kneeling on the jungle floor around him. "Ite, missa est. Go forth. And be safe, my sons."

The most important aspect of the mass in the midst of the jungle, as far as Kane is concerned, beyond the comfort it gives those who believe, and those who don't but wish they could, is the large number of soldiers in the cluster. More than ever before. An indicator of the pervading fear that this op isn't going to be an easy one.

"Hey diddle, diddle, right up the fucking middle," Sergeant Carter complains about the operations order in a low voice only Kane can hear. "They teach that at West Point?" Carter is from Detroit, made his latest rank in Germany and this is, surprisingly for the stripes, his first tour in Vietnam. But he gets some experience points for his tough childhood.

"They taught us Caesar, Napoleon, Grant and MacArthur, to name a few," Kane says. *"They all did right up the middle one time or another."* And Kane remembers from his lessons that Grant in his memoirs regretted only one order out of all the carnage he commanded in the war—the final, frontal assault at Cold Harbor; right up the middle.

Kane looks at the objective; he can see as far as the dense surge of green that marks the base of Hill 875. *"Not much choice."*

"Why are we taking the hill, sir?" Carter asks.

"Because it's there." Kane regrets the flippant answer. Carter, and the rest, are putting their lives on the line. He tries to explain. *"A Special Forces CIDG company made contact on the hill. The general wants us to take it."* As far as the plan, Kane isn't thrilled. Two companies, Charlie and Delta up, with Alpha in the rear, two up-one back, classic army tactics since men had been whacking at each other with swords. Except the NVA are anything but classic.

"Why not just blast it with arty?" Carter asks.

Kane tires of the questions to which there are no answers. After five months Kane is a veteran. He has more time in-country than Carter and most of the men in the reconstituted company of mostly replacements.

Kane looks at the trail that runs through the position. They'd marched on it this morning and the attack is going to follow it up the hill. *"I want an OP with an M60 behind us,"* he orders Carter.

Carter frowns and Kane knows he's thinking his platoon leader is putting a valuable machinegun pointing in the wrong direction. But memories of Ranger School always hover in Kane's brain. He can practically hear Chargin' Charlie Beckwith screaming: 'Don't be stupid!'

"Get the OP out with a 60 and check the men, sergeant."

Kane was moved to Alpha company after the disaster at Hill 1338 in June. He's the senior platoon leader in the company. It's disconcerting that he's commanding Ted's old platoon but no one in it remembers Ted.

Kane is a very different man from the one who'd experienced his first combat that day. Physically, the change is startling. He's lost weight that hadn't been apparent he could lose. He has practically no body fat, his body is all lean muscle. But it's in his mind that he's changed the most and the window into it, his eyes, are deep and withdrawn.

As Carter heads one way, Kane goes to the other end of the platoon. He kneels between two men. *"Canteens full?"*

Both young soldiers nervously nod, eyes wide.

Kane looks over their gear. Both are FNG, fucking new guys. Kane doubts either of them shave. He inspects their weapons. "Listen to your squad leader. He'll take care of you. Do what he says and you'll be fine."

The FNGs nod.

Kane moves down the line dispensing advice and as much encouragement as he can muster, which is almost nonexistent.

Why are *they taking this fucking hill?*

Because it's where the enemy is.

*****

Fierce fighting ahead has been going on for an hour at the head of Alpha company. They'd been going uphill behind Charlie and Delta which have been engaged for even longer. In trail position, Kane's platoon has not made contact yet. But that changes in an instant.

Bugles blare behind them and Kane instantly knows what that means. It's a trap.

The sound of the firing intensifies. Kane recognizes the sound of B-40 rockets and recoilless rifle fire, which means the NVA are dug in. Jets scream overhead, dropping heavy bombs on Hill 875. Artillery fills the gaps between air strikes.

Kane is behind a log, firing his M-16 on semi-automatic, actually aiming. He sees the enemy occasionally, a rarity. Khaki figures flit among the undergrowth and broken jungle. He implicitly understands they can also see him, but he's always known they can see him. It is usually their advantage having the Americans blundering into them. But now they're attacking.

He hits some of those figures, but it's not something to spend a moment on in the heat of battle.

Keep shooting. Issue orders. Hold it together. Updating the company commander on the radio.

Kane glances left and right, checking his men. Two soldiers are fetaled in their hole, not firing. "Carter!" Kane yells, getting his platoon sergeant's attention. He points at the two.

Carter slithers through the mud and undergrowth to the hole.

Kane can barely hear the radio over the sound of battle; the new company commander is calling in fire. Danger close. 'Grab them by the belt buckle'.

That's the NVA's tactic to reduce the American's artillery and air power superiority. Get so close to the Americans it can't be used.

Except in the direst of circumstances.

NVA pour out of tunnels and advance through the jungle.

This isn't the Sky Soldier plan.

This is the NVA plan, long prepared, waiting for the Americans to blunder into the trap. The paratroopers are in the midst of tunnels and bunkers and long-planned fields of fire. Surrounded. Charlie Beckwith would be swearing up a storm at the stupidity.

The NVA charge, some of them screaming, some insanely laughing, firing their AKs. To the left, a platoon CP, command post, is overrun, all the Americans killed at close range.

The company commander is standing, firing his pistol into the air to keep men from running; to prevent a complete rout.

Kane drops a magazine, slams another home. Eighteen rounds, he thinks as he starts firing, one part of his brain counting rounds, most of it considering the diminishing tactical options. The perimeter is dissolving, men fading uphill toward the dubious safety of Charlie and Delta.

"Hold the line!" Kane screams, but his voice withers beneath the screaming of bullets, artillery and jets.

There are too many NVA.

An M60 machinegun is firing nonstop thirty yards away, farther down the trail at the OP. It's the only thing saving Alpha from being completely overrun. Someone is making a stand.

For the moment.

"Hold the line!" Kane yells.

The handset jerks out of Kane's hand. He turns to see the cause. Blood is pumping from the ragged, gaping hole in the center of what used to be the RTO's face.

The RTO's wound saves Kane's life as a round snaps underneath the front lip of his helmet and plows along the right side of his head and punches a hole through the rear of the helmet.

Stars explode in Kane's brain and he's knocked off his feet, steel pot flying.

Kane falls on top of his RTO. Kane is barely conscious, his head ringing. Although his ear is only inches from the soldier's mouth, he can't hear the man's desperate, whispered prayers. He does feel the RTO's final breath.

Kane's blood mixes with the RTO's.

Kane looks up. Jungle, a tiny patch of sky, the canopy shredded by the artillery. Blue sky. A bird flies past. Kane envies it. He can't get his body to respond. A fire alarm is ringing in his head.

The sky is blocked by a brown face. Strangely, the Vietnamese smiles, revealing a gold tooth in the center. The Vietnamese says something but Kane can't hear him. He can only see the lips moving.

Bullets snap overhead. Artillery thunders. Kane hears that distantly, on another stage. The M-60 is still burning rounds, a last stand.

He's going to die. He knows it. The Vietnamese looming over him is going to kill him, just like Ted. He pulls his West Point ring off. Drops it into the blood and piss-soaked mud.

The brown face disappears and Kane feels a tug on his LBE. He's being dragged. Uphill.

He realizes the man is a Montagnard CIDG. Kane tries to help, to push with his feet, but his body isn't working.

The M-60 goes silent.

"Friendly!" the Vietnamese is calling out and Kane finally hears the word.

They're passing bodies. American corpses litter the trail that runs uphill toward Charlie and Delta.

"You not too heavy," his savior says, pauses, smiles once more. He raises his voice. "Friendly!"

Bullets going in both directions crack past the retreating Americans. Alpha has fallen apart.

Kane wants to stand, to issue orders, save his platoon, save the company. Save his men. He can't get to his feet.

He's pulled once more. Through the mud, broken vegetation. Over an eviscerated body smearing blood and gore.

"Friendly!"

They pass between two wide-eyed, frightened paratroopers. They're pointing their M-16s downhill. This is the perimeter of Charlie and Delta.

Another five meters. Stops. The brown face is in front of him again. Grabs him by the shoulders and sits him against a tree, facing uphill. Fingers probe the side of his head. He can barely feel them.

"My arm! My arm!" someone is screaming close by. "Where's my arm?"

Artillery. Bombs explode, the earth shakes.

What circle of hell is this?

"Mom. Mom. Mom." The voice is insistent.

Kane wishes it would stop. His right eye fills with blood. The casualty collection point is thirty feet away, near the company CP. Too many bodies. Too many.

Father Watters pulls a paratrooper to the collection point. Someone tries to get him to stop, to make him get down, but Watters shrugs him off and heads back to the perimeter.

"Dai Yu?"

Kane focuses on the CIDG.

The man taps his chest. "I'm Thao."

"Thao," Kane whispers.

Thao points at the wound. "Lot of blood, but head strong. You be okay."

"'Okay'?" Kane repeats.

A chopper flits overhead, cases of ammo and medical supplies tossed out, and away fast, bullets following, tattooing the metal.

Kane puts one hand against the tree. Tries to get to his feet, collapses.

Thao points to the casualty collection point. "I get bandages. You stay. Okay?"

"Right." Kane's not sure he actually says the word. Everything is echoing.

Thao scampers off, dodging wounded, empty ammo cases, the dead, broken tree trunks, discarded helmets and other debris of war.

His men need him. Kane has to get back in the fight. He tries to wipe the blood out of his eye but his hand has little strength.

Thao is back. "Easy, Dai Yu." He wets a piece of cloth with his canteen and wipes Kane's face, surprisingly gentle amidst all the violence.

Thao has a syringe of morphine.

"No," Kane tries to wave it off. He has to stay alert. Lead his men.

He doesn't feel it when Thao hits his thigh with the morphine.

Thao clears Kane's eye of blood. Father Watters is on his knees fifteen meters away, cradling a dying soldier in his arms, his head next to the man's ear, whispering Extreme Unction.

A jet screams by, angled across the axis of the hill, drops its bomb. Danger close.

The ground convulses. More screams.

"Weapon," Kane says to Thao. "My weapon."

Thao nods. "Many weapons here. Wait, Dai Yu." He doesn't have to go far. He returns with a blood smeared M-16.

Thao points toward the sound of the bugles and the AKs and the screams. "I get more wounded."

How can anyone be alive there?

How can anyone be alive here?

Kane grasps the M-16, uses it as a crutch to get to his feet. The surviving officers are gathering near the casualty collection point, coordinating the defense. Kane takes a step in that direction. Feels a whisper of something along his spine. Stops and looks up.

A jet is inbound. But it's coming from the wrong direction, along the axis of the ridge instead of across like the others.

The last thing Kane sees, silhouetted against the flash of the exploding bomb, is Father Watters making the sign of the cross over a dying soldier.

THANK YOU FOR THE READ!

Made in the USA
San Bernardino, CA
19 June 2020